Jane Was Here

Sarah Kernochan's Previous Work:
Dry Hustle

JANE WAS HERE

A NOVEL

SARAH KERNOCHAN

GREY SWAN PRESS

Publisher of Fine Books   Marblehead, Massachusetts

Grey Swan Press
www.greyswanpress.com

Cover designed by Norman Moore
Cover photograph by Phoebe Lapine

100% acid-free paper
Printed in the United States

LIBRARY OF CONGRESS CATALOGING-IN-PUBLICATION DATA
Kernochan, Sarah.
      Jane was here/Sarah Kernochan–1st ed.
          p. cm.
      1. Mystery–Fiction. 2. Reincarnation–Fiction. 3. Title.

Library of Congress Control Number: 2011926165

ISBN: 978-9800377-2-2

0 9 8 7 6 5 4 3 2 1

To my parents,
Jack and Adelaide Kernochan
I'll be seeing you.

*T*he night is pale, humid, with a few begrimed clouds. The moon has hung around so long it's ignored, unremarkable as a thumb-tack.

On this July night, the girl soon to be known as Jane enters the village of Graynier.

It has grown since she was here last, though that was too long ago for her to remember. Back then there were only a few hundred people in Graynier.

It had never been one of those quaint New England hamlets, with neat white clapboard houses, town hall and Presbyterian church presiding over a cozy green, a registry spanning back to the Puritans.

Graynier came into being because of the glass factory. Built in 1828 at the foot of Putman Hill, it harnessed the gush of Pontusuck Creek for its great wheel. Workers arrived; their houses sprang up on haphazard dirt lanes. The factory owner's mansion went up. His progeny built a cluster of modest Victorians to face the wooded hills, turning their backs on the working-class neighborhoods, repudiating community. The workers' progeny established shops and took up the better professions, valiantly trying to confer an air of prosperity on the village...But Graynier was built on glass, and everyone felt that impermanence underfoot.

The factory no longer exists.

She remembers so very little, she cannot comment to herself

how this and that have changed since the old days. Yet it was her home, this much she knows. That certainty produces in her a wild joy, thrashing like a bird against the curtain of fatigue sweeping over her body.

She wants to know everything, all, and at once.

Better that she does not: too soon for her to know the appalling events of the past. And the future she is rushing toward, sweeping the town's inhabitants along with her in a frightful flood of justice, is also obscured—as it should be.

Some of the people who were present for what happened all those years ago still live here. The one who pushed her from the womb. The one who carried her on his shoulders. The one who taught her arithmetic. The one who kissed her first. The one who fell in love with her. The one she loved instead.

And the one who killed her.

That one is somewhere here: a small life that shimmers and pulses in the night—or so Heaven must see it, for, in spite of that terrible deed, all life is sacred. But her killer would have no more idea of that than a mole snuffling about its starless underworld.

And Heaven would have her be ignorant as well, as she walks into the village of Graynier, in the valley between two hills, under a vapid moon.

PART ONE

CHAPTER ONE

At 3 a.m. Hoyt Eddy wakes up in his truck. The Shicker Shack's neon sign is shut off; his pickup is the only vehicle left in the bar's parking lot.

Mosquitoes bob and weave inside the cab as he scratches the bites on his arms. Maybe they took one too many hits off his over-bourboned blood. He twists to peer through the rear window into the truck bed. Sure enough, his dog Pete is gone, bored with waiting for him to sleep off the night's booze-a-thon.

Hoyt whistles. Pete catapults out of a dumpster, shaking off pizza crusts and wet coffee filters from ruptured garbage bags. He jumps into the pickup bed while Hoyt starts the engine.

Might as well stay up the rest of the night, Hoyt decides, pulling onto Route 404: have a glass of that Malbec he stole from Jack Meltzer's wine cellar, read the 1893 pocket edition of Byron's poems he bought for twenty-five cents at the First Methodist Book Fair. He likes the tiny print and age-dappled pages of the worthless volumes that sometimes turn up at church sales, especially oddities like nineteenth-century treatises on angling, or housework. He has an entire wall he has read of books like these, and another wall he intends to read.

Jack and Audrey Meltzer are arriving in two weeks to enjoy their dream house. As their caretaker (Hoyt Eddy Property Management, LLC), Hoyt is responsible for making sure everything is as it should be. That means he will have to rescue the place from ten months of neglect. He has to start work early in the morning.

He will spend the week preparing the estate: cleaning gutters, poisoning ants, roaches and the mice that have gnawed through the home theater cables. He will bomb wasp nests he's left untended to grow as big as basketballs; he'll repair cracked windows and punctured screens; bring in migrant workers from the motel (paying them a meager wage from the outrageous amount he charges the Meltzers for lawn care, using the name of a fictitious high-end nursery) to mow, trim, and weed. He will skim snakes from the pool; tie rags around burst pipes; dump copper sulfate into the lake to destroy the carpet of green algae which has vividly claimed it, and in the process kill whatever fish haven't mutated since the last time he threw chemicals their way. All must appear shipshape.

The illusion has to last through September. After Labor Day, Hoyt can let the elements and the pests have their go once again at Maple Manor. Once more vines will crawl under the roof, leaves blow into the garage, mice strafe turds on the kitchen counters and make their homes under the bedclothes. Snow and ice will wall off the driveway.

Hoyt does have a plow attachment for his truck, and he does bill the Meltzers for snow removal, but winter is mainly his time for uninterrupted reading and drinking. Once or twice during the season he will snowshoe into the property from the road, leaving aimless loops of tracks around the house as he notes damage he will address, in an eleventh-hour dash, next July.

Rehearsing this calendar of chores in his head, Hoyt's attention is elsewhere when he reaches the curve in the road.

A woman comes into view, walking in the middle of his lane, her back to his headlights. Hoyt's reflexes are slow: dreamily he records the thin hair wafting with each of her strides, her clam-digger pants, the duffel bag in her hand. Then, sucking air, he wrenches the wheel left to avoid hitting her.

At the same moment, in the opposite lane, a pair of low-slung headlights swings around the curve. Car and truck collide with a thick crunch.

MARLY HAD ALSO BEEN at the Shicker Shack earlier, though she left before Hoyt arrived. She hadn't wanted to go. But Chuck Mosher kept shooting looks over his wife's shoulder, his eyes jerking back and forth: *Marly...door...Marly...door.* Clearly he was nervous about having both ladies in the same room: the woman who bore his children and his name, and the one he fucked on bowling nights when he was expected home late.

Taking the hint, Marly had left. But it was a shame: there were at least six other guys at the Shack who were glad to see her. Gil Reynard, with his cute grin and maxed-out credit cards (she always has to buy drinks). Oly Gustaffson, back from Iraq with his amazing finger prosthesis; Oly's boss, who sells carpeting, and whom she mixes up with Harold Bourjois the mortician because they both smell of formaldehyde; Brink Banner, manager of a cold-storage warehouse near the freeway (a place nowhere near as cold as his wife, he once told Marly).

Actually, the entire town of Graynier is filled with men who exploit Marly's good nature. A cheerful person, Marlene Walczak always tells herself that if times are tough, they could be tougher. Her daughter Pearl may be overweight and illegitimate, but she could be morbidly obese and an orphan. Men might ram away at Marly like a plunger in a toilet, but at least they're not mean and disrespectful; they're fond of her. She loves seeing that little lamp switch on in their eyes when she swings into the bar after work. You can't fake that appreciation; it's almost as genuine as love.

"There are worse things," she always says, spinning her skimpy straw into gold. "Be thankful for what you have."

After leaving the Shicker Shack, Marly went to The Hut, where she bumped into Van Farkle, who was all a-twitch for some pussy.

Turning down his generous offer of the reclining seats in his Camry, she managed to wangle an invitation to his house.

In the past Van had enjoyed having her over; he would record their goings-on with the mini-cam he had mounted on the ceiling. By now, though, he had more than enough tapes of them scrambling around the waterbed; they were all pretty repetitive after a while. It took some effort to convince him that coitus in the home was way preferable to coitus in the Camry, something she'd learned empirically from slamming against the gear shift and cup-holders only the week before.

It was a good thing Van had woken her at 3:00 a.m. and told her to get the hell out. Otherwise her daughter Pearl would have discovered her mom's empty bed in the morning, and they would have both been late to work. Giving Van's meaty shoulder a kiss, Marly had gotten dressed quickly and jumped in her car.

Halfway home to the trailer park, she swung her Cavalier around a corner, and saw a young woman walking in the opposite lane.

For a split second Marly registered the girl's slight silhouette, rimmed by a big bright halo of light.

Then the halo turned into the headlights of a truck, which swerved suddenly, plowing into Marly's car.

HOYT GETS OUT of his truck, his hand on the back of his neck. In the collision, his head snapped forward and back; now bolts of pain are flashing through his cervical spine.

The first thought he has is about liability. Though his pickup looks fine (except for a little paint damage), the other car, a cheap compact, has taken the brunt, its fender flattened, its hood buckled, one light gouged out. The driver will be angry—or worse, injured. Hoyt braces for accusations, police reports, blood alcohol tests, defendant's hospital bills, insurance claims.

His second thought is defensive. It wasn't his fault. There was someone—a girl—smack in the middle of road.

Where is she?

He peers around quickly. It hurts to turn his head. There's no one on the road now; maybe she continued walking and passed beyond the streetlamp's pool of light.

The other driver gets out of the car. Hoyt tenses.

Then he sees it's only Marly.

Dazed, she's holding her neck, too. "Hi, Hoyt." She musters a meek smile. "Was—was that my fault?"

Hoyt relaxes. Why not let her embrace the blame, as long as she's willing? "You took the curve too wide. I couldn't avoid you." It's always fun to fuck with Marly Walczak's head.

Marly is looking about in confusion. "There was a girl standing in the road. Did you see her?"

"I saw someone. Nobody there now."

"Oh my God! You don't think I hit her?"

"You would've heard it."

While Marly checks along the roadsides for a huddled little body in clamdiggers, Hoyt searches under the vehicles. They both find nothing.

"Hoyt..." Moonlight plays on Marly's anxiously creased forehead and the sooty mascara whorls around her eyes. "Please let's not report this. My insurance was canceled last week 'cause the payment was late. I was going to put a check in the mail Friday when I get paid."

"Suits me. You got the worst of it, anyhow."

Her engine starts right up. As she inches it onto the road alongside Hoyt, the fender drags noisily, its headlight looking like Quasimodo.

"You're good to go," Hoyt says heartlessly.

"You know, my neck doesn't feel too good." She catches herself complaining. "Still, it could have been a lot worse!"

On the drive home, Hoyt keeps an eye out for the girl they both saw. But she seems to have vanished.

CHAPTER TWO

Around 3 a.m. Brett finishes the Little Rompers Nursery School website design, inserting his secret signature: a tiny pumpkin in place of the 'c' in the copyright notice circle. If anyone accidentally clicks on it, guitars explode and the Smashing Pumpkins holler, *"Despite all my rage/ I'm still a rat in a cage..."* So far his employer hasn't caught him at it.

He emails the link to his boss, rubs the sweat off his glasses with the hem of his T-shirt, and scratches a mosquito bite, pink on the pallor of his arm. It was probably a mistake to set up his workspace in the top-floor garret. The summer heat rises and clots under the rafters; when he gets up from the rickety ladder-back chair, unbending his long frame so his head grazes the eaves, he is momentarily dizzy. But he'd wanted to be within earshot of his son's bedroom, in case the boy has a nightmare or something and calls for him.

Not that Collin would.

Their first summer together, begun only a week ago, is already a disaster. Maybe Veronda wanted it that way. When he went to pick Collin up in Norwalk, she stood in the driveway with her fierce acrylic nails crossed over the boy's chest like a mother bear's. Gold eyes like a bear, too. Parting her claws, she handed Collin over to Brett. Her parents were on hand, for good measure, their baleful stares reminding him that he'd cut short their daughter's college career by impregnating her, thus forcing her return home to Connecticut.

Brett took his son's hand. It hung limply in his grasp as he led the boy to the rented van. "Bye, sugar bunny," called Veronda's mother. Brett knew there would be cold carnage if he returned their grandson dinged, dented, or white-ified at summer's end. The sinister whine of weed whackers on a Saturday reminded him of the hell he would descend unto at the hour of judgment for having boned a good black girl. This despite the fact that Veronda had been the one to straddle him, to cover his meager mouth with her lush pillowy lips, and later to shock him with her nasty laughter when he said he loved her.

He'd paid monthly support, sent Christmas presents, telephoned on Collin's birthday, but the message from Norwalk was always the same: *pay and pay but stay away.* We'll let him come to the phone and that's it.

The boy's conversation was all grunt. Brett gave up calling.

This past year, though, the recriminations changed: Brett learned that he was selfish, he had no interest in knowing his own son, he never asked to visit, he had a good job and unfettered freedom as if he'd done nothing wrong, as if Collin didn't exist! Brett took the blows and awaited fresh instruction. It came in June: he would take the kid for eight weeks of father-son bonding while Veronda went to Ghana to understand her roots.

Now, his hands sliding over crumbled wallpaper, Brett gropes his way down the staircase to the second floor. The dingy floorboards yelp under his bare feet as he pads cautiously down the corridor to look in on Collin, as a father would.

As it happens, Brett can't look in on his child because he can't see him. The boy's bed is swathed in mosquito netting hung from four posters. The kid is veiled from view—and that's the problem.

From the moment he got into Brett's van, Collin had vanished into silence, turning his face away as if telephone poles, freeway shoulders, blurred woods were of intense interest. Brett kept glancing at his son, admiring his amber skin and fluffy brown curls, the pretty eyes that were always averted. The only motion came from the boy's hands, continually pulling on his fingers, as if trying (in vain) to make his knuckles crack.

The poor kid is nervous, Brett thought. Maybe separation anxiety.

He waited to feel waves of fatherly, if not love, then solicitude. He imagined the waves would start gently, and grow to a pounding surf by the end of the camping trip.

Except father and son never went camping. For six hours Brett drove north in the rented RV—stocked with backpacks, tent, headlamps, freeze-dried chili—finally pulling up in a southern New Hampshire trailer park near a recommended trailhead.

He turned the engine off.

With feigned confidence Brett said, "Let's hook this sucker up," something he'd gone to a chat room to find out how to do. There had better be a Wi-Fi hotspot somewhere, as promised by the park's website. He had to keep up with the office for six weeks somehow.

Then the kid piped up: "I don't want to go camping."

"Oh. Why didn't you say anything?"

Collin's response was not to say anything.

"I was scared my first time too. But after you get through it, you feel really good about yourself."

"I'm not scared. I just don't like it."

"How do you know if you've never done it?"

"I can tell I don't like it." The boy spoke in the measured tones of an adult pretending patience.

Brett glanced anxiously at his cell phone. No bars. Maybe camping wasn't a good plan. "What do you like to do?"

"I don't know."

"Okay, at least you know what you don't like. How about kayaking?"

"No."

"We could find a river and ride down the whole way in rubber tubes. That's awesome."

"No."

Brett was running dry on ideas. "We could rent some mountain bikes."

"No."

"What do you do in the summers? Do you swim?"

"No."

"Do you know how to swim?"

"No."

"What if I teach you?"

"No."

"Are you afraid of the water maybe?"

Collin hesitated. Had Brett hit a nerve?

"I don't like swimming," the boy said, his tone final.

"Do you like sitting here? Because we're not going anywhere until you can think of something you'd rather do than hike into the wilderness with your dad." He said it lightly, but maybe ten-year-olds didn't compute irony. Were those tears glimmering under the long lashes, or the reflection of the setting sun?

Brett drove to a motel called the Hay Rick. There was one vacancy. The rest of the rooms were engorged with girls in muck boots, gathered for a big horse show.

Brett brought in a bucket of chicken to share and did his email while Collin watched four hours of TV.

In the morning, Collin came to a decision. "I like fishing."

"What kind of fishing?"

"I don't know." The kid had never done any; Brett hadn't either. Going online, he looked it up. "There's fly-fishing, rock-fishing, spinning, deep-sea fishing, trawling..."

"Deep sea," said Collin. The boy who didn't like to swim saw no irony in wanting to fish in deep water.

It took four hours to drive to the shore, and three more driving along the coast, looking for an affordable room in the fishing villages and beach resorts. The prices were horrendous, and most places were full.

Toward nightfall, they turned inland, southwest into Massachusetts, aimlessly following a blue-line road through wooded hills until they passed a sign that said "GRAYNIER."

Suddenly Brett wilted; his energy seemed to rush away. He could not drive a minute longer.

The only motel in town was run by the Poonchwallas, an Indian family. The teenage son registered them while the younger girl, Gita, eyed Collin's exotic hue with interest.

In the room, Brett fell asleep immediately on the stained bedspread. Collin watched TV.

After a while he peered between the window curtains. The girl Gita was sitting in an aluminum folding chair beside the sad little pool, bouncing the heels of her plastic clogs on the concrete and watching the door to his room.

He let himself outside. She jumped to her feet. "I knew you'd come. I was sending you messages in my head."

She looked a couple of years older than Collin; compared to him, she knew everything. Abashed, he waited for instructions, a doglike trait he unknowingly shared with his dad.

"Are you baptized?"

"I don't know."

"Then I'll do it." Taking his hand, she led him to the pool steps.

"I can't swim," he said. But he followed her down, his pajama bottoms ballooning as his bare feet slipped into the water.

"I'll teach you that, too," she said.

In the morning Gita boldly announced to Brett that she and Collin were going to play together. He looked at Collin, whose eyes were wholly fixed on his new friend.

Leaving the boy with her, Brett drove to the shore, trading in the RV for a compact. He scoped out apartments, boat rentals, fishing tackle. When he returned to Graynier to fetch his son, Collin declared, "I want to stay right here."

So Brett found a Victorian house to rent just down the street from the motel: decrepit, no TV, but cheap. Graynier was probably an equal number of hours from the seashore and the inland lakes: freshwater fishing if the deep sea didn't work out...

IT'S TWO WEEKS LATER, and they still haven't been fishing. Collin doesn't seem remotely interested; he plays every day with Gita. Brett has no idea what they do together, but he's here to meet Collin's needs, and Collin needs to play with this strange girl. So Brett spends his days designing his websites, strolling through Graynier, wondering why he likes the town so much and cares for his son so little.

There isn't much to Graynier. Walking in one direction along Graynier Avenue, also called Route 404, you skirt Putman Hill where a glass factory once stood, long since torn down. About two miles further is the Graynier Outlet Center. The interstate streams nearby, a single exit emptying customers from all over the state into the mall. Here they can buy overstock from big-city labels: Boss, Nautica, Lauren, Karan. Most of Graynier's inhabitants work at the mall.

Walking in the other direction, you return to the heart of Graynier, which is noteworthy because there is no heart. No center. Businesses are scattered among residential neighborhoods, with no attention to zoning. Wandering down the anarchic streets, Brett marvels that there's no design or reason for anything to be where it is. Why is the body shop next to the beauty shop? Why is the bank between a mobile home on concrete blocks and the bungalow of Madame Bertha, a palmist? Why is the town hall outside of town?

He finds it poignant somehow. His heart goes out to poor, chockablock Graynier, and it becomes his companion. Otherwise he would fall prey to an intense loneliness.

Brett has never felt this lonely before. Usually he enjoys working in solitary, one project after another claiming his waking consciousness. His romantic relationships—only two, actually—begin with a girl thinking what she needs is a quiet, unquestioning mate, and end when she decides she doesn't need a quiet, unquestioning mate, or "doormat" as the last one put it.

But now he is wracked by the loneliness of living with his son. Collin's rejection hangs there every day, uncontested, unrebuked, expanding with the heat. Brett takes to working late and sleeping late.

Collin is all but living at the Poonchwallas' motel.

BRETT TUCKS THE MOSQUITO netting under his son's mattress to close any gaps. Returning to the corridor, he passes the closed door to a bedroom whose fungus smell kept them both from choosing it. He assumes the house's shabby neglect is due to its owner, a retired Catholic minister who has gone to visit his mother for the summer. Maybe the Reverend has renounced all worldly pursuits like vacuuming, or maybe he reveres all God's creatures including germs.

Exhaustion propels Brett into the third bedroom, where he lies down, the ancient mattress making a crunchy sound (he suspects it's filled with straw). He likes this room, despite its sorry thrift-shop furnishings. The carefully handcrafted wood paneling is aged to a deep silky chocolate. The floor's hand-hewn pine planks were fitted lovingly tongue-into-groove, probably by the same craftsman. Brett discovered the flooring the first night, after a sneezing fit prompted him to roll up the foul braided rug. He also replaced the book on the bed stand, swapping *The Book of Common Prayer* **for** *The Ultimate Book of Sudoku.*

He's aware that he's still clothed, but the lure of sleep is strong. He sinks obediently from beta to theta...

Not three minutes have passed, when his breath stops. His lungs refuse command, will not inflate. His limbs are iron, mouth gaping, frozen, even his thoughts paralyzed by terror. All he can see is the ceiling, a parabola of light shining on it—from where? He knows he turned the bedside lamp off.

A man enters his vision, bending over Brett and looking intently into his face. Long gray hair curls over the high stiff collar of the man's coat; behind rimless spectacles, his eyes are tired.

"God rest your soul, good man," he murmurs. The pads of his fingers touch Brett's eyelids, drawing them down. Suddenly Brett feels his essence rush through his open mouth and rise to the ceiling, where he can now look down on the scene.

He sees the source of light: an old-fashioned kerosene lantern on the bed stand. The man in the dark coat is still bending over Brett's form, obscuring the face. Brett understands, with strange emotionless ease, that the man is a doctor, and that he—Brett—is dead.

The body's legs under the sheet seem wasted away: Brett can make out every knob and taper of the bones. As the doctor shifts, Brett sees the upper half of the body in the bed.

It's not Brett's face.

It belongs to some other man entirely, the flesh withered, no more than a cobweb covering the cranium, the eye sockets cavernous. The sheet drawn up to his bearded chin is flecked with blood.

Horror floods Brett: all at once he feels himself sucked back to the man's open mouth, through the bracelet of teeth, filling up this body that is not his.

With a great jolt, his heart lunges to life. Eyes flying open, he gasps for oxygen, jackknifing upright in the bed.

He flicks on the bedside lamp. The mirror on the wall opposite shows a rangy young man with his mouth open, frightened out of his wits. Brett is in his own body again.

Mouth dry, he hauls ass to the bathroom for a drink of water. It calms him slightly. How long was he without oxygen? He knows a little about apnea, a sleep stutter that can cause heart attacks and sudden death. Did he, for a brief moment, die?

And who were the people he saw in his room?

They must have been the usual senseless, random personnel of a bad dream, he decides, after another consoling glass of water. There's nothing to fear; they've vanished now. If he can putter around for a bit, maybe he can get back to sleep.

Remembering he left the dinner plates soaking in the kitchen sink, he goes downstairs to finish cleaning up.

SEVERAL MOSQUITOES HAVE drowned, nestled in the suds. He pulls up the rubber plug and waits for the cloudy water to drain. His eyes lift to the window.

In the small backyard stands the figure of a young woman, staring back at him, her face lost in moon shadow.

CHAPTER THREE

Brett steps back in surprise, turning to yank the chain on the overhead lamp; the light goes out. With the kitchen gone dark, he can see outside more clearly.

He surveys the patch of abandoned garden, the scalloped wire border, the single iron chair, the flagstones thrust up at angles by the roots of a lone sycamore.

The woman is gone.

Then: a soft rapping on the glass of the front door.

He walks to the entry, his heart thumping; flips on the porch light. Through the etched daisies on the frosted pane, a shadowy head waits. He could call out, "Who's there?" but he knows who it is.

He opens the door.

The first thing he sees are her eyes: light gray and solemn, full of request. Long muddy-blond hair tangles about her thin face; clam-digger pants and an ill-fitting wrinkled blouse hang on her slim frame. She holds a pink nylon duffel. She's maybe a few years younger than he, about five-six to his six-three. And she is pale, so pale, as if fed on moonlight.

She speaks, her voice low and a little husky, as if she has just woken up. "I'm Jane." She watches him hopefully.

"Hi. Are you looking for someone?" Warily, he scans the street for a possible accomplice.

"This is my house." A simple statement, without accusation.

Brett shifts awkwardly. "Oh. Well, Father Petrelli's away. I'm just renting. My lease is 'til mid-August." Maybe she's the owner's daughter. No, impossible: he's a Catholic priest. His niece?

But the girl is shaking her head. "I don't know him. Nor anyone, truly." An odd word, "truly." For a young person, her manner of speaking is strangely prim. "Yet I am sure, this is where I was born, here in this very house."

"Did you live here before he moved in?"

"I must have." She gazes at the house facade. "It resembles exactly the picture in my mind. Sir, if you please, may I come in?"

Her presumption is irritating. "It's after three a.m., do you mind? Come back in the daytime." He starts to shut the door, but she clings to the knob, panic flaring in her eyes, her cry shocking the silence of the empty street: "Please—please! I have nowhere else to go!"

"Shh!" Worried about his son upstairs, he steps forward to warn her away, leaving the doorway open. She flits past him into the house.

By the time he recovers, she's halfway down the hallway. Eagerly she assesses the walls and floor and fixtures, as if she's considering buying the property.

"Hey! You can't just barge in." He helplessly follows her into the front parlor, where she is already setting her pink duffel on the sofa.

"Here is where I belong," she declares, surveying the room. "I confess I see nothing familiar. Except..." She is peering over the cheap plaid sofa at a peculiar wooden box wedged in the corner. "It's possible I remember that."

He folds his arms testily. "Okay, what is it?"

She turns wondering eyes to him. "I don't know, sir."

"The name is Brett. And it's very late for games, so, sorry, but you'll have to leave."

"But...I live here."

"No, you don't. Not anymore. I have a lease."

"But I am so tired." She sits on the sofa before he can protest. "I have walked a long way."

His curiosity gets the better of him. "From where?"

"That's of no consequence. I won't be going back there ever again." Removing her shoes, she rubs her feet. The skin curls away from the pink sheen of a blister.

"Is there someone I can call who can pick you up? Don't you have family?"

"Perhaps I did have, once." She swings her feet up, tucking them under her. "I imagine we sat in this room after supper." She nods to the bay window overlooking the street. "It's an agreeable place to watch the people walk by."

Brett has a sudden thought: she's adopted, come in search of her real family. He gentles his tone: "Jane, are you looking for your birth parents?"

She makes a dismissive gesture. "You refer, I presume, to the two people who conceived me? I know where they are living, and want nothing to do with them. No." She fixes her earnest gaze on Brett. "Truly, I am looking for myself."

Brett sighs. He's arguing with an amnesiac, a mental patient, someone having a breakdown, or a stoner. Whichever she is, short of carrying her bodily to the door and dumping her back into the night, there seems no way to get rid of her.

Curling up on her side, she settles her head on her pink duffel, her eyelids drooping.

He tries another tack. "Can I get you some water?"

"Yes, thank you," she murmurs.

Brett retreats to the kitchen, crossing to the wall-mounted phone. His hand pauses on the receiver. If he calls the police, they will hold her in custody, contact her family or whatever home she walked away from. Maybe he would be returning her to some dire situation, abuse: some peril that prompted her to flee.

He needs to know more before he decides her fate. Filling a

glass with water, he returns to the parlor.

She has fallen asleep, knees drawn up, her shallow breath muffled in the folds of the duffel.

If he can remove the bag without waking her, there might be an ID inside. Setting down the glass, he kneels beside her.

"Jane," he says in a normal voice, testing. She's too deep in slumber to respond.

Up close, he can see the lavender halo of fatigue around her eyes, the delicate lashes shivering imperceptibly as she dreams, her lips slightly puckered, like an infant's seeking milk. Gently he takes hold of the duffel's strap, his other hand reaching to lift her head and slide the bag out.

Without warning her fingers uncurl, blindly seeking, and wrap around his wrist, dragging his hand to her cheek. Her eyes open, glimpsing him briefly through the clouded film of sleep.

Brett remains paralyzed, even after her lids droop closed again. His hand stays pressed to the softness of her white cheek. Suddenly, unaccountably, he is drenched in tenderness.

Every cell's invaded: he loves her as if he already has loved her, as if he started loving her long before he opened the door.

MANY DAYS FORWARD, he will wonder about this moment, when he questions once again why he let her stay on in the house. He will tell himself: it's like that moment when you're walking along and a little stray dog crosses your path. It was abandoned long ago, and years of dumb suffering have taught it that there is no rest anywhere, and yet it casts one sidelong look your way, a feeble spasm of hope.

The second your eyes lock, you know that from now on this animal belongs to you. Its need puts the flame to your love. And you stick your hand out, offering an end to its wretched wanderings.

Come. You are already thinking of what name to call it. *My Jane.*

CHAPTER FOUR

Even at a distance Hoyt can see the skunk, the black and white punctuation at the end of the green lawn, as he pulls up his truck in the Meltzers' driveway. He can tell by the animal's flattened shape that it spent the night in the cage trying to dig out or arching up to test the metal bars overhead with its webbed toes. Now it is lying down, weary and dull-eyed, head squeezed against the corner, with no appetite for the barbecue-sauce-smeared slice of bread that enticed it into the cage. The knowledge of its doom has spread like noxious gas through its body, leaving the animal with only enough energy for its last stand.

He shuts Pete inside the cab, where the mutt writhes with excitement. He takes the lid off the rubber trashcan in the truck bed, releasing the miasma of skunks gone by. Next he grabs a plastic tarpaulin, holding it in front of his face and body as he walks across the lawn to the cage. The skunk scrambles to its feet.

Mephitis mephitis, Hoyt thinks.

He has a head full of Latin, from prep school, law school, and earlier, when he was a kid and wanted to be a vet, studying the phyla of fauna obsessively, species and subspecies, markings and habitats. All that academic knowledge has devolved over time into a low-lying mental sludge that randomly belches up a stray fact once in a while, like the Latin name for skunk: *mephitis mephitis.*

Hoyt still knows everything he knows. But there are ineffable pleasures in playing stupid. If he had his way he would pass without pause into genuine and sincere stupidity, commensurate with his position in life. Unfortunately his intelligence, the fruit of his early industry, refuses to die, like the stink that is about to explode from *mephitis mephitis.*

Hoisting its tail, the skunk unleashes its spray on the tarpaulin. Hoyt uses the plastic to cover the cage, picking it up and returning to the truck. Fumbling through the tarp to open the cage door, he upends the cage, and the skunk plummets into the garbage pail. Hoyt fastens the lid over it.

Later, at home, he'll dispatch the critter with a .22 CB, single shot to the head, then hand over the pelt to Googie Bains, an aide at the nursing home and amateur taxidermist.

The Mistress of the Manor (Hoyt calls her MOM) has no idea he shoots the skunks and raccoons he traps on her property. She has asked him please to release the creatures in some other vicinity, a "humane" act that only makes them somebody's else's problem. Typical: MOM sees nothing contradictory in driving twenty miles in a gas-guzzling atmosphere-choking SUV to buy organic vegetables.

Hoyt just ignores her. Her husband, not Audrey, hired him to be caretaker, and Jack Meltzer understands that pests must die. And there is no more humane method than a bullet to the *medulla oblongata.* It's what Hoyt would choose for himself, if he had half a mind. (In fact, if he did have half a mind, it would be a mercy and a pleasure to blast out the remainder.)

Opening the cab door, Hoyt releases Pete. He'd bought the mutt from a shelter and now he charges the Meltzers fifty dollars a month for Pete to chase away Canada geese. Tearing across the lawn, Pete scatters the birds from the putting green, pursuing them to the artificial lake, where it bounds ecstatically into the water, content to churn and bark all day long until they get the picture.

Hoyt's neck still hurts from last night's collision with Marly Walczak. Maybe he should buy one of those foam cervical collars.

Meanwhile, he has to make his rounds.

Of the estate's thirty acres, twenty are wooded and ten cleared for the 10,000 square-foot country-French-style manor, the tennis court, lap pool, fishing lake, horse barn (never occupied), formal garden, remote-controlled waterfall, great lawn, and topiary maze.

The latter, MOM's creation, never fails to crack Hoyt up: that anyone would want to construct a claustrophobic labyrinth in the middle of such open splendor. Bathed in sun and sky, the property is perched on a high hill above Graynier, opposite its smaller sister Rowell Hill, boasting views of two counties beyond. So what does the Mistress of the Manor do but put up a maze of eight-foot hedges to hide in? "It's a beautiful place to meditate," she claims, though the only evidence of transcendental activity Hoyt has ever seen is a bong and a book of soggy matches hidden behind a stone bench— probably belonging to the Meltzers' 13-year-old daughter (currently at theater camp), who won't be coming up this summer.

For three weeks the region has seen no rain; patches of the lawn have turned brown. He turns on the underground sprinklers, which he really should have done every day of the drought. He will have to leave the sprinklers on all night to coax the grass back.

Hoyt is helplessly devoted to the art of negligence. Audrey Meltzer has pointed this out a hundred times to her husband, but Jack Meltzer always gives his caretaker the benefit of the doubt. Jack just flat out likes the guy. He's impressed and amused that his property manager can quote Chaucer and draft a will. Sometimes he invites Hoyt in for a drink, opens up a prize bottle of Meursault or Medoc from his wine cellar, and they shoot the shit, which leaves Jack with the agreeable feeling of fraternizing with a salt-of-the-earth local without having to lower himself. Hoyt is his intellectual superior, he doesn't mind admitting. Also a hell of a raconteur, a decent fellow, and honest.

Leaving "decent" and "honest" aside, Meltzer is mistaken that Hoyt Eddy is a local. He is the son of Hamilton Eddy of the Boston Eddys, a well-heeled, Catholic, hard-working, entrepreneurial family. Hoyt's father ran a mutual fund, and begat six boys, of whom Hoyt was the youngest and—conceived during his parents' divorce—the least welcome.

Absorbed into the father's new household, Hoyt's older brothers were overseen by his second wife, a brisk, rosy woman with four sons of her own. (These later turned out also to have been sired by Hamilton Eddy.) Hoyt was left with his mother Maeve.

Hoyt's earliest memory is of lying in his crib and seeing the shape of his mother's head beating rhythmically against the bars as she kneeled on the floor, sobbed and prayed. In place of any lullaby was the unchained melody of Maeve's prayers; her hiccupping cigarette-roughened voice pleading with God, Jesus, and the Holy Spirit, to take away her sins, cleanse her of hatred, and murder Hamilton Eddy and his bitch in their bed.

As Hoyt grew up, his mother's church-fueled hysteria landed them both on the streets. She'd given away the divorce settlement money to the parish and then entered a cloister, briefly putting Hoyt in a foster home. But when the nuns found out how crazy she was, they showed her the door. Collecting Hoyt, she moved them into a homeless shelter for a few weeks, and from there to Seattle, where she got a job at a florist's. She seemed to be waking up from her nightmare.

Then, when Hoyt was thirteen, she disappeared.

He continued going to school, living on what food she had left behind in the apartment, not telling anyone what had happened. Evenings, after football practice, he used his bus pass to travel all over the city, searching for her in every Catholic church and shelter he could find.

He loved Maeve. He was her little husband, her soul mate, her soldier; "my sword," she said. Forgiving her, picking up after her, soothing her rages, forcing her to eat, letting her sleep in his bed when she couldn't settle—he had no idea who he was without her.

A year after her disappearance, a post card arrived from Asia, forwarded by the Seattle post office to Boston, where Hoyt was by now living with his dad. Maeve wrote that she was working in a Catholic mission in Cambodia; she was at peace with herself, and asked Hoyt's forgiveness.

Hoyt was in no mood to forgive. Uprooted from a life of drama and chaos, he was in shock: marooned in a highly regulated, even-keeled household of over-achievers. Everyone was his own man here. Everyone slept in separate beds. No one had ever held his mother's head under the shower, washing clumps of shit out of her hair where she'd smeared it in penance for her sins. His brothers and half-brothers had Hamilton Eddy, his firm hand, sober love, and high expectations.

Ham Eddy's other sons kept their eyes trained forward, rarely talking to Hoyt, marching to collect their prizes and degrees with regimental precision. Ham had his own reasons for averting his eyes from his youngest son. Hoyt knew too much. He too had been sucked into Maeve's crazy, throbbing allure, had waded into the same muddy bog. And young Hoyt knew that Ham had the same weakness, that bent toward her madness. Not only had his father coupled with it, he still secretly pined for its tyrannical rhythms.

Submitting to the Hamilton Eddy program of hard, character-building work, Hoyt tried his best to make his dad proud. He was a quick study, nimble with words, brighter even than his brothers. But his heart was flayed, a salt tide of hormones surging into the wound. His grades rose and fell spasmodically; he became hostile to authority.

At sixteen, he was diagnosed as hyperactive and prescribed medication, which he sold to other students, since he was already embroiled in a passionate romance with paint thinner.

His exasperated father sent him to work on a country road crew in southeastern Massachusetts for the summer.

Hoyt seemed to thrive on outdoor labor and the community of laughing, cursing, shirtless brutes. He loved the hot hazy air, the exorbitant July foliage, the smell of wet tar, the filth that covered him until the evening shower and headlong collapse into bed.

The advent of August found the crew repaving a minor route near Graynier. One night at a bar, scarfing buffalo wings and brew with his fellows, Hoyt caught the eye of a waitress ten years his senior. She brought over the check, and the other guys grinned in Hoyt's direction. "The trust fund baby's buying tonight," someone said.

The waitress was late on her rent and must have thought the rich boy might leave some gratitude on her dresser if she did him up good, a hope fanned by the fifty dollar bill he threw down on the check.

"Do you have anything smaller?" she asked.

"No." He didn't even look her way.

"Well, do you have anything bigger?"

The men guffawed. "Reach in his pocket and find out!"

Hoyt's face burned redder than his sunburn. Up until then, he had successfully avoided women, still poking the embers of resentment toward his mother. But something, maybe the waitress' boggy odor, drew him back into the treacherous delta of womanity. Egged on by his cohorts, Hoyt spent the night in her little room above the bar.

Three nights later, when the road crew moved on to the next county, he left the waitress nothing except the memory of his ropy, sunburnt muscles, his blue, prematurely haunted eyes, and how odd he was, both insolent and shy. For his part, he would remember how she made him a man. He still held onto his misogyny, but he had discovered that a woman could be hammered down to size with the skilled use of his blunt instrument. It was almost a duty to do so: to neutralize the foe.

Inspired, he knocked up three girls back at school in quick succession. After the third request for abortion money, Ham Eddy gave up on Hoyt. Tired of raising sons, he decided to cut his losses. Though he agreed to pay for the rest of Hoyt's education, there would be no more beyond that: the boy was hereby disinherited.

As if chastened, Hoyt immediately applied himself to his studies, and never faltered. As his years of education extended from high school to university to graduate school, his master's degree in European literature was followed by a law degree, and Ham Eddy began to feel the prickings of fatherly pride despite himself.

Then Hoyt moved on to business school for two years, studying human resources management. Next came agricultural college, two years in animal husbandry. By now his father suspected he was being hustled. When Hoyt tried to enroll in divinity school at the age of thirty, Ham retracted his promise, cutting his son off for good.

Once again, Hoyt found himself undefined. Who was he? For all of his childhood he'd been an adjutant to his mother's fury: a page to her rage. Then from sixteen to thirty he'd become the vengeful scholar, determined to have his old man pay through the nose for a never-ending education.

Now it was time to put his abundant knowledge to some use. He had no particular ambition. Where should he live? He was a campus rat. What attachments did he have? His male friendships were fleeting, and he had never fucked any woman long enough to fall in love. Who was he? Where did he belong?

He pictured himself hanging his attorney's shingle in a quiet, affordable town, not too much work, plenty of time to himself to reread the classics and walk back country roads in the snow; under a canopy of green trees in the summer.

His thoughts wandered back to Graynier. For three days there, he dimly remembered, he had felt himself emerging as *something*—a man, a free working man. He remembered the smell of the leaves, the tar, the beer nuts, and his own sweat, pungent and eager; remembered a woman who lived above the bar; the excitement and anticipation as his manhood came forward to greet him.

Could he force time to yield up that moment again?

Another force was pulling him back to Graynier, one he wouldn't have understood even if he had been aware of it. Something darker, baser, unnamable, like the suck of a bog, like a mother's mud embrace.

Buying a small bungalow at the foot of Rowell Hill, he had started out full of enterprise. He rented an office in town for his law practice, posting his ad in the community bluebook and The *Graynier Gazette*. He introduced himself at churches, town meetings, high school sports rallies. He was handsome and magnetic—too good for the sorry little town, really. Jobs began to trickle in: a property closing here, an estate filing there.

He made the rounds of the bars, handing out his card at the Graynier Saloon, Shicker Shack, The Hut, and O'Malley's Mare.

One night on his way home he stopped off at the Mare to chat with the owner, Russ. It was Saint Patrick's Day; the place was crammed with singles. At one end of the bar, a trio of women wearing plastic leprechaun hats took turns shooting glances at him. At the opposite end, a small middle-aged man of Indian descent was giving a hicky to a scrawny flaccid-breasted fortyish blonde in a green sweater.

Spotting his mortgage officer across the room with a couple of cute bank tellers, Hoyt took his glass over to their table. A woman stepped in his path.

"Aren't you gonna say hi?"

It was the hickeyed blonde in the green sweater. She was smiling broadly; he noticed a back molar was missing. She struck a challenging pose, one hand coyly covering the burst vessels on her neck. Apparently she thought this was provocative.

"I'm meeting friends," he said.

"Aren't we friends?" she teased. "Whoops, more than friends, I'd say."

He remembered there was a ten in his pocket, change from the gas station. He proffered the bill. "Go have another on me," he said, hoping to get rid of her.

Instead she roped her arms around his neck, pulling him in tight. "I can't believe it's you. Hoyt! You came back!"

Despite himself, the pressure of her deflated tits against

his ribs woke up his dick.

The next thing he knew, she was weeping with happiness. "Ohmigod, ohmigod, ohmigod." She snuffled tears back up her nose, taking her hand away from the hicky to fan herself.

He looked at her wet, hope-filled eyes, the wrinkled lids powdered blue, her lips coated in some sticky petroleum product. Even through the odor of whiskey and sawdust he knew her scent. She was the waitress of his sixteenth summer.

Somewhere in the back of his mind he had known, when he moved to Graynier, that this encounter might happen. He had been content to leave it to chance, but now he wondered if he had sought it all along, wanting a reprise of the past—so that she might answer the question a second time, and show him what kind of man he was.

But he hadn't reckoned on her aging badly.

She fumbled in the purse hanging from her shoulder, handing him a photo. "Look. Guess who!"

He glanced at the picture of a grim overweight adolescent girl. "That's Pearl," she said. "She's your daughter, honey."

He smelled bait, saw the trap. He lifted cold eyes to hers. "The hell she is."

Her smile vanished as he thrust the photo back at her. "Hoyt, it's Marly. Don't you remember me?"

"No," he lied. "Somehow you know my name, but that hardly makes us acquainted." As she rocked back, he observed her clinically, verifying the wound. Then he flashed his handsome grin. "However, we can fix that. What's your name again?" And smacked her lightly on the rump.

Later, leaving Marly's bed while she slept, he stumbled over the dog in the corridor, falling against Pearl's door. The girl, fourteen then, stuck her head out: "What the fuck?"

Hoyt apologized, barely glancing at her as he moved off.

Outside, he stood in the gray dawn light. Marly had indeed answered his question a second time. Now he knew what kind of man he was: a man who didn't give a shit.

What was he doing here, in this town of all places? He felt suddenly that he would never leave, as if he were condemned to the spot. The hills leaned in, the sky pressed down; here he would stay.

Graynier was his home because it held his truth. He belonged here in this shithole because he was shit. He neither gave a shit about the whore he'd knocked up nor the fat kid who might or might not be his. He would go on banging Marly, now and then: it didn't mean anything. His feelings were dead.

And, being dead, required burial. He went back in Marly's trailer and swiped a bottle of tequila.

TURNING ON THE JETS in the Meltzers' steam room, Hoyt strips off his clothes. He sits on the tile banquette to sweat out the skunk odor, swigging from a bottle of Jack Meltzer's Meursault.

The wine fails to anesthetize the pain in his neck.

Images of the accident return. The girl suddenly appears in his truck lights; he rakes the wheel to the left...the car out of nowhere...the smash. His neck in a hot noose of pain.

He curses Marly. He drinks. He curses the girl in the road. He should have pasted her to the grill.

Later, he lies naked on the Meltzers' bed, letting his body dry in the breeze from the balcony.

He imagines MOM walking in and catching him. Opening her mouth to scream. He clamps one hand over her mouth, inserting the other between her legs. His fingers find her cleft, squeezing forth the juice until she groans for release. He throws her onto the bed, straddles her, grips a fistful of her hair to hold her head steady, guiding his member to her mouth. She opens to receive it...and laughing, he empties his bladder on her face.

Hoyt's laughter subsides. He listens to the birds outside—larks, a phoebe, a raucous jay—as he strokes himself. His penis is unresponsive, pickled from the long bender begun that gray dawn in the trailer park.

And that's the way he wants it. Deny them the satisfaction—take away their bone! If Jack Meltzer had any sense, he'd do the same. Instead, he has to lie here just like Hoyt, awaiting the will of the Mistress of the Manor. Under the white canopy, between four posters, the swagged bed curtains like white thighs, his head in their vise, he is doomed to his cage.

Mephitis mephitis.

CHAPTER FIVE

Collin clings to the slick obsidian rock. Foam-topped waves furl toward him, one after another and another. The sea rises like a chest filling with breath. He pounds his fists on the rock, *Let me in!* But he knows what will happen. He has been stuck in this dream before.

The rock will change into a house, and he will continue to bang on its door, screaming over the waves and wind, but the door will stay shut and he will remain locked outside.

And locked outside the dream is his body, limp as a corpse on his bed. The body's mouth will open, and his screams escape. His mother will come into the bedroom, wake him up, and take him in her arms. And still he won't feel safe. For days after, the memory will cling: shut out of his home, engulfed by a relentless tide, choking on water. Dying.

His silence, his wariness, his privately held terrors make him a strange child to his peers, his teachers, even to his mother and grandparents. "Seems confused, possibly has a learning disability," the school counselor notes, suggesting tests and meds.

But why shouldn't he be confused? There's the matter of his skin. As long as he has been alive, he has heard from his family: black is best. "You come from kings," they say, then glance at each other, which he interprets to mean *even though you're not actually black.*

Once again, he's locked out of the club, his cries ripped away by the wind.

Gita Poonchwalla is the first person to open a door, to make him feel he belongs. In fact, he is crucial to her plans.

"You're the Tawny One," she always says. "The one I've been waiting for."

This morning his father wakes him from the dream, calling "Breakfast!" from downstairs. Collin still isn't used to Brett's voice: the flat cadence, the absence of vigor. No "Git yo' black be-*hine* down here!" like his grandmother, or "Don't you be missin'at *bus* now" like his mother.

His college-educated mom always switches to another voice if some white person needs handling. She can "go Webster" as she puts it, speaking in the careful, armored tones of a newscaster, her eyes going hooded if that person gets a false idea about her friendliness.

Collin wishes the whole skin thing would just fade away. Gita Poonchwalla says anything is possible through prayer, so Collin recites the "*Our Gana Mother of Fire,*" then the "*Yenu Krisnu Fills My Soul,*" as she has taught him. Then he makes a silent plea: *let Jane be gone this morning.*

But when he goes down for breakfast, she's still there.

Jane is the whitest person he has ever seen. Way past white, as if she's from some realm where there's no sun at all and the inhabitants produce their own eerie glow like fireflies.

Collin slides into his chair. He notes the paper towel folded like a triangle beside his plate. He smells Canadian bacon frying, French toast and coffee. Pots of different jams sit in the middle of the table.

It was never like this before Jane came. There was only the cereal box on the table, and Collin fetched his own milk, spoon, and bowl. Later his father would come yawning downstairs to open a Coke and unwrap a granola bar.

Jane lifts her eyes to Collin. "I'm still here," she says, seeming to read his mind. Unfolding her paper towel, she smoothes it on her lap as if it's fine linen. "Did you sleep well?"

Collin grunts, instead of saying *No I didn't, I had nightmares 'cause you took my room.*

The day after she arrived, his dad took her upstairs to offer her the middle bedroom. "Jane is going to stay a while," he told Collin, who was trailing them suspiciously.

"Why?"

Brett paused on the landing. "Because she needs a place to stay until she...figures things out."

Meanwhile Jane passed the middle room without looking in. Instead, she walked right into Collin's room.

"Hey!" Collin trotted anxiously after her.

Inside his room, Jane was turning slowly in circles, a crazy smile on her face.

"This is my room!" She pointed to the wall opposite the window, where a bookcase stood. "My bed was there. I remember!"

"Jane used to live in this house," Brett explained to Collin.

She added, "Perhaps if I sleep here, I shall remember more."

"Collin, you don't mind switching rooms," his dad asked— *told*—him. "The other one's bigger."

"It smells gross!"

Jane stooped to examine the baseboard molding. "There was a mouse hole...gone now." She turned again to Brett. "Yes, I am quite convinced this room is mine!"

So Collin moved into the stinky room, which didn't smell any better after Brett vacuumed the whole upstairs and even cleaned the bathroom. Later she had him open up the weird box in the living room, which unfolded into some kind of keyboard instrument. They stood around mystified, and then Brett dragged Collin out with him to show Jane around town.

What wouldn't he do for this complete stranger? "It's like he's voodoo'd," Grandma would say. How long before Jane puts the spell on Collin?

He chants the "*Our Gana*" to himself for protection.

Across the table, Jane stares at him, her gaze like a chill hand around his heart. Suddenly the dream returns: the dark rock, the rising tide, the door, the choking, the fear—

"Dad!" Slipping off his chair, Collin tries to escape into the kitchen.

His father blocks the door, holding a plate of French toast and bacon. "What's the matter?"

"Can I skip breakfast? I'm not hungry."

"Sit down, Collin. We have a guest."

He pushes away his fear and sits again, staring straight back at Jane. He'll study her and make a report to Gita, who is very interested in evil.

Brett fetches the coffee. "Thank you," Jane says. Then they're all looking down at the food on their plates.

"I've never made French toast before. I got the recipe online. Wasn't so hard. Collin, be polite and eat."

The boy takes a bite, watching Jane from the corner of his eye. She picks up her fork and knife, cutting the toast into neat little squares.

"I also did a search on that keyboard contraption," Brett continues. "It's a *seraphine*. Does that ring a bell?"

She repeats the word quizzically, "Seraphine...no. I only remember playing it. Although I've forgotten how."

"It works off pedals and bellows. They started making them around 1830. After twenty years everyone started switching to harmoniums."

He's showing off his brains, Collin thinks. His mom calls Brett a "propeller-head."

"What are your plans today?" Brett asks Jane.

"I believe I shall walk a while."

"I was thinking the same. I'll get some work done, then we'll go out."

She's meticulously dividing each square of toast in two. "I prefer to be on my own this day. When I walk alone, without design, my thoughts will sense a loosening of the reins, and wander where they will. It's a most pleasant delinquency."

Brett seems stuck for a response. *She be buggin' out, talkin' at Websta shit*, Collin thinks.

She continues subdividing her breakfast. His dad's eyes are so slapped to her face, he doesn't seem to notice that for all her motions she isn't actually eating, the bits of toast reduced to a pile of pebbles she brushes to the side of her plate. Collin didn't see her eat yesterday either. Doesn't eat food, bloodlessly pale...

All at once, Collin knows what she is. *There's a vampire in our house.*

"Where's your coffin?" he blurts.

His father looks shocked.

"I have none," Jane laughs, disconcerted. "What a curious question."

"Collin, you're excused."

Heading upstairs, he hears Brett apologizing to her: "Bizarre thing to say. Sometimes I can't fathom that kid."

Collin used to think things would get better between his dad and him. He liked that Brett sometimes came into the bedroom at night, lingering on the other side of the mosquito net, showing a father's concern. He was impressed by Brett's fingers flying over the computer keyboard as he created web pages. Brett even asked him to keep a secret—that he used to be a master hacker until one of his friends got arrested, though he still sometimes breaks into bank accounts for fun. Collin actually stopped hating his dad's skinny arms and halting conversation.

It would have been easy to erase the gap. He could have just leaned his head on Brett's shoulder, slipped his hand into his father's, smiled up into his eyes, and reversed the misery of the summer; he held that power. Collin had planned on using it when he was ready. And then his father's love, safe harbor, would have been his.

Then Collin could tell his own secrets. About Gita and the spiritual mission they've embarked upon together. About his only friend at school, Khansee, an adopted boy from Laos who speaks incomprehensible English, wears very dark glasses to avoid getting seizures from the fluorescent lights, and every year since third grade sends Collin a meticulously hand-drawn Valentine signed "A Mysterious Friend Ha Ha." He could tell how when his mother's out he likes to lay out her silk scarves on her bed and roll in them, then fold them perfectly afterwards and put them back in her drawer. He could even tell Brett about the drowning dreams.

But it's too late. Now that Jane has arrived, his father is all hers, offering his neck to the demon.

Gita will know what to do.

BRETT FRETS ABOUT his son's foul temper. Yesterday, when he asked Collin along to show Jane around town, the boy was sullen, dragging his feet and glowering the whole way.

Jane herself didn't seem quite present as Brett pointed out the tabernacle, the maples, the stumps of elms dead from disease; the library, the car wash, the historical society, the nursing home. She nodded distantly, her gray eyes darting around, seeking something familiar—without success, it seemed.

A text came from his boss as they were wandering down Graynier Avenue. Brett angled his cell phone against the hazy sunlight to read the message. On impulse, he surreptitiously turned the camera on Jane, capturing her almond-shaped face, solemn eyes, mousy blond hair pulled back in a knot, as she stood against a backdrop of splashy green leaves and the vertical of a street sign.

Later, near the foot of Putman Hill, Brett suggested they turn back. But Jane's attention was riveted on an empty field across the road. A banner in the grass read: "ST. PAUL'S FAIR AUGUST 9-11 GAMES RIDES RAFFLE."

Jane turned to Brett and Collin, her brow furrowing. "Something was here in this field. Something of importance."

She glanced this way and that, like a hound searching for a scent.

Collin emitted a huge sigh. "Can I go to Gita's now?"

"No." His father's focus was on Jane, whose eyes filled with tears of frustration. He put his hand on her slender shoulder. "What's wrong?"

"Fragments come to me and I don't understand them. But they have a certainty—I *know* them to be true, as I know my name is Jane and I was born in Graynier. If they come not from my memory, then where?"

"Why can't I go?" Collin piped up. "This is retarded."

Brett wheeled on him sharply. "I'll let you go when you show some basic courtesy toward our visitor."

"She's not a visitor if she's staying," Collin retorted.

HIS SON HAS a point. "How long do you plan on sleeping here?" Brett asks, watching Jane crowd the French toast rubble onto her fork and lift it to her mouth.

"Until I understand everything." The fork lightly clicks against her teeth as her lips close over the food.

Women are forever taking advantage of him. This one won't even provide straight answers to questions he has every right to know. Instead she gives charming evasions, which fascinate him, weakening his resolve. He will have to take a hard line. "You're welcome for as long as you want, if you help out on the rent."

She looks up eagerly. "I shall give you all I have."

"You don't need to give me everything..."

"I have 62 dollars."

"That's it?"

"Alas."

Alas? Who talks this way? "Where are you from, anyway? I mean, before you came back here."

Her light, cool hand covers his; her gray eyes are affectionate. "It doesn't matter. I'm here, and I belong here, and with your kind forbearance, I'll stay."

Later, when Brett is washing the breakfast dishes, her words echo: *your kind forbearance.* She speaks like some ersatz "maiden" with a tankard at a Renaissance fair. Or someone out of an old book.

His mind trails to high school sophomore English, when all the girls were sighing over *Wuthering Heights*, a book that made the boys go bulimic, and what was the other one? *Jane Eyre*. Another Jane.

After Collin goes to Gita's and Jane goes for her walk, Brett has the house to himself. He calls the rental agent to ask who owned the house before the minister.

She has no idea. "Father Petrelli has lived there as long as I've been alive, and I'm thirty."

No way is Jane that old. She couldn't have been born in this house. What could be her motive to lie? (To gain entry; she needs a hideout.) She might be a runaway (but she looks a little too old to be a minor). There might be people looking for her. It would account for her secretiveness. Her name could be something other than Jane—for Jane Doe?

Brett goes into her bedroom, which she has left so tidy it could be unoccupied but for the pink duffel shoved deep under her bed. He gets down on all fours and pulls the bag out.

Emptying its contents onto the floor, he sifts through several pairs of underpants, cheap rayon skirts and blouses, a purple anorak, and a long nightgown, all with tags still attached from a Dress Depot outlet. Also a travel case with toothpaste, toothbrush, tampons, shampoo and body wash; a folded Massachusetts map; and three 20s and two singles: $62 exactly.

No credit cards or identification.

Inside the duffel he discovers a small zipper pocket in the inner lining, which holds a set of Toyota car keys on a ring. The ring's medallion is a laminated photo of a lounging tabby cat, looking surprised by the camera flash.

Brett calls the nearest Dress Depot outlet; a helpful manager deciphers the location of Jane's purchases through the store code on her price tags: Deer Run, Pennsylvania. He finds Deer Run on an internet map: it's a small town off a major route in the Poconos. It might be her home, or a place she passed through on her way to Graynier.

The duffel has given him enough information to coax the

truth out of her, if he goes about it carefully.

"I WAS THINKING of taking Collin on a trip to the Poconos. Do you know that area?"

"No."

"Well, but have you ever been through there?"

"No." Jane is back from her walk, dusty and depleted, gulping down the glass of orange juice Brett has brought into the parlor. They sit together in the breeze from the standing fan.

Thinking of the cat photo on the key chain, Brett says, "Maybe Collin needs a pet. What would you want, a kitten maybe?"

Her eyes smile over the rim of the glass. "I should want a little mouse. To live in the wall, and visit me sometimes."

"You never had a cat?"

"No." Suspicion flickers across her face. He's pushing too hard. He changes the subject. "Looks like you got a touch of sunburn," he remarks. "I'll buy you a hat at the mall. They have a lot of nice shops. Do you like Dress Depot?"

"Is that a shop?"

"You've never heard of it?"

"Truly not." But her expression is cagey. He's aware the clock is running out on his inquest.

"Anyway, you should see the mall. Want to drive my car? You have a license, right?"

She frowns. "I have never driven a car."

"You could get you a learner's permit and I'll teach you."

"No, thank you." She rises from the sofa. "I shall take my bath now."

After Jane goes upstairs, it comes to him: *she's Amish.* There's a community in Pocono country where they speak in an anachronistic dialect and don't use cars but horse-drawn buggies. *My mind senses a loosening of the reins,* she'd said.

He grows excited as all the pieces come together: she has just escaped from a culture rigidly stuck in the past. She had to ditch the homespun clothes and buy new outfits from Dress Depot, so she could blend into the outside world.

He would solve the riddle of the Toyota keys later.

Are her people out looking for her? Would they have notified the police? Or do the Amish have their own police? How long before they catch up with her? How long to reach Graynier from Pennsylvania in a horse and buggy?

How long does he have before someone takes her away?

He can't pry further into her secret or he will lose her. She is hiding out with Brett because instinctively she knows he is the kind of man who will protect her. And so he will. In time she may trust him with the truth. Maybe even come to love him.

He will hold her delicate, pliant body in his arms, childish and chaste. *My own Jane. Mine.*

CHAPTER SIX

*J*ing-a-ling.

Marly wakes up just before three a.m. The heat is fetid inside the single wide trailer. Her nightgown is pushed up around her armpits and damp with sweat. For a moment she can't think of what woke her.

Then she remembers. It was the tinkling of the bell on the gate outside. Someone either arriving or leaving.

It must be Russ going off, because he's no longer beside her in bed. She waits to hear his delivery van start up, the tires rolling off the grass onto the blacktop, the vanishing thrum of the engine as he hightails it home to his wife.

Pook rises from his station at the end of the mattress and totters over to lick her face, scattering the hard little poops he deposited earlier on the sheet. Eighteen, blind and incontinent, the terrier needs to be within 10 feet of Marly at all times; her smutty odor orients him.

Whenever she puts him out of the bedroom, an accordion gate keeps him from going into the kitchen and jumping on the banquette, and from there to the counter, where he would ravage cereal boxes and choke on party-mix. The gate exiles him to the narrow corridor running past Pearl's bedroom (door always closed) to Marly's room (door always ajar). Pook knows from bitter experience that if he stays in this corridor, he will be stepped on by Marly, or her hefty daughter, or one of Marly's men groping his way to the bathroom.

The dog's hearing is still excellent. After whatever man is on top of Marly makes that loud moan or curses enthusiastically, passes out or puts on his clothes and leaves, Pook knows he can hop on the bed and go to sleep enveloped in the familiar odor of sex.

Jing-a-ling.

Did Russ forget something and come back? Marly doesn't hear his boots on the front step, or the pop of the latch. Sliding out of bed, she stands up, her head starting to pound. Ever since the collision—with Hoyt of all people!—she's been living on Advil. Might be whiplash or something. No, just a headache, she tells herself. And: it could be worse.

Pushing the burlap window curtain aside, she peers out. She can't see anyone outside. Russ' van is gone. The gate is closed, the bell still.

Marly is puzzled. Only some living thing opening or jostling the gate would cause the bell to ring. The fence keeps Pook from roaming, but the merry tinkle of the bell she installed signals the approach of company, the departure of company, the flow of life.

Now she's awake, and hot. Maybe if she cracks a beer and watches TV in the kitchen, the string of infomercials will send her back to sleep. In another five hours she and Pearl have to go to work.

Glancing at her bureau, she is gratified to see a few folded bills there. Russ always leaves something—unlike Seth Poonchwalla, who seems to think that she should pay *him* for the honor of receiving his seventeen-year-old uncut manhood. Seth's father is not much more generous, plus he leaves marks on her neck.

Marly never discusses money, leaving it up to the men to decide if she was worth rewarding. It makes the money seem more like a gift, a pleasant surprise. Marly doesn't consider herself a prostitute, a delusion that keeps her sunny.

Turning on the light above the sink, she removes a can of Miller Lite from the fridge. Pain flares in her head as she pops the ring on the can, peeling the tab back. The ring breaks off in her hand, a thin spout of foam shooting from the can.

After she tosses it in the sink to spend itself, she notices a bead of blood appearing on her finger: the metal flap on the can must have sliced it.

About to run cold water over the cut, she hears a tinkling sound outside.

Jing-a-ling.

The bell on the gate. For the third time.

The hairs on her arms prickle; from the bedroom, Pook growls. Switching on the outdoor light, Marly pushes the front door open, stepping out into the yard.

Crickets grind away. The moon confers a monotonous tint to the neighborhood: swing sets, barbecue grills, rubber trash cans, droopy hydrangeas, basketball hoops, and her maimed car. Getting the headlight fixed cost her plenty; the bashed-in grill will have to wait until she wins the lottery (it could easily happen).

She checks the white plastic picket fence. The gate stands open just a few inches, barely enough for a cat to slip through. Between the time Marly peered out her bedroom window and popped a beer in the kitchen—five minutes at most—someone unlatched it.

Warily she looks around the tiny enclosed yard, dread brushing across her skin like a trailing spiderweb. No sign of anyone.

Then she feels a wetness on her palms. She glances down.

A strange, dark liquid covers her hands.

Scrambling back into the kitchen, she studies her arms under the well of light. The liquid is red, thin and warm as blood. Before her eyes, the stain spreads quickly, flowing upwards, against gravity, over her wrists and branching up to her elbows.

"Oh!" She wrenches the sink faucet on, whimpering. The beer

tab must have sliced her finger deeper than she realized—though she feels no stab of pain as she splashes water over her arms, rinsing the red off.

She turns her clean hands, looking for cuts. Her skin is whole, unruptured. No gash or wound anywhere that could have produced so much blood.

Noticing red smears on her nightgown, she wrestles it off in disgust, stuffing it in her laundry and putting the bag by the front door. She'll take it to the laundromat tomorrow after work.

Sleep will erase everything bad, she knows: sleep and the light of day, letting a person bounce out of bed with a positive attitude.

You won't get off that easy, the pounding in her head argues. She takes four Advils, climbs back into bed and hugs Pook to her heart, waiting for oblivion.

THE GRAYNIER BED & BREAKFAST is a splendid old mansion; Marly is proud to walk into it every day. When Graynier Glass ruled the town, the house was Philip Graynier's; now old Mrs. McBee runs it as an inn.

In the breakfast room, several inn guests are helping themselves to the buffet. Mrs. McBee summons Marly to her table where she always takes her morning tea.

The other employees may call Mrs. McBee a "stingy, dried-up old coochie" behind her back, but Marly refuses to think ill of her. The old dear puts an extra twenty in Marly's pay envelope every Christmas. Twenty's not nothing.

"Gabriella just phoned me," says Mrs. McBee bitterly, wired as usual on three cups of Oolong. "She's going to have a baby, she says."

Marly's co-worker is a peppy petite young Brazilian woman working three jobs. "Wow. That's so great." Marly eyes the coffee urn; after last night's weird events, she needs a strong caffeine infusion. McBee doesn't offer her any. "How far along is she?"

"She is having her baby *today*." Mrs. McBee's lips press together; she exhales sharply through her nose. "I never noticed she was pregnant, did you?"

"No, ma'am." Marly must admit that Gabriella had looked plumper during the past month. But no more than you'd be after a couple of milkshakes. *She hid it better than me,* she thinks. Marly had gotten fired from her barmaid job in the fourth month.

Name: Pearl Amy Walczak. Weight: 7 lbs 2 oz. Recorded Time of Birth: 5:38 p.m. Mother: Marlene Josefina Walczak. Father: Unknown.

Mrs. McBee fumed, "That means the child will be an American citizen. That's what they're all after. More mouths for the taxpayers to feed. Last night I wanted to watch *Hello Dolly* and it was in Spanish! Well, you'll have to do her rooms today in addition to your own."

A few hours later, after Marly finishes her ground floor rooms, she stops by the front desk to beg some Tylenol from Frankie the receptionist. "Got a punishing headache, hon."

Wheeling her cleaning cart down the second-floor corridor, she wonders, *Why am I being punished? What have I done to deserve this? Crumpled car, whiplash, bleeding, migraines...*

Then she scolds herself: *God must have a reason. God doesn't give you more than you can bear. You've been through worse times.* Too many to count, but she won't dwell on them.

Gabriella's rooms await. Marly's plastic clogs shuffle behind the cart; the ancient oak floorboards, with their dark, buttery sheen, crack and snap as loud as a rifle shots.

A guest sidesteps her cart, averting his eyes. She can't remember his name or when he was last here, only that she spent an hour in his room after work. He wore a lace thong and told her to call him Joanne.

Mrs. McBee doesn't know she has the only one of the Top-20 New England Country Inns with a whore on staff. Marly's patrons are discreet. She likes to think she's doing her little bit to enhance the place's popularity.

Starting in on Gabriella's rooms, Marly feels the pain in her head intensify, bumping around her skull like a trapped balloon. She rushes carelessly through her duties: slipping paper bands over toilet seats without cleaning them; refilling hair conditioner mini-bottles with body lotion; kicking dirty towels under beds.

In her final room, something rackets in the vacuum cleaner. Shaking the tube out, she finds a gold brooch with a broken catch. Pretty, though: a wreath of two roses entwined. Which proves her point: just when you think things are bad, heaven sends a little something to cheer you up.

Marly slips it into her pocket. Maybe Pearl will like the piece. Not that her daughter gives a hoot about her appearance; every morning she leaves the house without a stick of makeup on. It's a crying shame, because she has such a nice face.

When she was born, the nurses said Pearl was the loveliest baby they'd ever seen. But from her first contact with the rubber nipple of a bottle of formula, it became apparent she'd swallow anything.

By middle school she was known as "Hurl." Even now Pearl deliberately fills up with food. She seems to have been born knowing the role she must play: that she must always embody her mother's mistake. And she must forever inflate, by eating and eating, into a bigger and bigger mistake.

On top of that, the girl is abrasive, casting a sullen pall wherever she goes. She has never made any friends. She feeds off her mother's good nature like a tick drinking blood. The more Marly grovels before her, the more contemptuous and self-lacerating Pearl becomes. Their tiny trailer crushes them ever closer together, until even the oxygen seems to seep away, suffocating them.

So gray a pall does Pearl cast that Valyou Mart is the only place willing to hire her. Valyou employs only the most demoralized and blinkered working poor, at punishingly low wages, and with a promise of advancement they all believe (in vain). Pearl works in the stock room, out of sight of the customers who had complained about her attitude.

Still, Marly has never lost faith in her daughter.

She urged anti-depressant medication on the girl. It had no effect. She sent pictures of Pearl to an extreme makeover TV show. When a pre-interview invitation arrived in the mail, Pearl opened the envelope and went into a rage.

"You can't have it both ways, mother. You can't go 'round telling me I'm pretty and then send me off to be blendered. Make up your mind. I'll go on the stupid show if you say to my face I'm ugly as bait. Say it! Say it!"

"Honey, you're very attractive. You just need to believe it."

"Then we have no problem. I do believe it. You know why? Because my mother tells me so every day of my fucking life."

AT SIX O'CLOCK Marly is waiting in her car outside the service exit. Pearl emerges, stripping off her Valyou Mart smock. She heaves onto the passenger seat and slams the door, twisting around to stuff her smock in the laundry bag on the back seat.

"How was your day?" Pulling away from the curb, Marly braces herself for a tirade.

"Sucked the big one. No thanks to the whore in Juniors who told me the stock smelled of smoke and 'You should've asked for a cigarette break,' even though they don't let you take a break for anything, plus I don't smoke. I'm tempted to pee on the stock because they won't let you take a bathroom break—like ever—and then she could complain that the stock smells like piss and for once she'd be right. Where are you going?"

Marly has turned off Route 404 onto Honeyvale. "I have to stop by the laundromat." Remembering the brooch in her pocket, she digs it out and hands it to her daughter.

"What's this?" Pearl turns the bauble in the light.

"An old pin I found. I could polish it for you. It might be valuable, I don't know."

"It's junk." Pearl tosses it out the window.

She goes next door to Madame Bertha's to have her fortune

read while Marly lugs the wash into the laundromat. It's crowded; people sit waiting for machines.

By the time Pearl returns, Marly has only just started sorting the clothes to put into the washers.

"This time Madame Batbrain told me I'm going to inherit a lot of money," Pearl reports, "but for it to happen I have to give her some money to bury in the yard, and it'll be multiplied by a hundred when the inheritance comes through..."

Marly hunts for the bloodstained nightgown; she'll treat it with spray before adding it to the load.

"...I guess the theory is, if I'm stupid enough to give her five bucks for a reading, then I'm stupid enough to give her a thousand so she can blow town. Skank. If I had a grand don't you think I'd blow town myself?"

Pearl notices her mother staring in a panic at her nightgown, flapping it this way and that. "What's the matter?"

"Nothing," mutters Marly, stowing the nightgown in the washer and pushing in the coin slot.

Last night, the blood from her arms had smeared all over the front of the gown, red on white—she saw it.

There were no bloodstains on the nightgown now. Not anywhere.

BY BEDTIME MARLY'S head pain has vanished, never to return. But in its place come the bad dreams.

She dreams about the pale girl she glimpsed just before the accident. The girl stands outside Marly's gate, a long old-fashioned dress draped over her thin figure, gleaming through the night. She lifts her chin, as if to peer at the stars, head straining farther and farther back, until the muscles on the neck give and Marly hears the sound of crackling, of bones separating. Suddenly the woman's head topples to one side, as if snapped off its stalk.

Marly cries out in the dream, then wakes to the sensation of Pook's warm tongue slithering over her hand, ardently licking its way up her arm. She raises herself with a groan, thrusting Pook away. She squints at the clock through the darkness: 3:42. Irritated by the callous red glow of the numbers, she turns its face away, closing her eyes and sinking back on the pillow.

The next minute, the dog is all over her outflung hand, lavishing his tongue on every fold and crevice.

"Pook!"

When she switches on the bedside lamp, the burst of light shows what Pook was licking with such relish.

Red blood, welling under her fingernails, springing up faster than the dog can lick it away.

CHAPTER SEVEN

She's back in the pool.

Seth looks out the window at his sister Gita. She thinks the chlorinated water will lighten her skin. Gita has a drawer full of bleaching creams; she's always adding extra Clorox to the pool, steeping in it for hours.

The various welfare families who live at the motel sit around the pool, dully sopping up the hot sun. Seth's parents are visiting family in Mumbai for three weeks, so he is stuck indoors at the reception desk.

His parents make the trip every summer; usually they take Seth and Gita with them, but this time both children refused.

Seth doesn't mind being Indian, but he hates India.

Gita is okay with India, but she hates being Indian.

Ironic, since only last year she was the world's most obnoxious Hindu, berating her parents for their hypocrisy in joining the St. Paul's Episcopal Church: "You throw away your whole heritage because you're afraid to be different!"

True, but the Poonchwallas like to feel part of the community, and church is a pleasant way to mingle with neighbors and feel accepted. They chose St. Paul's because in mid-August it holds a fair with rides and raffles, and the whole town attends; and the date coincides with the festival of Ganesh, the elephant-headed son of Parvati and Shiva, so the Poonchwallas feel they have only cheated a little on their religion.

"You think being a Christian will make you white!" Gita told her parents, running off her mouth about Krishna and Vishnu at every meal, as if they needed to be taught their own faith. For months she threw herself into worship and meditation, painting a bindi above her unibrow and stumbling around in a sari, until the school asked her to stop.

Of course, Gita would sell her soul to be white.

After the Hindu thing came Gita's holy roller, born-again phase. She rode her bike to First Calvary of Innocents on weekends. Once when it rained, she asked Seth to drive her. He went along because he'd heard that the Pentecostal girls were brilliant at oral sex: all that speaking in tongues. This turned out not to be the case. And the service was bogus beyond belief, like a rave without the Ecstasy—crumpin' with a cross—not to mention non-stop solicitations for money, which he had to lend his sister.

The fun part was when some parishioners testified about their struggles with dope addiction. Seth knew them all.

He's their dealer.

After a month of getting washed in the blood of the Lamb, Gita switched to the Unitarians, taking the bus to Sunday services ten miles away in Quikabukket. There was a mosque nearby, so Gita stuck her head in there too, but they wouldn't let her in.

Eventually, she stopped shopping.

She has something going on, though. Tacked to her bedroom wall are pictures she drew of weird mutants, some kind of private pantheon he can hear her praying gibberish to.

Wack job.

Their parents walk on eggshells around Gita. They seem frightened by both their children, who say and do as they please with sullenness and disrespect, the hallmarks of American adolescence. Frightening children are yet another cost of fitting in. Mother and father have only one condition: that the children excel in math and science. Since both kids post stellar grades in all their subjects, humiliating their peers, the Poonchwallas can feel as if they've gotten back at America.

Seth has a hardon again, something that happens so often the fabric of his tight jeans has gone threadbare and faded from the strain.

If he lived in India, he could be married by now. Even little children get married there. Then he would have someone to fuck whenever he wants—three, four times a day even.

He presses his penis against the handle of the desk drawer. He has got to get laid. One of these nights he'll swing by Marly Walczak's.

He looks up to see the mulatto kid come through the gate, waving eagerly to Gita and stripping to his swim trunks to get in the pool with her. He's here every day. Maybe those two should get married.

"VAMPIRES DON'T EXIST," says Gita. Collin lies splayed on his back in the dead man's float Gita has taught him. "But it could be Shaarinen taking the shape of a vampire to scare you. Shaarinen gets his power from fear. He needs it to take different shapes to make evil."

She keeps her hand under his body, not touching, just poised there in case he panics. But somehow she removes his fear with the power of Gana, the woman god. That makes Gita the personal enemy of Shaarinen; she goes around evaporating all the fear he has taken the trouble to create.

"How do we know for sure that he's Jane?" Collin asks.

"When I see her, I'll know." She tosses aside her long thick black hair, the ends coiling like king snakes in the water. Drops of sweat cling to her moustache. He can't help but be impressed by the implacable eyes, swooping brows, the fierceness jutting from the soft nascent curves of puberty, like rocks tearing through dough. She thumps her hand on her heart, just north of her budding breasts. "It feels like someone's cold hand reaching in, right here."

"I felt it when she looked at me!" Collin is so excited he starts to sink. Gita's hand meets his back, lifting his body back to the surface.

"I have to see her myself." She adds, "You can't go around deciding everyone's Shaarinen. You're new at this."

Collin has trouble keeping up with her religious instruction. The strange names of her gods (Gana, Yenu Krisnu, Hotis) reverberate in his mind as vivid colors: magenta, lime, and gold; not at all like the gray uncertainty of Father, Son, and Holy Ghost. Their names create pungent flavors in his mouth, like the spices in the Poonchwallas' kitchen: cardamom, turmeric, mace. *Gana, Yenu Krisnu, Hotis.*

Gita has told him the legends and drawn their pictures, but Collin still has difficulty remembering who they are and what they do—except for Hotis, who has two penises where breasts should be and two breasts between his/her legs. Somehow he/she (Hotis is both male and female) and Yenu Krishnu (the Tawny One) are part of Gana the Mother. Only Shaarinen is separate, an outsider.

It all makes sense when Gita is talking, but as soon as she stops, it goes right out of Collin's head.

He wants to bring Gita to the house to see Jane today. Not that he has any doubt Jane is Shaarinen: that cold hand has squeezed his heart not once, but twice.

The first time was today at breakfast, and the second time was after his father sent him upstairs. Collin put on his clothes to meet Gita, then crept into his dad's bedroom to swipe some change left on the bureau.

"Put it back." Suddenly Jane was behind him.

The coins were already in his hand when he whirled around. His heart froze; he was in the presence of Shaarinen for sure. He thrust out his chin. "Dad said I could."

"Surely you know God's commandment, 'Thou shalt not steal.'"

But Gita had said it was all right: the money was for tithing.

Tightening his fist, he tried to push past her.

Jane stepped to the side, blocking him. "I will give you some of my money instead." She brought some crumpled dollar bills out of her pocket. "It's already stolen."

"You took it?"

She nodded shyly. "I had little choice. Therefore let me be the sinner, not you."

"A lotta shit over three quarters and a dime," Collin muttered, but he replaced his dad's change on the bureau and took the money from her.

He is justified in hating Jane, he thinks as he and Gita wade to the shallow end of the pool. She's nothing more than a thief.

"Stealing is peanuts for Shaarinen," says Gita. "He'll commit any crime, 'specially murder.'"

She isn't interested in inspecting Jane just yet; today she has planned for them to bike all the way to the Jewish synagogue in Huxberry Heights. Gita will talk their way inside. (Usually she pretends she's writing a school paper on religion.) While the rabbi's back is turned, Collin will take something.

When they staked out the Catholic church near the mall last week, Collin snuck into the sacristy and stole a set of bronze altar bells. Gita rejoined him a block away after she finished interviewing the priest. She said Gana would be pleased by the offering.

Their best heist was pedaling up Putman Hill to the big Meltzer estate and creeping onto the property to steal one of the tiki torches lining the path to the pool. Afterwards, they brazenly coasted down the hill with the torch balanced on Collin's handlebars. Later they lit the wick and, by the light of the propane flame, chanted to Gana until the smoke detector went off in the vacant motel room they were using.

The mission is going well. They'll both be rewarded when they've presented Gana enough offerings.

Unless Shaarinen intervenes.

"There he is!" cries Collin.

Gita's eyes follow his pointing finger to the sidewalk across from the motel. Peering through the chain-link fence that surrounds the pool, she sees a skinny, pasty young woman walking down Graynier Avenue.

"Jane," whispers Collin. He glances eagerly at Gita. "Do you feel anything?"

Gita starts to shiver as Jane walks out of sight. Wading out of the pool, Gita wraps herself in one of the motel's skimpy sandpaper towels. Her teeth are rattling, shoulders trembling.

"Gita...are you okay?"

"Shut *up*. I got a tummy ache is all." After a long moment she stops shaking. "Let's get the bikes."

"You sure you're not sick?"

Ignoring the question, she's already headed to the parking lot. "We're gonna follow her."

AFTER CRUISING EVERY inch of Graynier on their bikes, with Collin pedaling Seth's old banana seater, they give up. Jane is nowhere to be found. A day wasted. Back to Plan A: tomorrow they'll head for Huxberry Heights and the synagogue.

All the same, Collin feels strong. Gita believes him that Jane is evil, and the hunt for Shaarinen is on. His new friend has the courage of titans. If she's not afraid, he won't be either.

He remembers how Gita helped him overcome his fear of water the first night they met. She led him down the pool steps, wading to the middle. The water came to his neck; the floor fell away steeply into the deep end.

"In the name of Gana the Mother of Fire, Hotis, and Yenu Krisnu the Tawny One, I baptize you," she whispered. Grasping the collar of his pajamas, she commanded him to hold his breath and step forward. As his toes met the abyss, she pushed his head under.

Flailing and thrashing, Collin sucked water, his eyes popping open.

He had a vision. Suddenly the bright underwater pool lights were gone: he was drowning in dim, murky water. He could see his legs, tangled in the skirts of a long dress he was wearing. One end of the sash around his waist was tied to a heavy object, which plummeted to the bottom as he struggled against its weight.

With a long bubbling sigh, he gave up, his mind going black. Dying, like in the dream.

Then he was hauled up to the surface, coughing water and gulping for air. Gita's face loomed close, blurry except for her fearless, pitiless eyes. "Dawg, you baptized!" she laughed.

CHAPTER EIGHT

Dispirited, Jane trudges along Honeyvale Road. Except for the house on Sycamore, and the empty field she encountered with Brett, she recognizes nothing in Graynier; not a single memory awakes.

It is like sensing the nearness of rain. The memories are present all around, but cloaked in vapor, and I extend my palm, waiting for the first drops. I pray God for even the smallest sign—some glimpse, some clue to my past. Without it, I shall be forever a puzzle to myself.

One drop of rain. Almighty, come to my aid.

No voice replies; only the half-hearted warbling of birds in the limp trees, and the sudden rage of cicadas.

The afternoon heat slows her steps; she's thirsty. Passing a shabby ranch home set near the road, she notices a sliding glass door left open on the sun porch. She draws nearer. The window shades are down; no car parked in the driveway.

"Hello?" Pushing the screen panel aside, she steps into the house.

In the kitchen she finds a half-empty carton of pink lemonade in the refrigerator; she opens the lip, drinking deeply. When she is finished, she refills the carton with tap water. She uses the toilet, then wipes her face with a moistened washcloth.

Back on the road, she passes a backyard body shop...a cottage with a sign offering furniture repair...trees swamped by bittersweet vines...

She spots a tiny gleam near her feet. Bending down, she peers closer.

Plucking the brooch from the gravel, she examines it: a wreath, two roses joined, each unfurling petal finely wrought of gold, their stems twisted together to complete the circle.

Pleasure fills her. *This is mine*, she knows suddenly.

When she turns the ornament, the pin arm swings free, bent, its catch broken.

Suddenly there is no brooch, no Honeyvale Road: all disappears. In the blink of an eye, she finds herself in a different place. Climbing a hill.

She's following a low wall built of fieldstones. She must turn her head to glance left or right, her vision framed by a horseshoe shape. *I'm wearing a hat,* Jane realizes. *A bonnet.* The slope on her side of the wall is wooded; on the other side, a crowd of sheep observes her progress from a cleared pasture, bleating insistently as if to urge her on.

She hastens her pace, eyes on the steep rise ahead. The little blue cape about her shoulders snags on the branches of trees. In one hand she holds a book with a black cover.

The stonewall is her guide. It is familiar; she has mounted this hill many times before. Somewhere at the top lies joy—and terror. Bliss and treachery, both entwined, like the roses on the golden brooch fastened at her throat.

And then a single word enters her mind. An odd sort of word.

POSTING JANE'S PHOTO online, the one he surreptitiously snapped with his cell phone, was a whim. Brett had already surfed the missing adult and teen runaway sites, looking for her picture and description, with the usual pleas from family, friends, police.

Nothing.

Many of the posts featured playback of the vanished loved one's favorite songs. He toyed with the idea of inserting the Rolling Stones' "Lady Jane" on his post, but decided that mentioning her name would be too big a clue. He wanted to receive information without giving out any; to satisfy his curiosity without enabling anyone to find her. In the end he settled on the photo, accompanied by the caption: "Are You Looking For Her?"

He checks it every morning. Only two cyber-strangers have posted comments: "no but wd like 2 nail her," "she lookin for me? hey babe write me @" giving a prison address.

On this particular morning, while Jane is out for a walk, he is startled to see a new comment: "This photo closely resembles a female, 23, 5'5", gray eyes, dark blond hair, missing 2-1/2 weeks, last seen 7/20 at the Winchester Mall in Deer Run, PA. This young woman is unstable and needs attention. Her parents are anxious to bring her home. Please contact rfancher@fancherpi.com with whatever information you have."

His heart thumping, Brett quickly deletes his post. He tries to reassure himself that there was nothing contained in the listing that could lead anyone to her hiding place.

It's hardly shocking that she has parents. It's the word "unstable" that throws him.

Ten days ago, on the humid night when she rapped on the door, his first intuition had been that she was a mental patient—but that was before he loved her. *Unstable?* More like mysterious: enigmatic and strange.

She's deluded as well.

"How old are you?" he asked her at breakfast this morning.

She feigned not to hear, teasing a lump of scrambled eggs with her fork.

"I'm twenty-eight," he offered. "You're younger than me, right?"

"How can it matter?"

"Because I think your memory is playing tricks on you," he says gently. "Jane, Father Petrelli has owned this place over 30 years. You could have lived in Graynier—just not in this particular house."

"No!" Fork clattering onto her plate, her hands became fists. "Truly I was born in this house!"

He held his ground unhappily. "That's impossible."

"It is not impossible if..." She hesitated, regarding him cautiously. "If I lived here *earlier* than Father Petrelli."

"But you can't be more than thirty." With her naïvely earnest gaze, she looked all of 12.

"Why not? Perhaps I'm 50," she mused. "Or 150."

"I don't follow."

"Why do I remember playing the seraphine?" Her voice was grave. "It's possible I was born a very long time ago."

Don't snicker. "You'd have to be, like, immortal."

She grew cool at his condescension. "Our souls are immortal. You may indulge me, at least, on this point."

Brett found himself on unexpectedly shifting ground here. He believed in the safety of numbers, the digital universe, not this woo-woo stuff. On the other hand...why not indulge her, her "memories," her illogical claims? Accept them on faith, fall into step, and help her in her weird quest.

How better to get inside Jane?

He agreed to take her to the town's Registry of Deeds tomorrow, where they could research the house's prior occupants, going all the way back to the age of the seraphine. Then she left for her walk.

Now he hears her calling his name, her sneakers drumming on the stairs as she rushes up to his garret. Logging off his computer, he checks his appearance in the screen's reflection, rakes his sweaty hair back.

She bursts in, flushed and out of breath. "I've had another memory!"

"Great. What?"

"I must find a *wall*!"

He's bemused. "Any wall?"

"One made of stone. It climbs up a hill. I shall recognize it when I see it. And I have a word! I heard it here—" she presses her hands to her temples, "—and very clearly, too."

"What did you hear?"

She catches her breath. *"Quirk."*

"Just...'quirk'?"

"Nothing more. Yet—truly it means something. I prayed for a clue, and now I have two! A rock wall. And quirk."

Brett has a word, too; it weighs on his mind. *Unstable.*

Chapter Nine

Hoyt brandishes a handful of remotes, testing the cable TV and DVD player in the Meltzer's entertainment room, the windows' motorized curtains, the sliding panel that reveals the screen. All working now.

In the dining room, one of the track bulbs is out. To change it, Hoyt climbs up on one of the antique dining chairs. His boot goes through the rush seat, and he tumbles cursing to the floor, his leg stuck in the chair. When he manages to kick the thing off, it breaks into kindling. He stows the pieces in the truck bed next to the rubber trashcan, where another trapped skunk thumps around inside.

His neck hurts like hell, worse than ever since the accident. Time for a drink. Red or white?

Returning to the house, he proceeds to the wine cellar, where he selects a bottle of Montrachet. Jack Meltzer, being an oenophile, thinks of this wine collection as the jewel of all his worldly effects, and Hoyt has been chipping away at it all winter. A while ago Hoyt decided there were lower, unexplored depths to which he had not yet sunk. Ineptitude and kickbacks were not enough: the time had come for blatant theft.

Reclining on a pool chaise as he drinks, he admires his week's work. The pool is crystal clear; the grass is on the mend, the underground sprinklers coaxing forth green shoots amid the dead brown. The one disappointment is the Montrachet, which fails to take the edge off his whiplash, now a blazing collar of pain. Only straight liquor will do. After he drops the wrecked chair off for repair, he'll stop at the package store. Calling Pete away from the Canada geese, he heads back to his truck.

At Iacovucci's Furniture Repair on Honeyvale, Mr. Iacovucci strips the grass away from the frame to examine it more closely. "I can refit the joints okay, but the seat's made of bulrush. I gotta order that. It won't match the other chairs, 'cause they're pretty old and the rush is new. Come back in ten days."

The same day the Metzgers copter in, Hoyt thinks, getting back in his truck. He's cutting it close.

Driving through town, he spots two kids pushing their bikes up a long hill on their way from Huxberry Heights. They look spent. He pulls over.

"Want a ride?" he asks. "You can stow the bikes in back."

The girl looks at the boy. Hoyt has seen her in the pool at the Poonchwallas' motel, when he goes by to score weed off one of the welfare families living there. The boy has an exotic look: tawny skin, wide nose, a cloud of light brown curls—perhaps some blend of Hispanic, Caucasian, and African, though his limp, recessive manner could mean Asian (or possibly just nerd) blood. He seems to be in love with the older girl; he never takes his eyes off her.

The girl nods her assent. Hoyt piles the bikes next to Pete and the skunk pail. The kids climb into the cab.

Hoyt pulls back onto the road. "Am I leaving you guys at the motel?"

"Yes, thank you," says the girl.

"You're Seth's sister, right? I don't know your name."

"Gita."

He nods toward the boy. "Who's your groupie?"

"Collin." She frowns, insulted.

He had meant it as a joke; maybe he has been offending people for so long, he can no longer converse without barbs. The two kids are huddled against the door. The Indian girl looks queasy, probably from the skunk stench on his clothes.

Giving them a ride was an unforgivable lapse of character. He's annoyed, his neck aching. He decides to convert his good deed into an opportunity to sow terror and disgust.

"And you know my name, right?" he asks Gita.

"You're Mr. Eddy."

"Good. 'Cause you know not to climb into a car with a stranger, right? I might have been a sexual predator. You could've been in for some inappropriate touching."

The boy Collin glances uneasily at Gita, but she looks unperturbed. A bold one.

"It's a good thing children don't get me excited," Hoyt goes on. "But someone else might have other ideas. Or maybe that person would be driving along without any ideas, but just seeing you two on the side of the road, with nobody else around, would inspire this person to an unthinkable deed. And he could seem perfectly nice to you. Much nicer than I am. And you wouldn't suspect for a minute that he'd be capable of harming you, until you're already in his car and he's speeding away, too fast for you to jump out, and then he reaches over and gives you..." Hoyt's hand pounces on the muscle just above Collin's knee, pinching it in a vise-like grip. "...*a horse bite!*"

Collin lets out a high-pitched girly yelp. Chuckling, Hoyt releases him. Gita calmly takes out her cell phone, punching in a number.

"Who're you calling?"

"The police."

"Be my guest. You'll look like a little fool. There's no statute covering horse bites."

She slaps the phone shut. "Let us out *right now.*"

Hoyt swerves to the shoulder and lets the kids out at the foot of a steep hill. He tosses their bikes onto the road. Jumping back into the cab, he starts to pull away.

"You suck!" Collin shouts after him, a belated show of audacity for his girlfriend.

Hitting the brakes, Hoyt leaps out. Collin dives into the bushes. The girl stands fast, pointing imperiously like Moses with his rod: "Get thee hence, demon!"

Reaching into the cargo, Hoyt pries open the garbage pail, and before she can dodge it, pitches the skunk at her feet.

THE LOOK ON the Poonchwalla girl's face when the skunk turned tail and blasted her! Hoyt is still laughing when he stops off at the package store to pick up a gallon of gin and some Tylenol. Still laughing when he parks at his house. Not laughing when he finds his door ajar.

He often forgets to lock it. The house, a squat 30s bungalow, is at the end of a deeply rutted dirt road, shielded by dense pines, in the shadow of Rowell Hill. People don't come out here unless they're invited and they've run out of excuses.

His mutt growls, hackles rising. Hoyt quietly sets the liquor store bag on the landing and retrieves the .357 Magnum he keeps in the wood box, pushing his door open with the gun's barrel. Pete shimmies impatiently through the gap and bounds into the house, disappearing into the kitchen. Hoyt hears savage barking, plates crashing to the floor.

A raccoon streaks out, headed for the door, Pete in pursuit. Hoyt steps aside to let them settle up outdoors.

He enters the kitchen. Shattered dinnerware crunches under his boots: the coon was probably feeding from the tower of dirty dishes in the sink. Still, the animal didn't open the front door by itself. Nor did it pull up a chair to his table and peel an orange onto a plate. Yet there they are, the curved scraps of orange rind, with seeds from the devoured fruit neatly grouped beside them. A drained glass of tomato juice, poured from the can in his fridge. A box of crackers from the cupboard, the salty crumbs scattered about. An empty cheese wrapper, the final affront. Someone made a meal here.

Hoyt's bowels churn; his skin fizzes; the alien presence feels everywhere, touching everything. Standing stock-still, he listens for sounds. The house is silent. Outside, Pete's collar tags jingle. Hoyt looks out the window to see him trotting to the woods, limp raccoon in his mouth.

Hoyt moves stealthily through the house, his gun cocked. No one is there. He returns to the living room, where the front door is still open; the first mosquitoes of the evening whine around his ears. Plugging the bug zapper in, he fetches the bag of liquor from the stoop, locks the door and retreats to the couch, where he wrenches the cap off the gallon jug, pouring three fingers of gin into a smudged glass on the coffee table.

Who was here?

He senses something altered in this room. He can't put his finger on it, just a feeling. The heaps of books around his armchair are undisturbed; the sofa cushion, which Pete uses for a bed, still lies on the floor.

Washing down four Tylenols with gin, he looks around for something to read.

On the coffee table beside his cell phone charger sits a book he doesn't recognize: a small bound volume with gilt-edged pages. He turns to the flyleaf: *The Holy Bible*, King James version, printed in New York, 1851.

He flips through the mottled tissue-thin pages, the march of miniscule verses. Though he doesn't remember buying the book, that doesn't mean he didn't. Often he buys a dozen moldy old volumes at a time, enjoying the notion of all the hands that have held them over the years.

He examines a gold insignia stamped into the leather. Not a cross, as befits a bible, but some weird variation:

Then he notices something inserted like a bookmark between the pages. He opens to the marked page. In the seam is a long lock of hair, a reddish brown shade, silky to the touch.

How long has it lain here preserved and undiscovered? Whose was it? Rolling the strands absently between his thumb and forefinger, he glances over the text someone has marked in thick pencil. The verse describes the angel Gabriel appearing to a virgin in Nazareth. A common enough passage.

Suddenly, the pain returns: a noose ripped tight about his neck. For a few seconds he is unable to breathe.

A second later, the pain abates. Hoyt feels dizzy, confused. About to reach for the gin, he realizes the lock of hair is still in his hand.

Its luster has faded, the strands now feel dry, coarse, wiry. Repulsion fills him, as if he holds the desiccated souvenir of a dead thing.

He tries to shake the strands off, but they cling to his fingers. Bolting to the kitchen, he stamps the foot pedal on the garbage pail, flipping the lid open. He scrapes the tangled hair into the bag, dumping orange rinds on top. The lid falls shut.

In a frenzy, he cleans the kitchen, the sun setting behind Rowell Hill as he sweeps up broken plates, washes dishes, wipes the table clean of crumbs and congealed spills. Tossing the sponge in the dish rack, he turns to leave.

The garbage pail catches his eye. He halts, disbelieving his eyes. The lid is lifting, forced up by a profusion of snarled auburn hair, which expands, growing over the brim, tendrils searching blindly for the floor.

As if it lives.

Grabbing the pail, Hoyt runs out the front door toward the woods, feeling the hair curl like brittle vines over his hands.

Dusk obscures the path through the trees. Veering off, he crashes through the underbrush, arriving at the edge of his junk pit: a shallow ravine where he chucks old appliances, paint cans, truck batteries and rusted lawn chairs. Hurling the contents of the pail down the slope, he stands panting, peering into the darkness of the pit.

Somewhere it's there, growing. Hoyt kicks dead leaves over the edge, to bury the horror, then gropes his way back to the house.

CHAPTER TEN

Marly waits until the congregation files out from evening service before approaching Reverend Crowley.

"Father, could I talk to you in private?"

The elderly priest doesn't seem too thrilled by her request, regarding her through cataract-filmed eyes. "Are you a parishioner at this church?"

"No. I mean," she adds shyly, "I don't go anywhere."

"Are you interested in joining St. Paul's?"

"Maybe. I don't know." She has not set foot in a church since she was a teenager, at Saint Anthony Parish, when Father Petrelli put his finger up her. But she needs to confide in somebody, and priests are supposed to help. "Please. It's something important."

He ushers her into his office, sits at his desk, and folds his hands, waiting.

Squirming in the chair across from him, Marly looks down at her own hands in her lap. Last night, she woke to find them spontaneously soaked in blood again. She had been thrashing in her sleep; there were red streaks all over the sheets. But when she returned from washing her hands in the bathroom—again finding no scratches, cuts, or wounds anywhere—the stains on the bedclothes were gone.

Her howls filled the trailer as she sat and cried. If she had owned a car with enough horsepower, she would have hitched up her home right then and dragged it into another town, another county—shit, another *state*—someplace where you could sleep without being woken every single night by horrible dreams.

Worse, her sunny disposition is being borne away like a bright beach ball in a riptide. Who is Marly without hope? Strangely depleted, sick within: a stranger.

Father Crowley rattles phlegm in his throat. "How may I help you?"

"I keep having this feeling," she begins miserably, "that I've done something really bad. I'm ashamed, and I don't know what for."

The priest remarks, with a touch of smugness, "If you haven't attended church for a long time, I imagine you've accrued quite a few sins."

"Well, some. But here's the thing—" Marly takes a deep breath, then shows him her palms. "My hands bleed sometimes. The blood comes out of my fingernails and then it runs all over the place. And then it disappears."

Father Crowley's eyes narrow. "Like Christ's hands on the cross? Are you referring to *stigmata*?"

"Kind of. I hadn't thought of that."

"Congratulations are in order, then," he comments dryly. "It seems you're a saint."

He regrets his quip when he sees Marly brighten, hope flickering absurdly over her face. He adopts a more compassionate tone: "I'm afraid our church gives no credence to stigmata, spirit possession, and the like. It's really more in line with Catholic belief. Why don't you speak to Father Petrelli?"

Her eyes fall to her lap again, the light of hope dying.

FIRST SETH POONCHWALLA has to go buy three cases of tomato juice, in the large restaurant cans, at Valyou Mart. But even after his sister soaks in a bathtub filled with tomato juice, she smells; the whole apartment reeks like bloody hell. Now he has to listen to Gita squawk and blubber from the bathroom while he sits at the computer in the motel office, trawling the web for more tips to remove skunk odor.

Next thing you know, he's driving back to Valyou Mart, this time to purchase thirty bottles of a feminine douche that online tipsters claim will do the trick. While he's at it, he'll buy a case of cold decongestant capsules: tomorrow he needs to head to his lab and cook up some more illegal product for clients.

Seth is a chemistry prodigy, with a passion for robotics. In a few weeks he will attend MIT as a freshman, on a partial scholarship. Student loans will bridge the tuition gap, which Seth plans to pay off quickly with the proceeds of his drug dealing.

This sideline had an accidental genesis. Three years ago, Seth's parents sent him to one of the motel rooms to investigate suspicious fumes in the corridor. He knocked, smelling acetone and ammonia. When there was no response, he used his master key.

Inside the room, 17-year-old Tyrone Perguson and his single, welfare mom lay passed out on the floor. Glass jars, surgical tubing, hundreds of matchbooks, and a dozen empty boxes of cold-remedy capsules littered the bed. Something was burning in an electric skillet on the bureau. Fluid from a plastic jug of engine starter had spilled across the carpet.

Tyrone and his mother had apparently been overcome by the pungent ether. Seth turned off the skillet and dragged the bodies into the corridor, where they revived in time to escape before the EMT unit arrived.

They slipped back the next day, avoiding eye contact. By then Seth had figured out, from the ingredients in the room, that they were trying to make methamphetamine. He was offended by their carelessness and lack of method.

Tyrone was in the same grade as Seth but they had never spoken (Tyrone was in the remedial classes). The next time they passed in the halls, he muttered "Thanks" to Seth.

Taking him aside, Seth gave him a short lecture on lab technique. Instead of getting his back up, Tyrone suggested they split the profits, with Seth doing the manufacturing and him selling. Two years later, when Tyrone was convicted on weapons charges, Seth inherited the whole of the business: an enthusiastic clientele of locals intent on murdering their brain cells.

Seth's crank is scrupulously made, and near to pure. For someone of his talents, the processing is easy, though laborious. He takes his time with the volatile ingredients—hydrogen chloride gas, ethyl ether, red phosphorus—keeping his focus monkish, revering the equations.

As for the law, he long ago moved his lab off the motel premises to a safe hideaway. Sales are conducted right at the reception desk when he's on night duty. He has some $20,000 in cash sealed up in the pool robot, crawling along the underwater floor.

Night is falling by the time Seth returns from Valyou Mart with the shopping bag full of douche. He chucks it inside the bathroom and closes the door against the horrendous stink.

"What am I supposed to do with this?"

"Soak your butthole in it."

He's outa here. Hanging a "Closed" sign on the motel office window, he disconnects the night bell. Feminine douches remind him of Marly Walczak. He decides to drive by her trailer for a free fuck.

He would like to pay Marly once in a while. Or buy her some shiny lingerie that would make her look younger, lift up her flattened little boobies. Bring her a box of fine chocolates, to flesh her out a bit. But Seth knows never to flash money around and attract the suspicion of parents, friends, or cops.

Summer lightning rakes the treetops as he turns into the "Whispering Elms" trailer park. Clouds clump low; the air bulges with humidity. A simmering breeze balloons the patio awnings on the single wides, carrying the odor of backed-up septics.

Old Dave Gottschalk, who has lived on disability since he shot one foot off in World War II, is out in front of his Airstream, cursing and kicking the satellite dish with his good foot. Further on, 12-year-old Dom Pizzarro and his middle-school mates have their amps all the way up, quaking his mother's pink RV while she sucks oxygen and cigarettes in the bedroom, a goner from emphysema.

Marly's car isn't by her trailer, whose front door stands wide open. Through the screen, Seth can see the glow of the hanging lamp in the kitchenette.

PEARL RUMMAGES IN her mother's bureau drawer, searching for the orange vibrator. The blue one doesn't show up well on camera. She has been taking pictures of herself to post on the internet: posing on her bed in a satin teddy, aqua with black lace, and a Ninja Turtle Halloween mask.

Her profile lists her weight at 325 pounds, which gets more responses than her actual weight of 230. There are a lot of chubby chasers out there. At first she writes back to her e-mail suitors in a sweet, seductive tone. Then, when the guy is hooked, she abruptly bombs him: "Choke on my labia you dirtdumb jizzbag hey loser stick yr sucky worm dick in a blender & press liquefy fuckass."

A few of them actually like the abuse. She suggests to those ones that they meet her in a secret chat room, and sends a link that takes them to the homepage of the FBI.

No orange vibrator. Pearl closes the drawer. Thunder rumbles close by; her skin tingles in the electric air. The faraway beep of the microwave reminds her that the nachos are ready. Anticipating the warm ooze of cheddar over salsa, jalapeno slices, ground beef, Baco-bits, and corn chips, she pads into the kitchenette. As she opens the oven, she hears the bell jingle outside on the gate, then Pook's bark.

It's too soon for her mom to be back from the bars.

Someone mounts the stoop to peer through the screen door.

"Hi." It's Seth Poonchwalla. "Is Marly in?"

Pearl strides to the door, slapping it open. "She's out." She blocks the door, a boulder on legs.

He stands dumbly in his camo shorts and wife-beater, black eyes startled, mahogany skin gleaming under the porch light. Lightning flits behind his head; fat drops of rain pock the steps. "Can I come in?"

"Your funeral." Pearl steps aside as he enters, making no move to hide her pink acreage. Let this dweeb get the shock of his life.

She doesn't notice Pook struggling to get up the steps, and closes the door on the dog.

The storm cracks open: rain cascades onto the roof. "If you think you're gonna wait for her," she heads back to the microwave, "I got no idea when she'll be back."

Seth slides into the banquette, eyes on Pearl's back: the folds of it, the burst of her rump below the skimpy lace hem.

"Smells good," he says, as she removes the platter of nachos from the micro.

"You can't have any." She sets the plate down on the dinette table and sits, buttocks claiming both sides of the banquette's corner. Her sumptuous breasts toss about like waves as she shakes pepper sauce on the cheese.

"Why not?"

"Beef in it. Sacred cow." Her eyes mock him. The tops of her aureoles swell above the black lace, like tender pastel-pink sunrises. They must be about nine inches in diameter. "Isn't that your religion?" she adds.

"I eat anything."

"Notice, so do I." Circling the platter with one arm to hoard it, she lifts a sauce-laden chip to her mouth, tongue snaking out to snap the rope of cheese restraining it. Butterfat and salsa wash over her knuckles.

His dick has never been so hard. He is ready to cut diamonds with it, and lay them at her feet. He wants to enter her with his whole self, pulling all her soft flesh over him like a stack of comforters, filling his mouth with her pale pink sunrises.

Pearl pushes the platter between them. "Okay, have some." He feels like weeping. She guides a wad of nachos to her mouth. "Mom's kind of crabby these days. She's not gonna want to see you." Her lips close around the food, forming a tiny mauve flower.

"What about you?"

Pearl frowns, chewing. "Whabbout me?"

"Do you want to see me?"

She swallows warily. "Depends."

Jumping to his feet, he yanks his zipper down. "I want to see you," he says. His rod unbends, prongs out. "Maybe you can tell." His eyes are a beggar's.

Leftover rain drips in the silence. Outside, Pook scratches at the door. There is a dizzy sense of transition in the atmosphere, something departing, and another something arriving.

Pearl clears her throat, her voice husky with confusion. "You must be desperate."

He wishes she could see his heart. "Bitch, don't you know you're beautiful?"

Rolling her eyes, she reaches for more food. "Yeah, right. I'm a sacred cow." Through her mouthful: "Go fug yourself."

Seth is stymied, his jeans halfway down his thighs and his member standing in a draft. Then he gets an inspiration. "I've got money."

Dotting the grease from her lips with a paper towel, Pearl considers. "How much?"

"I've only got twenty on me. But I can get more."

She cleans out the inner pockets of her cheeks with her tongue, not answering.

He presses on: "A lot more. A hundred dollars."

"Is that what you think I'm worth?" Her look is plaintive; suddenly he feels her vulnerability. She's a virgin, he realizes.

"Two hundred," he says.

WHEN THE SKY goes inky and the rain begins, Marly switches on her low beams, turning her battered Cavalier onto Route 404. If she can't get help with her problem from the church, she'll just cheer herself up at O'Malley's Mare. Russ will be behind the bar, Chuck and Oly playing pool, Gil Reynard watching baseball. Waiting for her.

Suddenly she swerves, narrowly missing some kid in a purple anorak walking beside the road. Marly can't see anything through this downpour; she switches her wipers to high speed. That's all she needs, another accident.

Checking her rearview mirror, she sees the girl receding down the road. Her headlights had only briefly illuminated the lower half of the girl's face before Marly swerved, not enough to tell.

Was it the same girl?

That would be too perfect.

The storm gushes and flares. Good: now people will stop bellyaching about the drought. The men at the bar will talk about the Red Sox line-up, grub prevention, foreign wars, dyke actresses, the price of tires. Never about love. It's up to Marly Walczak to lay them down one by one, the males of Graynier, stroking their hearts to awaken vigorous love. That's what she's here for.

Running through the rain from her parked car, she swings through O'Malley's door. The same grins greet her, the same voices shouting come-ons above the honky-tonk.

Suddenly she's rocked by a repulsion she has never experienced. Here are the same drunk assholes; the same meaty hands all over her tits; the same beer tasting like carbonated armpit. All at once she sees herself nailed into her mattress by a procession of contemptuous men, her hands flung wide and bleeding from the fingertips. Waking countless mornings with the horrid crust of semen on her thighs. Used goods, marked down and degraded.

Negative thoughts—banish them! Things could be worse! She gropes, by habit, for things to be grateful for.

What, for her leaky trailer, demeaning job, slave wages? Her lumbering foul-mouthed sourpuss illegitimate daughter?

The repulsion will not be quelled; she feels like she's drowning in it. In a heartbeat she's back outside, panting for air.

The rain abruptly stops. In ten minutes it will have evaporated. There will be no relief from the drought.

AS PEARL AND SETH lock themselves in her bedroom, Pook wanders along the fence in the rain. Looking up suddenly, he searches the void with milky eyes, confused by an unfamiliar smell.

He hears a voice, a gentle command: *Lie down.* He obeys, rolling onto his side. A point of light grows in his vision, like a star, joined by others, pricking through the dark.

The dog pees with excitement, imagining his sight is returning. Instead, all the senses fade: the odors of weather, home, and intruder; the sensation of ribs pressing into the wet earth with each breath; the sound of that breath diminishing; the taste of minerals as his tongue lolls onto the dirt. The points of light cluster and revolve. Pook gradually relaxes; all is as it should be.

Good dog, says the voice.

Pook floats into the meadow of stars. *Good dog.*

This is where Jane finds him: a small still-warm shape stretched on the grass inside the white plastic fence. Stilling the bell carefully with one hand, she pushes the gate open and crouches beside the dog. Her purple anorak drips rain onto his body.

Lifting Pook, she carries him to the screen door and peers inside. Hearing no voices, she steps inside quietly, as she has learned to do when entering strangers' houses.

She lays him on the kitchenette table next to a plate of half-eaten nachos, murmuring, "Poor little fellow." Then she opens the refrigerator to find what she came for.

THE BELL ON the gate tinkles.

In the bedroom, Seth lifts his mouth from Pearl's nipple. "What's that?"

"Must be Mom's home."

He pulls out of her, feeling a sweet estrangement. He sits back on his heels; holding her thighs apart, he gazes, stunned, into her manifold mystery.

Pearl has never bagged a boy's heart before; for the first time she knows the thrill of ownership. Sliding the window screen aside, she helps Seth slip out, watching him stumble off into the night.

A high, heartbroken wail echoes through the trailer.

Pearl quickly throws on a wrapper and hurries to the kitchen. Her mother stands bent over Pook lying across the table.

"My baby," Marly whimpers. She can't bear to touch him, already knowing his fat little tummy will have no spring; his pink ribbon of tongue is hard as wire. Rainwater has pooled around his body on the formica tabletop.

Muddy sneaker prints lead to and from the screen door.

Marly turns on Pearl, her voice thick with rage. "Who did this?"

"I don't know, I was asleep."

"Somebody killed him! Someone was here! Look!" Marly points to the counter beside the refrigerator. "They ate my yogurt! They drank my root beer! They killed my dog! Whoever did it, I'll shoot the fucking sonofabitch!"

Chapter Eleven

The stabbing pain in Hoyt's neck wakes him early. He stumbles into the bathroom to take some Tylenol and put on the foam collar he bought in the pharmacy. The day is already sweltering.

Padding naked to the kitchen, he helps himself to a breakfast of toast and gin.

Outside, a car door slams. Peering out the window, he sees Marly get out of her banged-up Cavalier and march up the path to the bungalow. What is the sorry bitch doing here? She looks strange. Hoyt is more used to seeing her in drugstore makeup, tight denim cat suit, and fuck-me-shoes—or naked. Today she's wearing dingy sweatpants and thongs and looks thinner than ever, distracted, disheveled, her complexion grayish. Her usual moronic smile is gone.

He slips into some boxers and opens the door.

"Hi, Marly. Gettin' any lately?"

She brushes past him into the house.

"Come in, why don't you?" He closes the door, answering himself, "Thanks, don't mind if I do."

She shifts from one foot to the other, eyes darting around the room. "Could you loan me a gun?"

"No." It's what he always says, no matter what Marly asks for.

"I know you got a bunch. You could spare one." She spots his revolver, still on the coffee table after the intruder incident. "That one."

"No. Go buy your own."

"My credit card's maxed. Hoyt, please. Somebody broke into my house a couple nights ago."

That gets his interest. "Really? How did he get in?"

"Pearl left the door open. And it was a woman."

"What makes you think that?"

"She ate my *yogurt*. What guy would do that?"

Hoyt frowns, scratching the stubble on his chin. "That's odd. A few days ago, I left the door unlocked while I was out. Someone came in, had a bite in the kitchen, and left."

"Then I didn't imagine it." She runs shaky fingers through her hair. "'Cause I've been hallucinating stuff lately. Scary stuff. I think it's from the accident we had. Something must've happened in my head. I can't sleep anymore, I get these nightmares—" She eyes his cervical collar. "Guess you're not having no picnic neither."

Hoyt thinks of the lock of hair slithering out of the garbage can, coiling in his hand. Maybe Marly's right, maybe their collision caused some sort of neurological damage to both of them—scrambled the visual cortex.

The agony in his neck is gathering again, ready to pierce the scrim of pills and booze. He is impatient to get rid of her. "You don't need a gun. Just lock your door."

"I need protection! She murdered my dog!"

"It's probably the pissed-off wife of some guy you're pleasuring. If she comes around again, invite her in and eat her pussy."

Marly glares at him, then makes a sudden dive for the gun. Hoyt pushes her away.

"Motherfucker!"

"Not quite. I will concede that I'm a dickhead."

She clenches her fists as if she's going to haul off and punch him. "I used to think you were a good person underneath. I accept that you don't give a rat's ass about me. But how you can ignore Pearl, your own child—"

"If you were so sure she's mine, you would've told her by now," he interrupts. "She's not, and you know it. And, as you rightly surmised, I don't give a shit." He heads to the bedroom. "See yourself out. I have to get dressed."

But she pursues him, hissing, "I can file a paternity suit. I should've done it long ago. I could force you to give a DNA sample."

Turning in the bedroom doorway, he reaches into his shorts and extracts a pubic hair. "Here. Knock yourself out." He hands the hair to her and shuts the door in her face.

As he throws on a T-shirt and jeans, he hears her car drive away.

Her transformation disturbs him. Marly was one of the few remaining people he hasn't completely alienated. Whenever he showed up at the trailer, in the days when his sap ran too fast for the liquor to quash, she allowed him in her bed, docilely enduring his insults. He never enjoyed exploiting her; he'd done so out of an inexplicable sense of assignment, as if they had a contract: he to hurt, her to receive hurt.

There's no woman left who can stand him now. It's not just that he's drunk and nasty; he is also a loser, blowing every job he has ever undertaken, from attorney to real estate agent to house painter to exterminator, racing downhill with a deliberation for all to see.

Returning to the living room, he knows the gun won't be on the table, and it isn't. He wanted Marly to have it: he just didn't want to appear to care. Give a woman an inch, and it morphs to a mile; and pretty soon you're Mama's little soldier, handing over your gun.

BRETT PAGES THROUGH the musty record books in the Graynier courthouse's registry of deeds. Jane pulls her chair alongside his, tilting her head close so she can read with him. She smells of lavender and, faintly, of onions: lavender from the French soap he bought her at the mall, onions from the Western omelet he made her for breakfast.

The pretty ribboned straw hat he gave her, to protect her fair skin from the sun, rests by her elbow on the reading table. He aches to give her more. Maybe a book of romantic poetry. She could tilt her head against his, as she's doing now—even lay her head in his lap while he reads Byron or somebody.

She likes his presents, but they don't bind her to Brett as he would like. Instead she spends more and more time away from the house. Out on her walks, she searches every day for an imaginary wall, as he waits, his frustration and anger building as the hours pass. Last night she returned well after dark, wet from the rain. Seeing her weary and dejected, he abruptly filled with tenderness, wanting to smoothe her tangled hair and kiss the tiny veins at her temples. He keeps holding back, both the anger and the caresses. There is a gentility about Jane; he feels there's some kind of etiquette he must obey.

The clerk sets down more volumes, indexes of land transactions tracing ownership of 53 Sycamore Street backwards from the present.

1977: grantee Petrelli bought the house and .4 acre lot from grantor O'Connell. 1961: Grantee O'Connell bought from grantor Nielson, who owned the house for more than half a century after purchasing it from Pease in 1903.

Brett photocopies each record of transfer.

"We have nothing earlier than 1826, when the town was incorporated." The clerk arrives with the final pile of heavy tomes, each dustier and dingier than the last. Brett's sinuses fill in protest.

Pease purchased from Sperry, 1877. Sperry from Upham, 1866. Here Brett succumbs to a volley of sneezes, ejecting a flood of mucous into a tissue proffered by the clerk. Upham bought from Jarley, who bought the house and lot in 1854 from the Estate of Benjamin Pettigrew. Pettigrew bought the empty lot in 1829 from the P. Graynier Holding Corporation.

"Pettigrew bought the lot without a house," Brett explains to
Jane. "That means he built the house sometime after 1829. His estate sold the lot with the house in 1854, which meant he still owned
it when he died."

"Benjamin Pettigrew," Jane writes careful notes in her elegant,
looping script. "Then it was he who bought the seraphine!"

"Not necessarily. Anyone could've bought it at any time, like,
at an antiques store." He's anxious to leave; his throat is constricting
and his chest hurts.

Disagreeing, she shakes her head stubbornly. "You said harmoniums were more in fashion by mid-century." Then she mused, "I
wonder if Benjamin Pettigrew lived alone, or if he had family."

The clerk advises them to check the census records at the
Historical Society. "The census lists the occupants of every house
by name. But you'll have to deal with Elsa Graynier. She's shy a
few screws."

THE LAST LIVING member of the Graynier family, Elsa Lucille
Grayner is something of a local legend. Most people in town consider her an eccentric nut, though generous and community-minded.
She lives in a white-shingled 1873 Queen Anne house on Graynier
Avenue, in a set of rooms above the Graynier Historical Society,
which she established and has curated since the death of her beloved
father, J. P. Graynier, twelve years before. The archive contains every
last Graynier document and artifact—most of them untouched by
anyone but Elsa, though sometimes a teacher drags in a gang of re-
calcitrant schoolchildren.

Because the history of Graynier is indistinguishable from the
history of Elsa's ancestors, she guards the museum with primal intensity, as if fending off extinction. Every day she wanders the museum talking to her father, whom she sometimes glimpses winding
the Ormulu clock in the corner. Evenings she listens to *Tristan and
Isolde*. Never married, childless, she will live out her family's doom
to its end: the twilight of the Grayniers.

Entering the foyer, Brett and Jane step on a mat that sets off a *ding-dong* inside the museum. Frosted glass sconces, and a ceiling fixture with a hobnail glass bowl, flood the hallway with light.

Jane points out the museum door's etched daisy panel. "Look. It's the same glass as our front door." Since she got up this morning, she has been jumping out of her skin, rushing Brett out of the house. He glances at her determined profile, her shoulders tensed as if her soul's salvation hangs on this errand.

A shadow moves behind the glass, and then a tiny, plump woman in her seventies throws the door open. Perspiration tinted with beige makeup stains the neck of her blouse.

"Hello! Come in! Welcome!" She motions them inside eagerly.

Glass fixtures blaze from every wall of the torrid, airless room. Five immense glass chandeliers hang from the ceiling; reading lamps with frosted glass shades line the tables. Glass-front cabinets are filled with goblets, plates, decanters, and bottles, clear or rendered in jewel tones of ruby, turquoise, canary, magenta, emerald. Artificial light bounces off every surface, lending an infernal glare to the massive oil portraits that hang between the lanterns and sconces.

"All made at the Graynier Glass factory," the woman chirps, sweating like a stevedore. "I'm Elsa Graynier. Would you like a tour?" She gestures toward a sign over a doorway: "THE HISTORY OF GRAYNIER GLASS."

"Thanks, maybe next time," says Brett.

"I'll take that as a promise!" Elsa wags a finger at him.

"Could you point us to the census records?"

"Certainly. May I ask for what purpose?"

"We're interested in the history of a specific house. We'd like to find out all the people who lived there from the time it was built."

Elsa lowers her voice confidentially. "Have you got a ghost?"

"Not that I know of."

"I'm relieved! I thought you might be researching one of those awful haunted house guides." Elsa leads Brett to a shelf of oversize volumes bound in red cloth. "Now, then! Where is the house and when was it built?"

He shows her the photocopied page from the Grantor's Index. As she studies it, he looks around for Jane.

She's standing beneath a 19th century oil painting, seemingly riveted by the portrait of a middle-aged couple in formal dress.

"It says Benjamin Pettigrew purchased the lot from Graynier Holding." Elsa looks up from the page. "One would expect that. The company owned all the property when the factory was constructed. Then it rented or sold lots to the employees. Pettigrew was probably one of them. I'll check the factory payroll records. You see if you can find Pettigrew in the 1850 county census." She passes Brett one of the red volumes. Its pages are suffused in dust; his nose starts flowing again.

"Who are the people in this painting?" Jane asks.

Elsa joins her beneath the portrait, gazing up at the seated man. He is gaunt, with fierce deep-set eyes and a flat head, dressed in black cutaway, tall standing collar and flowing cravat. "My great-great grandfather Philip Graynier, who founded the glass factory. Indeed, he created the whole town."

"And the lady?" A handsome woman stands, dressed in a lace cap, capacious skirts and leg-of-mutton sleeves, her hand resting on her husband's shoulder.

"That is Evelyn Graynier, my great-great grandmother." Elsa bustles to a glass cabinet to remove some antique ledgers, leaving Jane to stare up at Evelyn Graynier.

Jane's eyes are fixed on the woman's lace collar. A brooch is pinned at her throat.

A gold wreath, fashioned of two roses.

Dust flurries up as Brett pages through the slim volume of the census: only about 5,000 county residents in 1850. Running his finger down the list of names, he marvels at some of them: "Alpha Daniels," "Submit Fowler," "Worship Hale." The columns beside each name list age, sex, color, profession, date of birth, property numbers, as well as the answers to such questions as: "Married within the Year?" "Over Age 20 & Unable to Read & Write?" "Deaf & Dumb, Blind, Insane, Idiotic, Pauper or Convict?"

At the P's, his finger pounces on an entry. "Got it. *Pettigrew, Benjamin L."*

"I just found him, too!" Elsa calls from the corner, an open ledger on her lap. "He was the superintendent of Graynier Glass. Quite an important position after all."

Jane tears her gaze from the painting and listens attentively. Brett slides his index finger across the columns. "Age: 51...Place of birth: Canaan, Connecticut...Number living in house: 4. Him, two daughters, and a 'female servant.'"

Jane approaches, peering over Brett's shoulder as he drops his finger down to the next name.

"The first daughter was '*Pettigrew, Rebecca, age 21.*' She was born in Canaan, too. Wonder what happened to the mother. The second daughter's name—"

Suddenly Brett wheezes desperately for breath. His chest is tight, as if the weight of a great stone is pressing on his lungs.

"Dear!" Elsa looks up in alarm. "Is something the matter?"

Frantic for air, Brett rushes out the door.

Jane follows him outside, where she finds him leaning against a tree, thumping his lungs and gasping.

After a few moments, the pressure on his windpipe eases. "Allergy—dust—gotta run home—my inhaler—be right back."

Elsa is removing the census book from the reading table when Jane goes back inside.

"If you please," says Jane, "I should like to study it a while longer."

Her long hair grazes the paper as she turns the pages, until she finds where Brett stopped.

Pettigrew, Benjamin.
Pettigrew, Rebecca.
Pettigrew, Jane.

Marking the name with her index finger, she gropes for her notebook with her free hand.

Pettigrew, Jane. Date of birth: March 2, 1833. Age: 17.
Sex: F. Color: W. Place of Birth: Graynier, Massachusetts

She copies the information into her notebook. Then, as she turns back to the census, her gaze accidentally falls on something. She lets out a cry of surprise.

"Find something?" Elsa bustles over.

"This." Jane's finger presses hard on a name directly under the P's, among the Q's.

Elsa leans over to read it, pushing her reading glasses up on her nose: "Quirk?"

Jane moves her finger across the columns. *Quirk, Efrem. Profession or Trade: Farmer. House Lot Number: 141.*

"Where is this lot?" Jane asks, trying to still the tremor in her voice.

Elsa is puzzled. "I thought you were looking for Pettigrew."

"I need to find this property. It's exceedingly urgent."

Elsa sighs. "I'll have to pull out the early maps, I suppose." She crosses to an architect's cabinet of wide, shallow drawers, opening one after the other, while Jane waits anxiously.

"Here's a surveyor's map from 1848," Elsa says at last, pulling out a wide sheet and smoothing its creases on the table. "That's just a couple of years before the census."

Jane bends to study the finely drawn demarcations, the ant-sized names and numbers fading into the brown-spotted paper. Elsa fetches a magnifying glass.

Lot 141 lies near the top of the map, 126 acres of cleared farm-land, its meandering boundary inscribed, simply: *Quirk.*

"This is on Rowell Hill. See here..." Elsa points to a tiny amoe-ba shape near the north border. "That's Pease Pond." She traces the southern property line running along the base of the hill. "And here, at the bottom, this is where Old Upper Spruce Lane runs now."

Just inside the east boundary, meandering up the hill, is a dot-ted line. Jane asks, "What does this broken line signify?"

"A wall. Probably to keep the livestock in."

Jane bounces up and down. "Of course! The sheep!" She starts laughing.

Elsa regards Jane as if she's a lunatic, then casts an impatient eye on the Ormolu clock. "I'm due upstairs for lunch with my father. May I put away the map now? It shouldn't be exposed to the air for long."

Jane points again to the dotted line. "But—is it possible—if one had a copy of this map, might one find this wall?"

"I can tell you, there's no farm there now. The entire hill is woods. The old walls must have fallen apart by now."

Jane's face droops. "Are you certain?"

"I should think so. I happen to own Rowell Hill." Elsa draws herself up. "Most of the land in this township belonged to the Grayniers; it's been passed down through generations. My father left it all to me."

Jane steps away from the map so Elsa can remove it.

"But I'll make a copy for you anyway," Elsa says kindly. She spreads the map carefully in the photocopier bed. "I've just remembered, last year I gave permission to some hikers to cut a trail up Rowell Hill. It starts somewhere at the end of Upper Old Spruce. The path may have grown over, but it's worth exploring. You might find portions of your wall still standing."

WHEN BRETT RETURNS to the museum, inhaler in hand, the museum is locked for lunch, and Jane is gone.

Chapter Twelve

Propped in a wheelchair on the porch of the Bayh & Bayh Convalescent Center, 97-year-old Iris DeRota is not aware of being on a porch. She is actually sitting in a beach chair beside a wise old clown. Their feet rest in the water of a slow, silver river too wide to glimpse an opposite shore. She looks down at her legs stretched before her: unblemished and well-shaped, as they were in girlhood.

Iris and the clown converse without speaking. He tells her, as he has many times, that she needs to stay a little longer. The wait doesn't bother her, but she feels a pang of longing: everyone is waiting for her, behind the sky, and she is eager to see them, to receive their applause.

Look who's here, says the clown.

Iris jerks awake, cracking open an eye: the known world comes into view. It has a flimsy aspect, like the scenery of an amateur production. The Graynier Avenue street sign, the whitewashed porch railing, the bodies and faces passing to and fro on the sidewalk: an insubstantial hodgepodge (or "whatnot," as Iris would say, if she could talk).

One of the aides, Googie Bains, calls her "Iris DeRutabaga." (Sometimes he amuses himself by jerking her nose to see if she'll yawp.) Today her aide is Brenda, who is inside at the moment, crushing Iris' meds into a cup of vanilla pudding. Brenda adores Iris, whose distinguishing virtue is being "no trouble at all." The old lady has the sweetest sparkling blue eyes, which crinkle agreeably whenever anyone smiles or baby talks to her.

Sometimes Iris stretches her papery lips into a grin, revealing handsome bridges. Though she only takes pureed food, the nursing home had them put in anyway. After hours of dentistry (which Iris obligingly slept through), the dentist sent a bill three times his normal fee to Iris' attorney in Springfield. The lawyer, whom Iris' family put in charge of a large discretionary fund to insure her last years would be comfortable (and who routinely awards himself three times his normal fee), paid the bill without a second thought. By usual arrangement, the dentist kicked back twenty percent to the Bayh & Bayh.

Born in Springfield, Iris married a man in dry goods. She produced four children and countless tea loaves. After her husband died and her children moved with their families to the West and Southwest, she spent many years at St. Joseph Eldercare in Huxberry Heights. Eventually the family attorney relocated her to a cheaper facility in Graynier. He pays Bayh & Bayh the same monthly rate as he used to pay St. Joseph's, and Bayh & Bayh kicks back the difference, receiving full reimbursement for such expenses as a dance therapist, flat-screen plasma TV, and cosmetic dentistry. The move may be a mercy, though; at St. Joseph's they were selling Iris' blood.

The clown calls this world the Colony. The other place, where he and Iris meet, is the Realm, although really the Colony is part of the Realm, the way an egg is itself and is separate from the cake but is also in the cake. Anyone who knows how to bake from scratch could understand that.

Look who's here.

She sees the girl. A few feet away from the nursing home porch, the young woman pauses to consult a map, the brim of her straw hat obscuring her face.

Then she lifts her chin, her gray eyes meeting Iris' blue ones.

The street scene fades, all except for the girl, who throbs with color and light. Iris has seen her before, in the Realm. "Jane," she says, her eyes crinkling at the corners.

The girl's eyes slide away; she folds up the map.

She didn't hear her name because I'm still speaking in my head. It has been a long time since Iris last spoke. *I'll have to make an extra effort.* Her lips form the shape; she takes a breath, concentrating.

The word comes forth, in a voice as fragile and bygone as dried blooms: "Jane..."

Too late. The girl has walked on.

Producing the one word has left the old woman exhausted. Her lavender-tinged eyelids sink.

My poor Jane. Why does she have to remember? Iris asks the clown. *Why wasn't her memory washed clean like everyone else before she went to the Colony?*

The clown answers merely, *An experiment.*

Very soon Iris can come back to the Realm, he promises, and she can watch her beloved girl from there.

Goodbye, my daughter.

CRUISING HIS POSTAL truck along Rabbit Glenn Road, Thom Sayre stuffs the last mailboxes: Mueller, Rossi, Gustafsson.

Hoyt Eddy passes in his pickup, not waving. Thank God Hoyt now rents a post box in town. Thom used to have navigate a mile of ruts to the end of Upper Old Spruce Lane.

Finishing his route, Thom heads back to the post office, honking at Bern D'Annunzio going the other way in his cop cruiser. They'll see each other that night at the firehouse, sit around with the other volunteers, cards and hoagies, no wives, no kids, couple of pedestal fans for a breeze. Most nights the alarm goes off at least once, especially in this drought, when everything is combustible.

He drives past the quarter-acre subdivision where Gil Reynard built that gigantic imitation-stone mansion. It still hasn't sold; even the bank can't get rid of it. Thom chuckles: wherever Gil heard there was going to be a housing boom in Graynier, that it was the new "hot" town for Boston weekenders who couldn't afford the Cape—well, he must have heard it from someone's anus. Maybe Gil misheard the anus; he's that dense. Or the drugs have fried him. Gil is hooked on something Thom can't remember the name of, not crack but something like it.

Thom knows everything about everybody in Graynier, or near to it: names, addresses, addictions.

He doesn't know the name of the girl he's passing now, but he has seen her often on his rounds. A young slip of a thing, face shaded by a straw hat with a plum-colored ribbon. Betty Haff at Meadowlark Realty told him the girl is staying with one of her renters, Brett Sampson: the tall dude with the mixed-race kid. Chances are she's Sampson's girlfriend. Definitely an outdoor nut, likes to walk off a lot of shoe leather, even in this heat.

He watches her in the rear-view. She's turning onto Upper Old Spruce. Thom has seen her going up and down so many different streets, she could be a terrorist drawing up a map of bomb targets—if there was anything in Graynier besides Gil Reynard's house to bomb.

Not fifty yards behind the girl is the mixed-race kid pedaling a bike that's too big for him, alongside Gita Poonchwalla on a bike too small. The Poonchwalla girl's been growing up a storm the past year, getting that sullen look girls get when they're going through the awkward stage. At 62, Thom remembers a time when the town had no Poonchwallas or Alvarezes or Ngs—names with no vowels or too many. There were only Italians and Scandinavians, descended from the immigrant artisans who worked in the glass factory, long ago.

Thom passes the two kids on their bikes. They disregard his wave, their eyes trained steadfastly forward.

GITA AND COLLIN hide their bikes in the pines, creeping among the trees to stay out of sight.

Gita is distraught. Jane is headed for Hoyt Eddy's house. Thus evil joins evil, and Gita's already difficult task is doubled. Spiritual sensitivity is her heavy cross; the ability to *know*, in every cell, when a malevolence is near. Sometimes the sensation is only a hot tickle at the base of her skull, sometimes a burst of flame in her breast, or under the surface of her skin, brightening like coals when she senses Shaarinen's presence.

He can enter and discard forms at will; temporarily inhabit a mortal being to commit his acts of violence, such as entering a black crow poised over roadkill, or the time he entered a punk who jacked cars from the motel parking lot: Gita was the one who caught him and called the police. By the time they came, Shaarinen had exited the kid's body.

So she has taken him on before. But the business with Jane is unprecedented; this time, Shaarinen is *fully incarnated*. Jane is not a borrowed body: this is the demon god himself, walking the streets of Graynier as a frail, demure girl in a straw hat. He is gathering his forces for an apocalypse of some sort. The knowledge is lodged like a fiery spear in the pit of Gita's stomach.

What began as a small point of inflammation (in fact, an undiscovered ulcer) has increased sharply since Jane arrived in town. Right now Gita is giddy with pain. She can easily control fear, but not hate. And hatred is tearing up her gut, smoking through her pores.

Gana, who hates evil, chose Gita to be her warrior for good. Yet just when Gita could bear the burden of constant watchfulness no more, and she prayed for release, Gana appeared at the motel: *fully incarnated* as the Tawny One, Yenu Krisnu, the predicted savior in a male child form. Gita could cry with gratitude at being chosen to tutor the boy.

Their mission must be completed before the end of August, when Collin has to leave with his dad.

By then they will have met their destiny: the cataclysmic showdown between Yenu Krisnu and Shaarinen.

Gita and the Tawny One advance, crouching, through the

woods, to the edge of the clearing where Hoyt's house stands. Pressing her burning stomach against the cool earth, she commands Collin to lie belly-down beside her on the carpet of pine needles so they can peer from under the tree branches.

They watch Shaarinen proceed up the driveway toward Hoyt's bungalow. Collin whispers, "The two of them are definitely working together." He hears Gita make a gagging sound. In surprise he turns to see her clutching her stomach, a yellow patch of vomit sinking into the earth. The smell of bile reaches his nostrils. "Gita!"

"Shh!"

Shaarinen turns and looks in their direction. His female form climbs the sloping lawn, toward the tree line. Flattening themselves against the ground, the children hold their breaths as Shaarinen comes to a stop right in front of their hiding place. His pale gray vacant eyes scan the woods.

Gana has thrown her protection over them; Shaarinen cannot sense their abhorrent goodness even three feet away.

The demon moves off, skirting the edge of the property. He keeps close to the perimeter of the trees, searching for something. Rounding the corner of the house, he disappears from view.

Collin scrambles to his feet.

"Stay down!"

"Don't we have to see what he's doing?"

"Wait 'til he comes back around." Gita seems paralyzed, curled up and hugging her abdomen. The color is drained from her face.

"You're all white."

"I'm being purified."

He waits respectfully. Maybe when the war is over, he'll be all white too, by the grace of Gana.

After twenty minutes, Shaarinen has not reappeared.

"Maybe he went in the back door?"

Gita sends Collin on recon. Staying inside the tree line, he moves toward a position where he can view the back of Hoyt's house, passing what looks like a dump: old furniture and truck parts chucked into a leaf-filled pit. Could be a portal! Gita says that demons use them to come and go from the Worldunder.

Completing his circle around the house, he calls, "He's gone!"

Gita emerges from their hiding place, looking revived. "I know, 'cause the pain in my belly's going away."

"But where did he go? We were watching. Unless he snuck into the woods back there. Maybe there's a trail we don't know about."

Gita eyes the woods behind the house. She does not seem to be feeling the warrior energy at the moment. "Shaarinen wouldn't have to sneak away. He can dematerialize. It's one advantage he has over us. You'll be able to do that too, one day."

Collin straightens up with pride. He is coming into his own as an avatar: already taller, braver, filled with purpose.

He picks up a rock from the driveway, hurling it at Hoyt's front window.

The rock smashes through the pane, shards of glass collapsing inwards. Letting out a whoop, Gita watches him take another rock from the lawn. His aim is sure and true. The air echoes with the crash of another window destroyed.

Gita and Collin grin at one another, no words necessary: Hoyt is as much their enemy as Jane. Grabbing a rake leaning against the tool shed, Gita moves to the kitchen door, swinging the handle with all her might against the glass panel.

They circle the bungalow, demolishing every window. The woods seem to shiver with each report: a crash, and then laughter. Not the laughter of children, but of a goddess and her acolyte.

CHAPTER THIRTEEN

Jane's sneakers crunch in the dead leaves, her socks snagging on greenbrier. When she started out, entering the woods in back of the bungalow, the trail was visible, climbing the hill diagonally. Passing a ravine where someone had dumped some junk, it switched back, continuing in a gentle zigzag uphill. But as Jane got higher, the trees grew closer together and the underbrush took over until the trail disappeared entirely.

For the last 20 minutes she has been climbing without guidance, fending off the thorny reach of blackberry bushes, tripping over roots and saplings. Conifers crowd out the birch and oak trees, carpeting the ground with their needles.

Granite rocks great and small protrude on the hillside, but do not constitute a wall.

She trudges upward, straw hat tipped over her eyes, gaze fixed on the ground before her, not daring to look behind. One glance will confirm that the way back is swallowed up, and she is lost.

Suddenly her head slams hard into a low-hanging branch. Rocked back by the blow, she loses her balance, tumbling into a thicket, her hip hitting something solid beneath a snarl of vines.

Rubbing her already swelling forehead, she extricates herself from the vines, tearing the strands apart. Her hip is bruised; beneath the tangle of vines is a pile of stones—the hard thing her hip encountered when she fell.

She scrambles unsteadily to her feet. Something directs her gaze back to the pile of stones. Though the smaller rocks are scattered about, beneath them is a sturdy base of large, heavy rocks.

She is looking at the remnants of a wall. A farmer's arduous labor, from more than a century past.

Brushing off the heaps of dead leaves, she discovers more such rocks. Looking up the hill now, she can trace the wall beneath the foliage vaguely creeping and crumbling upwards.

Farmer Quirk's wall! In a burst of exhilaration, she is almost running up the steep incline. Where will the stones lead? Something of great importance waits at the top—so her vision said! She gasps for breath as she climbs, salty sweat trickling into her open mouth.

The crest of Rowell Hill is up ahead.

Throwing off its camouflage, the wall emerges wholly, real and intact, crowned by a glory of green moss. The terrain levels out; Jane slows to a walk, taking more care to step over the loops of vines, skirting the prickly shrubs. She is intensely thirsty.

She glimpses a bright expanse of sunlight through the trees—an open area. Heart pummeling her ribs, she rushes toward the light. As she parts the pine branches to step through, she finds herself in a small clearing. In its center is a shack.

JANE DRAWS NEAR a small, primitive lean-to made of weathered planks: perhaps an old hunting shelter. The roof seems recently tarpapered, shaded by the overhanging branches of chokecherry trees. The door hangs tilted on loose hinges, a long-handled ax and a spade propped beside it.

Pressing her ear to the door, Jane listens for sounds of someone inside. She hears only the drilling of a woodpecker nearby, the katydids simmering in the trees. Lifting the door's hook-and-eye latch, she peers inside.

A single room. The flooring is made of the same splintered wood as the walls; a built-in bench covered by a narrow mattress and folded blanket are its only furnishings. There are no windows, only a hinged flip board that props open to serve as hunter's lookout. Arranged neatly against the wall are a kerosene lantern, folding camp stove, some butane canisters and plastic gallon jugs of distilled water.

She enters eagerly, unsealing one of the jugs and gulping down water as fast as she can. Pausing for breath, she lets the water splash over her face and clothes.

Looking around the room, she feels no stirring of memories; her instincts are silent. Is this her journey's end? Is this mean little shack the answer to her soul's eerie unrest?

She curls up on the bench mattress to collect her thoughts. Fishing Eleanor Graynier's brooch from her pocket, she clasps the talisman between praying hands, closing her eyes: *Why was I brought here? Help me understand what I'm to do. Heavenly Redeemer, send another memory, a vision, an answer...*

Sleep comes instead.

THE SOUND OF CRASHING in the underbrush outside jolts Jane awake. Something approaches. Sucking in her breath, she waits helplessly.

A light tattoo of hooves on dirt, crossing the clearing, fading.

She opens the door in time to glimpse a herd of deer, a regatta of seesawing white tails, bounding away through the woods. Following the deer's progress, her eyes stray to a heap of stones strewn over the clearing's opposite perimeter.

How could she have missed it? Quirk's wall does not end at the clearing, and it beckons her onward.

Glancing at the long shadows extending over the ground, and the slanting light through the trees, she sees the sun is low. No time to venture further; she must turn back and retrace her way down, God willing, before dark.

"I MUST GO BACK tomorrow, to follow the wall further."

Brett applies iodine to Jane's scratches where the branches flayed her face and arms as she stumbled down Rowell Hill.

"You should've waited for me." He dabs the cotton ball to her cheek, the warmth of her breath on his wrist, the flowery smell of her soap. They sit on her bed, a province not permitted him before tonight.

"You disapprove." She pulls away. "Yet I am so close to remembering. I can feel it." She glances at the doorway, suddenly aware of a pair of eyes on them.

Collin flits out of sight; they hear his bare feet pattering back to his room, his door shutting.

"Your son feels a certain antipathy to me."

Brett wants to stay on point. "I don't like you wandering about the woods all alone."

"But I have a map." Slipping under the covers, she slides her feet down, playfully nudging him until he is obliged to get off the bed. As he lays a cold pack on her forehead for the bruise, she chatters on. "It will help my concentration to be alone. I must be mindful every second."

Messages abide in everything God places in the world before us, she tells him. Every crumb of earth, every blade, leaf, rock and cloud signifies, "if we could only learn to read them!"

Brett has never seen her so pretty and beguiling, her cheeks' customary pallor yielding to bursts of pink, as if life and spirit have broken to the surface. He wishes that she could always be so happy, and that he was the cause.

Jane settles back on the pillow. "I shall hardly sleep, waiting for tomorrow."

Brett offers to read her some poetry to help her sleep.

"I should enjoy that very much."

He fetches an anthology of the romantic poets he got this afternoon, driving all the way to the nearest library in Quikabukket. She listens intently to some poems of Shelley and then Poe, asking him to read several times over the one called "Ulalume."

> *And we passed to the end of the vista,*
> *But were stopped by the door of a tomb –*

By the door of a legended tomb;
And I said – "What is written, sweet sister,
  On the door of this legended tomb?"
She replied – "Ulalume – Ulalume –
'Tis the vault of thy lost Ulalume!

The romantic poets are a real gloom-and-doom crowd, Brett thinks, disappointed; he could come up with better poetry himself. Like, *Jane, oh oh Jane...You steal my heart again...and again...*

He looks up from the page. She is sleeping. Removing the cold pack, he touches his lips to her cheek, and to the sweet dent at the corner of her mouth. *Oh, Jane...*

CHAPTER FOURTEEN

When Hoyt lifts his head, he is in pitch blackness, hunched over a table. His mouth tastes of bile and tannins. His brain stutters to life: he is at Jack Meltzer's desk in the study.

Groping for the desk lamp, his hand collides with a glass bottle. It topples. He switches on the light; red wine is spilling onto the keys of Meltzer's computer.

Righting the bottle, Hoyt swabs the keys with the hem of his T-shirt, waking the computer from sleep mode. The screen brightens to reveal the *Wikipedia* article he was reading when he passed out.

It all started earlier that day when he'd picked up the Meltzers' chair at Iacovucci's. The repairman had turned the chair over to show Hoyt where he'd had to glue the joints. "Tell your client no one should sit on this," Iacovucci said. "These chairs aren't just old, they're crap."

That was when Hoyt noticed, inside the seat frame, a strange insignia burned into the wood: a variation on a broken cross. The same symbol that was stamped on the cover of an old Bible. The same book containing the lock of auburn hair that had multiplied and clung to his fingers.

"Any idea what this mark is?"

Iacovucci's snowy eyebrows lifted over his bifocals. "That means it's a Gabriel Nation chair. Crazy what some people pay for them—they're rare, made upstate by some nutty 19th-century commune like the Shakers, except with zero talent for furniture. That's why you don't see many of these, on account of they fall apart so easy." Iacovucci eyed Hoyt's cervical collar. "So what happened to you?"

"Whiplash." Hoyt's pain was increasing every day; the foam collar didn't seem to be helping any more. Alcohol worked better, along with a modicum of weed.

By late afternoon he was hanging out in Jack's study, chugging a bottle of the Meltzers' best Bordeaux and sucking on a joint as he surfed the Web for wildlife porn. He liked to watch the big-loined animals going at it: elks, Kodiak bears, lions. Also hot, bundled king cobras.

Halfway down the bottle, and a charred roach all that remained of the marijuana, Hoyt found himself typing "gabriel nation" in the search bar. Following a link to an antiques site, he read a short paragraph on the insignia:

> "The Gabriel Nation cross, with its base bent to the left signifying the angel Gabriel's position at the left hand of God, and its apex touching the scalloped canopy of heaven, symbolizes the highest spiritual state which can be achieved during mortal life."

Wikipedia offered a few more details:

> "Gabriel Nation, a short-lived Christian utopian community, originated in Beller, Texas, in 1849 under the leader-

ship of Levon Artzuni, an Armenian immigrant. Two years later, when Texans proved hostile to his ministry, the charismatic Artzuni moved a small group of followers to Hovey Brook, Massachusetts."

Hoyt knew Hovey Pond. It was about fifty miles northwest of Graynier, near Marlborough. The town had a massage parlor whose Friday "Wild West" nights made the trip occasionally worthwhile.

"Declaring himself the messenger of the angel Gabriel, Artzuni preached that the divinity of angels was attainable by humans: through prayer, ecstatic trance, and conversion of sinners, concepts he drew from the evangelical religious traditions of the South. What gave the group its notoriety was Artzuni's claim that virginity was a prerequisite for all members, without which one could not aspire to angelic beatitude.

"For a time, Gabriel Nation was tolerated in Massachusetts, until disaffected locals spread rumors that Artzuni himself had divested some female converts of their virginity, and local outrage forced the group to move on. Whether they would have eventually died out like the Shakers, who also promoted celibacy, can never be known, since all the followers of Gabriel Nation perished of famine en route to the Pacific Northwest in 1857."

For a moment, Hoyt was with the little band of believers, huddling with their demented leader in some godforsaken mountain pass as doom howled in. He shivered: it was a feeling like when he was ten years old, hunkered down with his scripture-spewing mother as the eviction notice was hammered to the door.

He touched his fingers to his eyes, suddenly aware he was

crying. Angrily he wiped the tears away, but they only flowed harder.

It was a mercy when he passed out.

AND NOW, REGRETTABLY, he's conscious again.

Hoyt shuts off the computer, getting to his feet. The blood booms in his head; his neck is on fire again. Ripping off the useless cervical collar, he chucks it in the trash basket and lurches to the door, leaving his mess on the desk for Honorata the maid. Tomorrow she'll clean everything up before the Meltzers copter in. Right now he requires neat liquor, fast.

He yanks open the glove compartment in his truck, his hand closing around the sleek, cool glass shape of deliverance. Twisting off the cap, he brings the bottle to his lips, throwing a slug of brandy *"derrière la cravate"*—behind the necktie—as the froggy froggy French put it. The thought hits him that he forgot to order a replacement for the missing tiki torch on the pool path— no doubt the work of teenage vandals. Ah, the Vandals. Sack of Rome, 455 A.D. Were they hormonal too, with acne? He drinks to them, those naughty Vandals.

Then he remembers Pete. Climbing out of the truck, he puts two fingers in his mouth and whistles for the dog. The night's humidity seems to suffocate sound. Haze drifts across a chawed-off moon as Hoyt walks up the driveway toward the lawn, whistling again. "Pete!"

Honks from the lake greet him, which means the dog is in the woods; the Canada geese wouldn't be back if Pete were around.

Taking the brandy with him, Hoyt strides out on the grass. Immediately he realizes his blunder. He'd left the sprinklers on—for two days? Three? Now every step he takes is in mush, the viscous soil sucking up his boots, the grass drowned. Halfway to the lake, his feet have sunk past the ankle; he can't pull either boot up.

"Pete! You asshole!"

The unseen geese chortle. The skunks must be high-fiving each other in the bushes.

Trying to pry his boots from the mire with all his might, he manages to drive them deeper. His stomach recoils as the mud breaches his calves. Cursing, he decides to undo his laces and pull his stockinged feet clear.

But first, a drink.

Before he can take a swig he is sinking further, as if in a slow elevator down...

With a sound like thunder, the ground below his feet opens and he free-falls, hurtling through a void.

He lands with a crash on his back and lies there in shock, staring at the stars above. His thumped brain burps up the German for star: *stern*. The stars are stern indeed, admonishing him: *Your fault. You left the fucking sprinklers on.*

He scrambles to his feet. He is standing at the bottom of a crater, a gaping sinkhole in the middle of the Meltzers' flooded lawn, the rim of its steep mud walls at least five feet above his head, far out of reach. Water droplets pelt his upturned face: the underground sprinkler pipes, sticking naked out of the collapsed soil overhead, drizzle on his head in further mockery.

If he can climb partway up the side, he can grab onto the pipes and hoist himself up the rest of the way. Clambering up the slope, he grasps at frangible roots, dislodging stones.

The wall caves downward under his exertions, melting away. Hoyt is back at the bottom, the hole bigger than before.

He gropes up the opposite side. This time when the wall gives way, he is sent rolling to the bottom with rusted metal scrap, loose chunks of concrete rubble, and what looks like a part of a toilet seat.

He realizes the contractor used improper fill, then neglected to compact it. The sprinklers' deluge only hastened a collapse that was long overdue. Flat on his ass and panting, Hoyt mentally hoists a glass to his fellow cheat, who really should be here with him celebrating at the bottom of the canyon.

Taking his cell phone from his back pocket, he dials 911: he'll rouse that circle jerk known as the Graynier Volunteer Fire Department. *No service*, his phone announces. Maple Manor's signal is weak; Jack Meltzer had brought in a brace of lawyers to defeat the installation of a phone tower on Rowell Hill, which would have compromised his view. Usually Hoyt can find a spot where there's a flimsy connection—but not here at the bottom of a twelve-foot pit.

Hoyt leaves the phone on, just in case someone might be able to get through from the other end. But no one knows he is here; no one lives nearby; and no one, in any case, cares. Everyone above is sweating through a hot summer night, but down here the bowels of the earth are cold, wet, and covetous, hoarding their captive. He's in for a long night.

Even worse is the prospect of getting sober. He feels around for the brandy bottle, hoping it survived the plunge. His hand contacts something smooth and round. But it's only a piece of plastic duct pipe amid the debris. He flings it aside and keeps digging, first methodically, then with a vengeance, dirt packing his nails, his arms scraped bloody by stones and scrap metal.

At one point he pulls forth a long femur bone. Perhaps from a horse, from the bygone days when this whole area was carved up into farms. In the deep woods behind his house, he has seen remnants of stone fences. Suddenly a straight, carefully-laid wall will appear, demarcating nothing anymore except maybe history.

Yes, plenty of history to be found in a ten-foot scrap hole. If he gave a shit.

He slumps back in defeat, gulping air heavy with decomposition. *Always knew I could sink lower if I tried.* He laughs bitterly, then settles in to wait out the night.

From time to time, Hoyt hears the light rumbling of more soil breaking from the walls, sifting to the bottom, covering his outstretched legs; he can feel the bumping of worms underneath as they collide with his body and reroute. He pushes away the thought that he is in his grave. Nothing to do, nothing to drink, and all thought is ill-advised.

HOURS LATER, HOYT wakes to the sensation that someone is looking down at him from above. He struggles to focus, but there is no moon to see by, the stars rubbed away by low-lying mist.

Gradually, he makes out a head hanging over the rim of the sinkhole.

The head is small, thick-necked, with flaps of long hair drooping down. Though he can't see its eyes, he feels an opaque gaze on him.

"Hey," he croaks uncertainly.

The presence starts to breathe fast. Staccato exhalations, like husky laughter: *Heh-heh-heh.*

Hoyt's hair stands up; his blood races as fear tightens around his heart.

A low growl forms in the thing's throat, growing louder, like a train emerging from a tunnel.

Then a bark.

"Pete!" Nearly swooning with relief, he stands and calls the dog. "Hey, boy! Go get help."

This is not a command Pete understands. He's not a TV dog. If he were, he would run, get rope from Hoyt's truck, clamp one end in its jaws, toss the other end down, and haul his master out of danger. But, Pete is stupid.

Or, alternatively, Pete is smart: there is no rope in Hoyt's truck.

If the mutt can't help him to safety, at least he can keep Hoyt warm. "Come on down!" He beckons vigorously. "Good dog! Jump!"

Crouching, Pete readies to leap. Then, gauging the distance down, he changes his mind. He whines an apology, does a couple of spins to denote frustration. Then the smell of night prey drifts by his nostrils. With a bound, Pete's racing away to better options than spending the night stuck in a hole with a man who has no food. Pete is too smart for that.

Hoyt sits on the ground, leaning back against the wall again and closing his eyes. He hugs himself to preserve his body's heat, every muscle tight with cold.

As he passes in and out of consciousness, the haze departs, uncovering the stern stars.

Whump. He jerks awake.

The bank opposite Hoyt is calving like an iceberg. *Whump.* Another chunk of wall slides to the bottom.

He sees something white embedded in the bank. A white head. Small, like a child's skull. And it has eyes.

He's got to be dreaming. He yells, hoping to wake himself up. Instead, his bellowing causes the dirt to shift again, sifting away from the head to reveal its white neck. And he's not dreaming.

Another layer of soil breaks away. Two small white hands appear, thrust out stiffly. They seem to reach for him.

Tamping down the terror building in his chest, Hoyt tells himself that if the thing is a skeleton, all it can do is frighten him. It can't move: it's inanimate.

Crawling to the opposite bank, he touches the white head. Its surface is rough and cool. As he comes closer, he can discern its features.

He knows that face! Roaring with fury, he grabs its neck, wrestling it from the dirt. Shoulders emerge—then a draped torso. Abruptly the soil releases the rest of it, and Hoyt falls backward, a four-foot, 100-pound chunk of heavy white granite on top of him.

A slender woman, broken off at the knees, palms extended, veiled and robed, long lank hair, with that repulsive pitying gaze... He knows it too well. There are many versions of the Holy Virgin. This one on top of him is the Immaculate Mary—probably a garden sculpture.

He remembers how his mother had all the Virgins, the way you collect action figures. Her statuettes were placed everywhere, even atop the washing machine. She prayed to them loudly. Sometimes she even crawled into Hoyt's bed with one of them clutched like a teddy bear. He would roll over in his sleep and be gored in the stomach by the Holy Mother's outstretched palms offering succor.

He was just a kid who loved his mom. He swallowed her beliefs whole, and so he loved the Virgin too, passionately. The Mother of God was beautiful, and without stain. She bore a divine boy without having sex. She was always there when you needed her. And also, indestructibly, when you didn't.

Mary's fall from grace came later, when his mother ran off. As months elapsed, Hoyt was reduced to scrounging for food in dumpsters, too embarrassed to call his father, dodging the landlord. Still he wouldn't admit that his mom had abandoned him. Instead, the Virgin Mother was his betrayer, with her lying crafty eyes, her false innocence, her palms lifted as she shrugged: *what do I care?* He threw every one of the Virgins down the trash chute, hearing them crash to pieces at the bottom. At night, sleepless in his mother's empty bed, he prayed, "Mother Mary, come to me so I can kill you."

Now, heaving the granite statue off, he smashes her to the dirt, snapping the delicate column of her neck. Her stone head rolls off.

Later, after he manages to fall back to sleep, his arm will reach for her, and cradle her head to his bosom.

CHAPTER FIFTEEN

Shutting off the sprinklers, Silvio Pereira calls to his three
nephews to stop unloading the mowers from the truck. The
ground is too soupy to carry the weight. As little and light as the
Brazilian is, his footsteps leave deep gouges in the grass, so he uses
the flagstones to circle the Meltzer house.

Rounding the corner, he sees the vast sinkhole out on the lawn.
His boss' voice is calling him from somewhere down in its depths.

On the second floor of the house, Sylvio's wife Honorata is
about to start vacuuming when she hears shouts. Crossing to the
window, she sees the men gathered around the pit. *Looks like a bomb
fell.* Mrs. Meltzer won't be happy. Maybe now Silvio will get Mister Eddy's job. Then the Pereiras can buy that three-bedroom house
on Lower Shad Street and bring her family up from São Paulo. She
watches the men lay down planks to the rim of the hole.

Silvio almost doesn't recognize the frightened, diminished
man at the bottom. Beneath the grime, Hoyt's upturned face is ashy;
his legs shudder beneath him as if he doesn't trust the earth to sustain him.

"Can you get me out of here?" Hoyt asks hoarsely.

"You make the grass too wet," Silvio says. "Now you gotta

big hole."

"Thank you for pointing that out."

Though Silvio has a twelve-foot ladder for window cleaning in the truck, he leans over the edge instead. "Mister Eddy,
you owe me money long time. When you gonna pay me?"

Hoyt's reply is barely audible: "Tomorrow."

"Now. Today you gonna pay me."

After he helps Hoyt climb out of the crater, Silvio follows him
to his pickup, where Hoyt makes out a check with a trembling hand.
Meanwhile the dog nonchalantly trots out of the woods, hopping
into the truck bed as Hoyt starts the engine.

"Mister Eddy," says Silvio, "what you want I do for the hole?"

"It's your problem. You're the boss now." Hoyt drives off without another word.

OFFICER BERNARD (Bern) D'Annunzio types up his report. Marlene
Walczak came into the station yesterday to complain that someone
had broken into her trailer. There have been five similar break-ins
over the past two weeks, all with the same pattern. The intruder
entered and left through an unlocked door, leaving few traces behind: a half-filled water glass, a banana peel, a bowl of milk with a
few Cheerios still swimming in it, an empty yogurt container in the
trash. One elderly lady found her bath towels damp and a ring of
soap scum around the tub. Bern extracted a long strand of blonde
hair from the drain. Since then, the Graynier Police have taken to
calling the mysterious intruder "Goldilocks."

According to Ms. Walczak, Goldilocks murdered her dog.
Bern leaves this out of his report; complainant admitted her pet was
about 110 in dog years. Complainant also looked a little crazy, with
all the telltale signs of being a meth addict: skinny, wired, paranoid,
bad complexion. She had a weird mole on her cheek, not round but
sort of smeared, as if someone had painted it on and then tried to
wipe it off. (Bern's cousin had something like that on her arm; the
doctors biopsied it, then scooped a deep hole in her flesh to remove

the tumor.) After she left, Bern's partner told him that Marlene was the town whore.

Bern is new in town, transferred six months ago from the country sheriff's office in Quikabukket. Graynier had never needed its own police, but now the town has a drug problem, and thus the new police station is temporarily housed in a Winnebago on Route 404. Bern is one of only four cops on the new "force," and none of them is cut out for investigative work.

They've petitioned the state to send in a plainclothes detective to ferret out where the meth is made and who the dealers are. Bern keeps expecting the guy to walk through the door.

A man comes in, about 70, too old to be him. He hands his business card to Bern. *Richard Fancher, Private Investigation.* He has driven up from Roanoke, Virginia.

Probably a retired cop, Bern guesses. Unsuited to the La-Z-Boy and floundering in excess energy, with a wife who hates having him underfoot. So the guy opens an office in his garage, puts up a website, more for pride than money. Not many bites; he'll give up in a couple of years. Then it's a short step to the geezer condo in Jupiter; he's already wearing the untucked short-sleeve pineapple-print shirt. His bones creak when he sits down, handing Bern a photo.

Bern doesn't recognize the girl. The picture is a print-out on a lousy printer with low ink. Soft-focus of a pallid, heart-shaped face on a thin neck. Hair could be blond or brown; she's half-standing in tree shadow, unaware she's being photographed.

"Runaway?"

"Yes and no." Fancher looks cagey. "Let's say she's an adult who suddenly went off on her own, and my clients want to know where she is."

"What makes you think she's in Graynier?"

"By now she may not be. But when this picture was taken, she was." Fancher slides another print-out from his attaché, a blow-up of the photo's top corner, zoomed in past the girl's shoulder. A blurred white vertical of a sign post, dappled by tree shadow; you can just make out the letters: "Graynier Ave."

"There's only one Graynier Avenue in all of North America, and that's in beautiful downtown Graynier, Mass," the old man finishes slowly, as if educating a doofus.

Bern doesn't appreciate Fancher's tone. He tosses the photos back to him. "Go by the post office and ask Thom Sayre. He knows everybody."

APPROACHING HIS FRONT stoop, Hoyt registers the jagged glass littering the steps, the missing window pane beside the door.

The vandal is back. Found the door locked, took his revenge.

Still dazed by his ghastly night in the sinkhole, Hoyt can't muster any outrage at first. Crunching through the glass, he opens his door.

Strewn over the living room carpet are shards of glass, glittering in the morning sun that pours through his empty window frames. Four windows have been smashed. Hearing the cheeping of birds in his bedroom, he goes in to find some sparrows and a cardinal ricocheting off the walls. The bedroom pane is shattered too.

The agonizing pain in his neck has returned. Grabbing a pint of bourbon from the coffee table, he hurls himself on the sofa and drinks for dear life, firing up his wrath.

Why me?

Starting with the road accident three weeks ago, something demonic has pursued Hoyt: like that mythical black swarm of she-flies, the Furies, who feast on the guilty.

Guilty of what? What have I ever done to deserve this?

He's not that interested in an answer. Revenge is all that matters. The vandal will be back, and Hoyt will be ready: locked and loaded.

WHAT DID I DO *to deserve this?* Marly stares at her mole in the hotel suite's bathroom mirror.

As long as she can remember, she has had a "beauty mark" on

her right cheek, a light-brown mole about the size of a pencil eraser. Then, a few days ago, it darkened. Now it is almost black, and sunk into the flesh, a depression whose ragged borders have expanded to the size of a nickel.

Why is God punishing me? Her car banged up, her trailer broken into, her dog gone. Every night, the terrible dreams. And now this evil-looking mole. That cop couldn't stop staring at it. How can she set foot in O'Malley's Mare? Who would sleep with her? She is rotting like a piece of fruit on the ground.

God never gives you more than you can handle. Things could be worse. At least the bleeding from her hands has stopped. At least she's not hallucinating any more.

She wipes away the tiny specks of food flung onto the glass by flossing guests, then goes into the bedroom to start vacuuming.

Since Gabriella left to have her baby, Marly has been cleaning the Ellis Suite, the biggest, fanciest room in the B & B. The master bedroom of the old Graynier family mansion, it holds all the original furniture: fringed Victorian chairs, stained-glass lamps, carved rosewood armoire and matching bedstead, a marble-topped bureau.

The last guest left the mirrored door of the armoire hanging open. As Marly swings it shut, her reflected image comes into view. She screams.

The face in the mirror isn't hers. It's an old man with muttonchop whiskers, his thick mane of white hair raked into disheveled peaks. He glares back at Marly. A deep whorl of puckered scar tissue forms a hole in his cheek under one eye.

Her screams bring the maintenance man. He finds her shaking uncontrollably, pointing at herself in the mirror of an old armoire, nobody else in the room.

"UNH," SAYS COLLIN, by way of goodbye to his grandparents, as he hands the cell phone back to his father.

Brett tries to stay alert. His in-laws' call woke him after only three hours' sleep, following a long night at the computer.

"What's going on with Coll?" George Linwood's deep, mistrustful bass rumbles in his ear. "All he does is grunt."

"Yeah, it's just his way." Brett rakes his fingers through his sleep-rumpled hair.

"*His way?*" Veronda's mother Olani is on the extension. "We know our own grandson. Don't preach at us what we *know*. What you been doing with that boy?"

He glances over at his son. Already dressed for the day, the boy looks away and retreats downstairs. "Lots of things," Brett answers feebly, wiping sweat from his brow. Even at eight in the morning, the heat promises a scorcher. "He's learning to swim."

"*To swim?* Collin never studied no swimming."

"Well, he says he can swim now."

"He *says?* Ain't you *observed* him?"

The front door slams. The kid doesn't even bother with breakfast anymore, hurrying out every morning to meet Gita.

George jumps in, "Who's supervising this swimming?"

Every day, Brett lets his ten-year-old son walk out the door unsupervised, and doesn't see him again until dinner. Worse, he's grateful; Collin's defection gives Brett more time to obsess about Jane.

Phone to his ear, Brett wanders down the hall. "He's got a friend. A girl from up here. They do lots of activities together."

"What's her name?"

"Gita."

"*Gita?* What kind of a name is that?"

What kind of name is Veronda? "Indian, I guess." He looks into Jane's room. Her bed is empty. When did she go out?

"What type of Indian? Whoopin' it up or the other kind?"

Every morning Jane packs up her belongings and tidies the room to look as if no one slept here. Ready to fly at a moment's notice. He checks under the bed: her duffel is still there. He breathes a sigh of relief, tamping down his chronic fear that she has left him.

Someone raps sharply on the front door.

"Sorry, I've got to go." Brett claps the phone shut, cutting off his in-laws and hurrying downstairs.

The stranger on the stoop is an unsmiling, square-set elderly man with an attaché. Despite his tropical-fruit-print shirt, he has an aura of official business.

Brett's heart dips: is he here about Jane? Has something happened to her? "Can I help you?"

"Are you Brett Sampson?" The man has a soft Southern accent. "Yes."

"Dick Fancher. I'm a private investigator." He offers a business card, damp with sweat. "I'm told that you've got a young woman staying with you. Is this her?" He hands Brett a printout photo.

Brett stares at the print-out snapshot of Jane, captured by his cell phone and posted, foolishly, on the web.

Fancher notes his dismay. "Can I come in?"

Chapter Sixteen

Brett Sampson is not a skilled liar. Dick Fancher, P.I., thinks it's a safe bet that the girl Brett calls "Jane" did *not* leave Graynier yesterday on a bus to Montreal. Neither does he believe that the girl showed up unannounced, a complete stranger, and Sampson just took her in without hesitation; or that he learned practically nothing about her during the three whole weeks she stayed with him.

Still, Sampson seems in no hurry to get rid of him. On the contrary, he wants to talk, or at least to listen. Inviting Fancher right into his kitchen, the guy sat him down, made coffee and French toast. After offering his phony information about the girl's departure for Montreal, he started plying the detective with questions: where was she from? (Wyatt Bend, Virginia.) Who were her parents? (Bill and Karen Moss.) Why were they looking for her? (She ran away.) All asked with a heated curiosity, bordering on obsession.

Fancher lets Sampson play interrogator, keeping his answers short to tantalize and draw the guy in further.

"What reason would she have to run away?"

"What reason did she tell you?"

"Like I said, she won't say anything about anything." Sampson shakes his head in frustration, not realizing he's just used the present tense.

She's still around; Fancher would bet good money on it. She might even be in the house, right now. He keeps an ear cocked for telltale creaks overhead, a toilet flushing, while Brett continues: "I mean, she's not a minor, right? So how can she be a runaway? She's free to go where she wants."

"Legally, yes. That's why the police aren't sitting here in your kitchen. But some kids—and a 23-year-old, in my book, is still a kid—they aren't so well equipped for freedom. They can't take care of themselves. And then we're not talking about an ordinary kid either..." Fancher trails off coyly, waiting as Brett grabs the bait.

"Why do you think Jane can't take care of herself?"

"You'd better get used to calling her Caroline."

"Fine, whatever! Could you please just tell me why you think she's unstable?"

"I never said she was unstable." Fancher had used that exact word in the message he left on Myspace. Brett must be the one who posted her picture.

"I mean...you said she isn't ordinary. Why?"

Look how he's jumping out of his skin. He's in deep, covering for her; maybe he's her boyfriend by now. Fancher decides to tell him everything. The more Brett understands about her troubled history, the more likely he'll give up her whereabouts.

"Could I get another cup of coffee?"

After Brett refills his mug, Fancher starts from the beginning.

"HER FOLKS THOUGHT they had a normal baby. But by the time Caroline was two, they realized she was different. Totally silent, avoided eye contact. Remote. Screamed when they touched her. They had her tested, fearing the worst, and sure enough the diagnosis came back: she was autistic."

Fancher watches Brett carefully as he talks. At the mention of autism, Brett's lips part very slightly, as if he's trying to keep his jaw from dropping.

"You must have noticed she was a couple cans short of a six-pack," Fancher drawls, testing him.

"I don't know what you mean." Brett closes his mouth firmly.

Fancher presses on: "You can imagine what that news did to them. These are decent, hard-working people of modest means, father's an electrician, mother ran a cat-care business. They already had three children. The prospect of taking care of Caroline overwhelmed them. And Wyatt Bend is a very small town; no experienced caregivers, no facilities for special-needs kids.

"At first the Mosses did their best, hoping Caroline would somehow snap out of it. The worst part of autism seems to be that the kid just shuts you out. You don't get any kind of response ever. Not a word, not even a smile. No love. She's in her own little world, humming, doing repetitive motion stuff like flapping her hands or banging on a wall. Anyway, by the time she was six they were looking to place her in a home. The nearest one was about 60 miles away in Deer Run, across the state line in Pennsylvania.

"They had to come to terms with the probability that she'd be spending her whole life there. The doctors told them, severely autistic people don't just 'snap out of it.' Her mom and dad visited her when they could, but I guess no matter how much you love someone, if you never get anything back, it's hard to keep it up. So eventually they went on with their lives."

As Fancher pauses to sip his coffee, Brett interjects eagerly, "But Jane talks. She looks in your eyes, she doesn't bang her head on the wall."

"That's the kicker. Caroline was in Deer Run for 17 years and suddenly—this was in June—Bill and Karen get a call from the doctor. He tells them: she's talking. I mean, she's talking normal, like you and me. She can read, and write. Somehow she absorbed a lot of stuff over the years without showing it, and suddenly she's ready to speak up. She understands where she is, and she's asking to leave.

"The parents are blown away. All their kids have grown up and left, and they've been enjoying the empty nest, and now the facility doesn't want to keep Caroline anymore because they say she's competent.

"The Mosses drive up to see her. The Caroline they find waiting for them, with her bags all packed, is well spoken and polite, but still very distant and not affectionate. It was like hugging a statue, Karen said. And now they have to take home this total stranger.

"So they put the bags in the trunk, and Caroline gets in the back. She sits real quiet while they drive her to a mall nearby to buy her clothes and toiletries and things, which Karen thought would be a nice way to get to know each other. Caroline goes along with everything, but she's not exactly talkative other than 'yes,' 'no,' and 'thank you.'

"Later the parents are waiting outside the dressing room while Caroline tries on some bathing suits. Karen takes a moment to go to the ladies' room. When she looks in her purse for some lipstick she notices her car keys are missing, and all her cash.

"She runs out and tells Bill she was robbed, and they get the store detective. Meanwhile no one's paying attention to Caroline in the dressing room. When they finally remember her, they realize she hasn't come out. They open the curtain, and she's gone. She left a note, which she must have written at the institution, planning her escape."

Fancher opens his attaché, handing Brett a photocopy of the note. Brett recognizes Jane's careful penmanship.

Dear William and Karen,

I extend my most sincere thanks to you for so kindly providing my comforts of the past twenty-three years. I trust you will accept with equanimity that, since I have reached the age of majority, your obligations to me are at an end. Truly there exist no sentimental ties between us. I have made certain of this, in order to spare you any pain over our inevitable parting. Please be reassured that I am fully able to make my own way in "the world." Kindly do not seek to find me, as I do not wish it.

> *With filial gratitude*
> *and most respectfully,*
> *"Caroline"*

Brett puts the letter down without comment.

"Kind of formal, wouldn't you say?"

"She does—did—have a sort of old-fashioned way of speaking," Brett admits.

"I'm told autistics sometimes have their own language. It's another way of putting up walls. Anyhow, she succeeded at disappearing. Because she stole their car keys, they couldn't drive off to look for her. So she gained a lot of time. The police were summoned to the mall, but they wouldn't conduct a search. Somebody needs to be missing a minimum of 24 hours, and there was no evidence of foul play. And the letter indicated she was exercising her right as an adult to skip town. When the cops were no help, the Mosses came to me."

Chin in his hands, Brett re-reads the letter before him.

"She's a sick pup, my friend."

Brett shakes his head without looking up.

"Come on, is this a normal letter you would write to your own parents?" Fancher taps the signature at the bottom of the note. "Look at the quote marks around 'Caroline,' like it's not her real name. More quotes around 'the world'—she doesn't acknowledge reality. She's made her own world, where she's Jane, and her whole family—mother, father, three brothers—they don't exist."

Brett won't respond, sliding the letter back to Fancher.

The detective sees that the more he presses his case, the deeper Sampson will dig in his heels. "Look, she needs help," he says gently. "Regardless of what she writes, she's not ready to be on the loose in a very confusing world. Not everyone's as good-hearted as you. She could wind up really damaged—even murdered. I've seen it. Just tell me where she is, son."

Brett folds his arms stubbornly. "I don't know. She was headed to Montreal."

"I think you do know. I also think you know what's the right thing to do. She belongs with her parents."

"She doesn't think so. It's pretty clear in her letter that she doesn't want to be found."

The fact is, Fancher's not sure the Mosses really want her back. Parents who are berserk with grief, they splash their missing loved one's picture all over the internet, the post office, nailing posters on trees, taking out a mortgage to pay for the search. This couple waited a week before hiring him, and haggled over his fee. He had the impression they were just going through the motions so it would look like they tried.

He tries a compromise. "How about I negotiate so Caroline doesn't have to return home? If I can just go back to her parents with the information that she's safe, and tell them where she's living so they won't worry, I think they'll honor her request to leave her alone."

Brett gets up, clearing the table with finality. "It makes no difference. I don't have any information."

All at once, they hear the front door open. Both have the same thought: *she's back.*

Vaulting from his chair, the detective bolts for the hallway, but Brett gets there first, blocking the passage with his tall body.

A deep male voice says, "Go get your daddy."

Fancher arrives in the entry behind Brett, peering around him to see a dusky-skinned boy standing on the stoop, a uniformed cop behind him.

Recognizing Officer D'Annunzio, Fancher quickly ducks his head back and steps into the parlor, out of sight. He trains his ears on the conversation in the hall.

"Mr. Sampson?"

"Yes?"

"I just picked up your boy walking by himself along Fallow Road. I didn't think it was a good idea for a kid his age to be running around unsupervised."

"Thanks, officer. I thought he was on a play date."

Listening as D'Annunzio takes his leave, the detective noses around the parlor. He spots a pink plastic hairbrush on the sofa. Picking it up, he notes long fine strands of blond hair snarled in the bristles. Caroline's.

He hears the door close, and father and son arguing in the hall:

"Why aren't you over at Gita's?"

"She was sick to her stomach."

"Then why didn't you come straight home? What were you doing halfway out of town?"

"Let go! It's none of your business."

"It darn well is my business. I'm your father. Just what were you doing?"

"Ow! Following somebody."

Fancher slips back into the hallway, in time to see Brett crouching at Collin's eye level and gripping the boy's shoulders hard. "Following who?"

"Jane." The kid pronounces the word with obvious hatred. Averting his eyes, he catches sight of Fancher for the first time.

The old man smiles kindly at him. "You know Jane? Does she still live here?"

His father jerks up straight. "You can't question him—"

"Yes," Collin answers defiantly.

Fancher smiles evenly at Brett. "Guess she missed the bus."

As Brett hustles Collin upstairs to wait in his room, Fancher collects his attaché from the kitchen. When he returns to the front hall, Brett is already there, holding the door open.

Stepping out obligingly, Fancher turns on the stoop. "My cell number's on my card. When Caroline gets home, please call me. I'd just like a chance to speak with her, nothing more."

Brett slams the door on him.

Walking to his car on the corner, the detective knows he needn't look further for Caroline. She will be coming back to this house.

As he opens the door, the car's broiling air greets him. He climbs in, wishing he had brought a cooler with some cold soda on ice. It could be a long wait.

CHAPTER SEVENTEEN

Jane drinks deeply from one of the plastic water jugs stored in the hunting shack, then studies the old surveyor's map again. It shows a body of water called Pease Pond not too far from the clearing. She can refill the bottle there, so the shack's occupant can remain innocent of her embezzlement.

Setting her straw hat's brim against the sun, she continues along the farmer's wall, empty jug in hand, following the farmer's wall.

Today the climb up Rowell Hill is easier; her lungs have adapted to the effort; a long-sleeved shirt and trousers tucked into her socks protect her skin from sharp twigs and thorns. Navigating the woods more confidently, she chants aloud from the poem Brett read to her (*"Ulalume, Ulalume"*), matching its rhythms to her stride.

She spies a gleam of silvery blue through the trees ahead and, jumping to the other side of the wall, she veers toward it.

Pushing through branches, she emerges into an open space.

A large pond, about thirty acres of limpidly clear water, spreads before her, the metallic sheen of reflected sun concealing its depth. Drought has driven the water from the pond's edges, leaving cracked mud, wilted weeds, and bleached, half-sunk cadavers of trees with naked branches rising from the surface like rigid white fingers. No breeze stirs the noonday; nothing moves beneath the water, save for the tremors of ghostly grasses as minnows weave in and out.

For some reason the place unsettles her.

Filling the jug, she wedges it between some rocks to retrieve on the way back.

She follows the tumbled stonewall on. Sloping gently downward, it travels through a stately area of pine woods. The trees close ranks like soldiers bristling with weaponry; Jane raises her hands to protect her face as she shoulders through thickly meshed limbs.

Suddenly her hat flies away, snagged by an unseen branch. She wheels, looking up to find it dangling from a spiny tuft, nearly out of reach. Its blue ribbons trail downward.

Blue? Her hat has a plum ribbon.

Standing on her toes, Jane tugs on the ribbons, and the hat falls into her hands.

The hat she holds has a straw brim curved like a horseshoe and a tiny nosegay of silk flowers sewn onto one side of its blue satin band. As Jane fits it on her head, the brim conforms to her face, almost meeting under her chin as she ties the ribbons into a bow.

It is her bonnet.

The stray tendrils of hair she brushes from her eyes are dark, an auburn color. Glancing down, she sees a long white skirt, feels the petticoats underneath jostling about her legs. Narrow laced boots of soft brown leather cover her feet.

Her blouse is white muslin with puffed sleeves, and a pale blue capelet covers her shoulders. She lifts her hand to her throat, where she feels something pinned. Her fingers encounter the familiar delicate convolutions of a gold brooch that, a moment ago, rested in her pants pocket.

I am myself! Her laugh of amazement dances in the air.

On the path, she seems to glide through the trees, following a now freshly built fieldstone wall bounding a pasture where sheep graze in the distance.

A disconnected voice chatters inside her head:

Almost there—hurry—is he waiting?—God please let him be there—ah, my angel—my one love —

How the sun beats! Mercy, I'm drenched—forgot my handkerchief—shade ahead, soon, soon—

My face hot and red—a sight—make myself pretty—fix my hair—bite my lips—

Hush! Vanity—stupid selfish me—must be pure—root out desire—attend the word of God—

Jane glances down to find a book in her hand, a Bible. A curious emblem is stamped on its black leather cover, something like a crucifix, yet not.

She nearly falls, tripping over a stout tree root. Straightening, she catches her breath and considers the path ahead. Farmer Quirk's wall twists and jogs; where it turns sharply left, demarcating the farm's northeast corner, Jane sees a stand of lofty white pines.

Suddenly she is rushing headlong toward the pines, breathless with anticipation, lifting her long skirts to allow her boots to skip over the ground.

Arriving in the center of the grove, she gazes about in a familiar rapture. She is standing in a circle of ancient, towering pines, a soft bed of pine needles beneath her feet. The trees' arrangement forms a natural glade, their long branches brushing the edges with fragrant shade.

Here is the place.

The stonewall continues past the glade, but Jane has reached her journey's end.

Overcome by the heat, she sits in shadows on a fallen log, setting her Bible on the grass.

The voice in her mind returns, very distinct now, a rush of chatter:

He hasn't come yet. I hoped he would be the first, so I might see his countenance light up when I arrive!—though he tries hard to conceal such improper joy. How I love that clumsy little wobble as he rises too quickly to his feet, hastily marking his place in the Holy Book before shutting it. But since I am first, I shall hide in the shadows—observe his impatience when he finds me absent—and when he sits to wait, I shall steal from behind and clap my hands over his eyes in play—though truly it is a pretext to touch my fingers to his dear, dear face.

But what if he does not come? Be still now! Show forbearance—the sun has put you all in a fever!

Removing her bonnet to cool her brow, Jane places it in on her knees, then gives a start: a plum-colored ribbon encircles the crown, and beneath the flat wide brim on her lap she is wearing trousers. Dead pine needles stick to her socks and dirty sneakers.

Dress, bonnet, and book, have all vanished, and Jane is marooned in a pine grove, without the faintest clue why she is here. She feels an awful wilderness within. Searching in her pocket, her fingers close around the brooch with the broken catch, for consolation, as if it can somehow conjure memory: *Come back! Show me more! I want to know everything!*

She must be patient. A sign will come if she waits here. The vision showed her this was a meeting place; a man will arrive— but who?

Only the rasping complaint of crows disturbs God's silence. At length she gives in to the serenity of the place, closing her eyes as she inhales the white pines' resinous scent.

Hearing a rustle, like that of a bird shrugging its feathers close by her ear, she opens her eyes.

The ground is moving. Frightened, she holds her breath: beneath her the earth rumples like an animal's hide shuddering off flies, and a patch of earth caves in at her feet; pine needles, loose stones, and dust slide down toward the center as if drawn into a funnel.

As suddenly as the slide began, it stops. Mere seconds have passed; the glade is still. A shallow depression a few inches deep rests before her.

Dig here. Something below invites, waiting for Jane to find it.

LATE AFTERNOON finds Jane trudging toward the house at 53 Sycamore Street, covered with dust, dirt wedged under her fingernails from where she'd tried digging in the glade. Only managing to displace a few inches of soil and stones, she abandoned her task, retracing her steps to the pond and washing her hands as the sun descended. Carrying the water jug back to the hunting blind, she spied the rusty shovel leaning against the side of the shack. She had forgotten it was there. No time today to return to the pine grove with the shovel; she would have to come back tomorrow.

Exhausted from her long trek, she doesn't immediately notice the car parked at the corner, the man waiting inside, his elbow resting on the open window. Her gaze slides absently to the license plate: Virginia.

She stops abruptly, sucking in her breath. The man's eye appears in the side view mirror, glancing at the street behind.

Jane ducks into a narrow alley between houses, hoping he didn't see her. Skirting backyards, she hurries to the wrought-iron gate behind her home.

Her mind races: perhaps the car from Virginia was nothing but a coincidence.

Or can it be they have found her?

CHAPTER EIGHTEEN

Hearing the back door open, Brett bounds barefoot down two flights, arriving at the kitchen doorway to see Jane bending over the letter on the table. Her grimy shirt clings to her skin in damp patches; sweat gleams on her face.

She looks up. "How did you get this?"

"From a private investigator your parents hired. He traced you here—wants to talk to you."

"I don't want to talk to him. And they are not my parents!"

Brett shoves his hands into his pockets to hide his nerves. "You were adopted?"

"There is no time for explaining." She moves past him, heading quickly down the hall.

"Caroline!" he calls after her.

Her shoulders tighten at the sound of the name, but she doesn't break stride, running up the stairs to her room. Brett finds her on her knees, tugging her pink duffel from under the bed. "You're Caroline," he says, aggressive now.

"I have been called that. But it's not who I am." Standing, she loops her bag over her shoulder. "I will go out the back."

"No." Brett blocks her exit.

"I must go!"

"You don't have to run away. The detective said your parents might leave you alone, so long as they know you're okay."

"I have no reason to believe it. Tell him I have had a change of heart and gone back to Virginia. I'll stay somewhere nearby here, and then come back when it's safe."

"You expect me to take that on faith? When you've totally lied to me?" Brett towers over her, glaring angrily.

"I haven't lied. You must forget everything he said," she pleads. "It will only confuse you."

"Put down the bag. You're not leaving and you're going to tell me the truth."

She drops the duffel, but is far from daunted. "I will say nothing if you force me to stay. Believe me, I know how to be silent."

In an instant, her eyes become dim and distant, her face slackening as a low hum issues from the back of her throat. She brings her palm up to her empty gaze, jerking her elbow back and forth so that her hand flops like a dead appendage. As she increases the rhythm, her hum rises, punctuated by giggles.

"Stop," Brett whispers, horrified.

Her arm lowers and the hum dies. With an impersonal smile on her lips, she turns her head to the doorframe, thumping her skull against the wood.

"Stop it!" Brett pulls her from the door. The flesh under his fingers feels curiously leaden, as if she is an inanimate thing in his grasp, with an oblique, painted stare. "Jane—Jane!"

As swiftly as she left, she is back, her eyes returning to his frightened face with their full spark. "That was Caroline. Have you had enough of her company?"

"Please," he releases her, "just tell me what's going on."

"I shall try to help you understand. But after, you must promise to let me leave."

"YOU HAVE ASKED for the truth. You have asked for facts. They are not the same. Caroline's life consists only of facts, but of truth there is none."

Jane sits very erect across from him at the kitchen table, hands in her lap. Intermittently her eyes dart to the back door.

"Here is your first fact. I was the baby born from the union of Bill and Karen Moss. I spent my first months in the natural daze of an infant, but soon I felt a certainty that I was *in the wrong place*. I remember how loudly I screamed when I saw my room was not my own, and the two people who hovered over my crib were not my mother and father. Even the name they gave me, 'Caroline,' was false.

"The facts of their world were not the truth of mine.

"This world in which I found myself a castaway was all wrong; yet it insisted it was right, with Bill and Karen always trying to touch me, to teach me, to bend me. Being helpless I could only pull back inside myself, as far away from them as I could manage. I refused to look at them, or to speak. I flapped my hands and spun in circles to keep them from touching me. I learned what behavior they hated, like loud humming and slamming myself against walls, and I stuck to it resolutely until finally they stopped trying to take control of my being.

"I was called autistic. So much the better. It got me away from that house and those people to a place where I was left alone, the Saint Albinus Residence in Deer Run. Fortunately for me, the staff neglected its patients, and if anyone tried to force a connection with me, I presented them with Caroline Moss, who stared into space, or spun in circles, or banged or hummed, until they gave up.

"There were a few others like me in the residence, those who simply would not cooperate with the world. We were called autistic, but we didn't see ourselves as the ones who were impaired. On the contrary, we were unusually strong. It took great self-discipline to maintain our remove. Now and then I would hear another one like me laugh, and I would laugh, too, because sometimes it struck us as so funny, normal people thrashing about in their complicated dramas, which seemed as nonsensical as dreams. But we couldn't look at each other and give ourselves away. The doctors wouldn't have appreciated the joke. It was really best not to speak at all.

"I cannot explain it, but from an early age I knew how to read, write, and speak. Perhaps I was born knowing. I concealed my abilities, and the staff believed me ignorant. But I was learning all I could about life on the outside from eavesdropping and from the television.

"Thanks to my spying, I discovered I could live independently as an adult when I reached the age of 21. I had a long time to wait, but it is nothing...to wait. When you have rejected that fabrication they call *real*, you enter a sphere without time. It's as though you find yourself suspended in pure sky, so that you lose all sense of up or down, forward or backward. The idea of time, of years passing, seems ever so quaint."

Though Jane is speaking precisely, thoughtfully, Brett feels more lost than ever; he can make no sense of it. Only a little while ago, he held power over her, blocking her escape: now he is once again limp in the filaments of a web that has held him since she arrived on his doorstep.

"Still, when the time came," Jane continues, "where would I go? Where did I belong? I was puzzling this question one day as I stood near a group of aides, when one of them showed the others a glass bowl she had bought for a dollar at a rummage sale. Turning the bowl over, she showed them the raised letters on the bottom: 'GRAYNIER GLASS.' She had done some research, and thought it might fetch a good price, as the bowl was probably from the 19th century. She said it was manufactured by a long gone company in Massachusetts, in a town called Graynier.

"The instant I heard the name, I knew it was where I came from. I stepped in and snatched the bowl. They tried to wrest it from me, but I held fast, and as my hands touched it a second name came to my mind: 'Jane.' How happy I felt! I found myself shouting it: 'Jane! I am called Jane!'

"I had never previously spoken. Naturally they were very shocked, even more astonished when I asked, 'How old am I?' They never bothered to celebrate the patients' birthdays in Saint Albinus unless parents were visiting. I asked this question loudly, over and over again.

"I was led into the doctor's office, all the while crying, 'Tell me how old I am, at once!' When she began to prepare a syringe to calm me down, I immediately quieted, explaining as reasonably as I could that I had woken from my 'sleep' and cared to know a few details of my identity. After the doctor was persuaded to open my file, I learned that I was 23. Two extra years wasted! I demanded to be retested for autism.

"It occasionally happens that an autistic miraculously 'emerges.' I convinced all the doctors that I had recovered and could function perfectly well in all respects that mattered to them. So they telephoned my alleged parents.

"All the while I hid from everyone my most urgent desire: to be *entirely myself.* I wanted to be Jane. All the years I had taken refuge from 'the world,' I had dismissed emotion and pain. Because these belonged to Caroline. But now I wanted them: Jane's feelings, Jane's suffering, to speak in Jane's voice, I—what is it, dear? Am I not explaining it well?"

Brett is pressing his hands to his temples. "I'm trying very hard to understand you. But it sounds kind of psycho."

Her gaze reproves him. "I had planned to tell you the truth at a later time, when you were ready, but you forced me to speak prematurely."

He opens his palms in surrender. "Who are you? I listen and listen, and it keeps changing."

"Who am I?" Reaching across the table, she places her white, cool hands in Brett's.

Suddenly it seems unimportant that she makes no sense, that she is mad. Her touch ignites his craving to own her wholly; let the world turn to ash outside.

"I am Jane Pettigrew," she says.

STANDING OUTSIDE the kitchen, Collin stills his body so the floorboards won't give him away. He heard Jane and his dad come upstairs (where Collin was exiled to his room after his blowout with Brett). When the two went to the kitchen, Collin stole downstairs after them.

He peers around the doorframe, careful to stay out of his father's line of sight. Not that there's much chance of being discovered, his dad is so hypnotized by the demon across from him, hanging on every word of her ridiculous story. Jane can say anything, and his father turns to candy she can roll around in her mouth and suck on.

If his dad wasn't so weak, Collin could love him. He wants to. But as long as the poor man remains in Shaarinen's thrall, his soul is gone. You can see it in his eyes. Collin is the only one left in this house with his wits about him.

And he has the goddess' mandate.

An idea comes to him. To escape the house without attracting attention, he must prepare himself for invisibility, a mind technique Gita taught him for tracking Jane. You focus the mind on scattering your atoms to merge with the background scenery so that you are present but imperceptible. (It was working pretty well on the road earlier, until Officer D'Annunzio interfered.)

Slipping noiselessly into the front hall, Collin lets himself out onto the street. He stops to reassemble his atoms, then proceeds toward the out-of-state car parked at the corner. He leans through the open driver's window, whispering, "Sir, hello?"

The old man asleep inside jolts awake.

"Hey there, hoss," the man blinks.

"You looking for Jane?"

The man sits up straight, looking embarrassed. "Is she back?"

"Yes, sir. She's in our kitchen."

"JANE PETTIGREW?" Brett repeats stupidly.

"Yes. Benjamin Pettigrew's younger daughter. This was my home almost two centuries ago."

A knock sounds sharply at the front door.

The two spring to their feet. Seizing her duffel from the floor, Jane bridges the distance to the back door in two steps; right behind her, Brett captures her arm, pulling her to him. Her body is vague and light in his arms as he clasps her tight, feeling the intricate web of her bones.

"You promised to let me go!"

She gives up struggling, wrapping her thin arms around his waist and pressing her cheek to his chest. He kisses the top of her head, and she raises her face to offer her lips.

Joining his mouth to hers, he understands what it was Jane meant: to enter a sphere without time. They seem suspended forever, heart against heart, in a welcoming universe.

The knock comes again.

This time Brett lets her pull away. She steps back, hand groping for the screen door.

"Jane, where will you go? How can I find you?"

Rummaging in her duffel, she thrusts a folded map into his hand. "Follow Quirk's wall."

Then she is gone, out the back door and crossing the yard at a run. As she vanishes through the iron gate, Brett is struck by a memory. *She has left me before. Disappeared.* He dismisses it as some kind of *déjà vu.* Still, the certainty remains, an echo in his cells. *She deserted me before.*

Insistent knocking breaks his trance, drawing him to the front door. He knows before he opens it that Fancher will be standing there.

"You're too late," he tells the old man. "Caroline took off. She decided to go back to Virginia. Maybe you can find her on the road."

Behind the detective Brett catches a flash of movement; someone else is on the stoop.

Collin steps into view: his son, the traitor.

CHAPTER NINETEEN

Jane makes up her bed by the light of a battery lantern in the shack, covering the hard wood of the floor with a folded blanket she found stored under the bench. Whoever left supplies in the hunting blind will return one day, she knows, so she will be careful not to disturb the placement of things, only using the blanket, the lantern, and the camp stove to boil water from the pond. Her clothing and all traces of her occupancy will fit into her duffel, which she will hide in a nearby tree after she leaves each morning. When hunger insists, she will slip down Rowell Hill to find a house where she can steal food.

Balling up her duffel for a pillow, every muscle aching from the day's exertions, she lies down to sleep wrapped in her purple anorak. Sensing her allure, mosquitoes drift through cracks in the walls, singing lascivious hymns through the thin nylon fabric of her anorak after she draws the hood over her face.

She curls up in the pleasure of reliving her first kiss from only a little while ago. But it was foolish to tell Brett where he could find her; he may unwittingly lead others to her hideaway. She will have to conceal her presence from him, too.

Perhaps she should have left Graynier, returning another

time when they have given up looking for her. But there is more to do here.

Feeling the billowy shifting of night currents, she hears the soft mincing step of a deer, approaching and receding, in the brush outside. The evening cicadas rattle away, owls hoot, a rabbit shrieks; in the darkness small creatures surrender their lives to the turbulent divinity infusing all that is.

In the morning she will take the shovel to the stand of white pines, and dig.

BURIED THINGS AWAIT *in the glade, under a carapace of jutting roots and stones. Jane will not have to dig down very deep before she reaches the leather satchel. Inside are letters: tender words on rotting pages, bound up with the ribbon of remorse.*

PART TWO

Dear Mr. Trane,

We most enjoyed your illuminating lecture last night at Graynier Hall. We should have preferred to congratulate you in person, but there was already such a crowd of comely admirers around you that our father, not wishing to wait, swept us away. Perhaps you noticed two very disappointed faces in bonnets (one blue, one claret) retreating to the door. Nonetheless (and paterfamilias permitting!) we will most eagerly attend your second talk tonight in order to hear more about Gabriel Nation.

Respectfully yours,
Miss Rebecca Pettigrew
Miss Jane Pettigrew

Dear Mr. Trane,

We were dismayed to learn of the abrupt cancellation of your second lecture. Had Reverend Duckworth not complained to Mr. Graynier, you would have found an enthusiastic assemblage of the curious, for indeed word of your eloquence has spread fast. We venture to explain that ours is a young town and unaccustomed to receiving speakers of uncommon intellect, tho' last year we were visited by Abby Kelley Foster who spoke of women's rights. (All of us women who attended cheered her pronouncement that we should not be kept "like dolls in the parlor" and deserve to receive our freedom in the same manner that abolition will one day unfetter all the slaves of our nation!) She, too, was requested to leave, and by the same consortium of backward ministers led by Reverend Duckworth, who rules the sour Presbyterians of our community. He wants nothing to do with modern free-thinking and will only countenance religious discussion as dictated by himself, everything else being apostasy, and therefore your speech espousing a new approach to spiritual union with Almighty God was particularly abrasive to His Reverence. He has succeeded in muzzling you by appealing to the prejudices of Mr. Graynier, who has never been seen in church and detests religion, who regards philosophers and reformers as troublemakers, and who has absolute power to boot them into the next county.

For truly we live in a little monarchy here and Mr. Philip Graynier is our King. He is owner of the glass factory, and without him there would be no town. Nearly everyone is in some fashion employed by him, even our father who is superintendent of Graynier Glass.

We hope you will not hasten from our village in spite of such rude reception. There are some here who are not as small-minded as others and who hunger for lively discourse. In our own household we were raised in the Unitarian church, which teaches tolerance and respect toward new spiritual ideas, as all paths must lead finally to God our Maker. Thus we would be honored to receive you for dinner in our home, if you would be so inclined, in this way to continue without harassment our learning about Gabriel Nation and your fascinating mission.

Please send your response by the same hand that has presented this letter to you, that of our hired girl Letty, a hand which can in addition make an excellent mutton stew!

Very respectfully yours,
Miss Rebecca Pettigrew
Miss Jane Pettigrew

Dear Mr. Trane,
  Please accept our deepest apologies. We are unable, after all, to have you to dinner tonight. We regret your inconvenience. We hope you enjoy a safe passage tomorrow to your next destination.
                                    Respectfully,
                                    Miss Rebecca Pettigrew
                                    Miss Jane Pettigrew

Dear Mr. Trane,
  Forgive me for slipping this letter inside the foregoing note (neither Papa nor Rebecca know I have done so, dear Letty being my fortunate ally) but I could not bear your thinking that I or my older sister are capable of such cold and discourteous conduct. Indeed our father forced us to write the note. In our fervor to have the honor of your company we sent you the invitation without consulting the head of our small household, never dreaming that Papa would not share our enthusiasm, since he expressed his approval for your lecture and intended enjoying the second before it was cancelled. Alas, in the intervening time, he has paid far too serious attention to vague and dubious rumors that concern Gabriel Nation and your leader Mr. Artzuni. In short, Papa decided that further association with your ideas would be insalubrious to his womenfolk and, thus mortified, we were instructed to withdraw our gesture of friendship.
  Forgive me again for addressing you in such a confiding manner when we have never met. You may think me bold, and I have been called so (as well as "impetuous," "headstrong," even "intractable") but I am proud of my epithets, since they merely signal that I am a young woman of independent mind, and as

such I may state frankly that you have been unfairly abused in Graynier and I greatly regret our losing you to other, more forward-thinking towns, where your message shall surely fall on more deserving ears. May the Lord bless your journey and grant you success.

Most respectfully yours,
Jane Pettigrew

Dear Mr. Trane,

Letty carried the news to us this morning of your distressing accident. (I rely upon her discretion as always to deliver this note to you in private.) It grieves me inexpressibly to hear of your injuries. It would have been more judicious to shoot Mr. Trumbull's dog than your poor horse. Many have complained to the old gentleman of the dog's unruly temper, asking him to secure the animal, and several times it has rushed at our own chaise and frightened our horse Betsy. Dear Mr. Trane, you must wish you had never laid eyes on Graynier for all the trouble it has brought you, and now I am told that you are forced to remain until your shoulder and leg have healed.

However, it is entirely your good fortune that Widow Seely has offered to shelter you during your convalescence, for no truer Christian nor sympathetic spirit is to be found in our town. You shall have everything you need, and more. She has long been an especial friend to me, indeed since my infancy. My mother died of the canker rash not long after my birth. Rebecca was sick with it, too, and if Mrs. Seely had not come to my father's rescue, caring for both invalid and newborn while he mourned my mother's passing, then I doubt you would now be reading this letter, for all the family Pettigrew would surely be in cold ground were it not for her ministrations. If your Mr. Artzuni preaches that we mortals may aspire to the station of angels, then he would certainly recognize in the good widow those angelic qualities which ensure her place in Heaven.

Thus I hope you will not be too lonely, for even if your sole companion for the next months is to be an elderly woman, yet she is the finest company, devout and very well spoken, and moreover you shall find an extensive library at your disposal. I have often borrowed some volumes from her, as books are hard to come by in Graynier, and sometimes Rebecca and I linger to read in her parlor those particular authors who are not permitted in our house. Our father does not object to young women's education but will not sponsor our entertainment!

Please believe in my sincerest condolences and wishes for a swift recovery.

Your unmet friend,
Jane Pettigrew

Dear Mr. Trane,

How kind you are to send such a prompt response with Letty, and how fortunate I am that the accident did not injure your writing arm! (I do not mean to make light of your ill adventure; indeed I am very sorry for your discomfort.) I shall now repay your favor by attempting to dispel the lassitude which you report has invaded your spirits. You are hereby enjoined to follow my prescription, sir.

Wake early tomorrow and ask Widow Seely to seat you on the green velvet divan in the front parlor, near the window which affords a view of Graynier Avenue. Once advantageously positioned, you shall glimpse the flow of characters who comprise

Graynier, in their natural order of appearance.

The first face to cleave the morning air is Captain Stallings, now north of ninety years on this earth (though only ten of these in Graynier – he came to live with his grandson who owns the dry-goods store). The old captain still takes pains to powder his hair, as you shall see from the white flurry on the shoulders of his greatcoat; and although his step is faltering and his future frail, he patrols Graynier Avenue, stem to stern, back and forth, from daybreak until his noonday dinner. If you should call a greeting to him, he will not answer, for he is deaf as a haddock (so Letty likes to say).

Now resume stirring your tea. By the time you look up, Sarah Jessup will be hurrying past with her basket of eggs and fresh butter to sell to the grocer. They will grace the larders of many in town, but not the Pettigrews, for we have our own chickens, and a cow, Emerald, who occupies a small shelter Papa built in the back. As a child, when my ceaseless chatter had driven all in the house to distraction, I went outside to sit on the milking stool and continue my prating, often giving her lessons from my McGuffey Reader. Thus Emerald learned her grammar and subtractions at nearly the same time I did. And when one day I was pronounced "precocious" (with disparagement), then I ran to tell her that she must be "prekishes" too. We both bear our scholarship with pride!

Only last month, dear Emerald produced no milk, and Papa began to talk of relieving her from earthly toil, until we discovered that someone was creeping into our yard before dawn and squeezing his own refreshment. Papa stayed up all night to apprehend the thief. It was a poor miserable Irish fellow from the shanty village, which you may have noted when you rode into Graynier. It is heartrending to contemplate how these people live. They came for the ready work at Graynier Glass, but the wages Mr. Graynier pays them are not enough to afford them even the meagerest improvements. Papa, who is the factory's head gaffer, has tried to persuade Mr. Graynier that healthy well-paid workers would increase his own prosperity, but His Majesty is unmoved.

Still, they stay on in their sorry matchstick dwellings. No one knows how many children are there, since so many die. Our thief needed Emerald's milk for his newborn baby, whose mother had passed away for lack of a doctor. Rebecca and I have been so upset by this that Papa now allows us to visit the shanties (in the company of one of the Ladies' Benevolent Society) to bring them food and clothes, the overflow of our God-given abundance, His name be praised.

But you must not listen to my digressions, or you will miss the next player to cross the stage: following Sarah Jessup with her egg basket comes a swarthy man with pendulous mustaches, Signor Iacovucci by name, who is the gravestone carver. He hastens to meeting, arriving at morning services before Reverend Duckworth has even opened the church doors. He greets each and every arrival with an elegant bow and warm smile, for he knows they shall all need him one day, and how much less anxiety they shall feel when they entrust their loved ones' epitaph to someone who seems almost a friend. They need not worry: truly Signor Iacovucci is an artist, creating from hard stone such soft images as drooping roses and weeping willows and hearts entwined. Papa had him inset a beautiful cameo of my mother for a new gravestone last year, crowned with a Bible verse. (I had chosen a lovely verse from "The Lament of Tasso" but my father would not hear of it, believing Lord Byron to be a reprobate. I vow only to marry a man who cherishes my beloved Byron as I do! Do have Mrs. Seeley lend you "The Bride of Abydos" if you have not read it.)

Not long after Signor Iacovucci disappears, you will see his countryman Signor Bruno stride by. He was the best cutter at Graynier Glass, having brought his skills all the way from Florence, but when he fell ill with quinsy, Mr. Graynier dismissed him. Now he carries a hand organ on his shoulder, and he will set himself outside the general store, where come the children who have been promised candy in return for sitting quietly in the church. He knows all manner of tunes to set them dancing, and whatever coins have not been squandered on sweets will find their way into his rumpled hat.

Now the mail coach rattles by your view. Perhaps it will brush against the branches of the trees, and loosen the horse chestnuts, which rain upon the ground. Schoolboys pounce upon them. They look about for some hapless soul upon whom to launch their missiles, but the only strollers to appear are Mr. Henry Beecham the apothecary with the milliner on his arm. Now, the milliner was once married to Henry's brother Clarence. Henry himself was a bachelor; they say he had long been in love with his brother's wife and could not imagine marrying another. Last year, Clarence died of a sudden, and Henry was finally able to claim his bride. Of course, some viper tongues of the village whisper that Clarence died from a dram administered to him when he was ill with pleurisy – a medicine prepared by his brother the apothecary! But I believe, as in the Greek saying, that if you speak evil, soon you will be spoken worse of.

Do not dwell on the couple, though their happiness is a pleasant enough sight. Attend instead to an oxcart lumbering by. The driver seems to be an upright skeleton. Nay, it is Farmer Quirk, bringing a load of barley straw for the stablery. Flung carelessly on top is a deer carcass to sell to the butcher. Beside Mr. Quirk is his wife, who is universally pitied. Unknown to him are a pair of shanty boys who have slyly perched on the back of his wagon, hidden by the mound of hay, and who have rode all the way into town thus. The schoolboys espy the two stow-aways, and hurl their chestnuts at them. Forthwith the shanty boys jump off the cart and the war begins. Do not open your window, or be pelted!

But do not leave your seat either, though my monologue may have grown tiresomely long. (Indeed, this letter's many pages may produce a suspicious bulge in Letty's apron pocket!) The boys will scatter anon, when a tall gray-haired gentleman comes along, escorting his two daughters. One is wrapped in a crimson shawl, and the other wears a blue pelisse and blue vel-vet bonnet with rose colored, watered silk lining. Pay utmost attention to this trio. Yield not to the distraction caused by a fancy barouche, pulled by a pair of sorrel prancers, which races by, its driver ignoring the recent town ordinance that forbids carriages to be driven through town at "an immoderate rate." Why should he obey? He is Ellis Graynier, who does as he pleas-es. If his father is king, then Master Ellis is the crown prince. Many young women (even my sister Rebecca!) think him hand-some. I am not of their number.

The tall gray-haired gentleman, who is my father Mr. Ben-jamin Pettigrew, pauses to tip his hat to his employer's only son. My sister (in the crimson shawl) stares at the fine barouche, wishing Master Graynier would look her way. And I – please watch carefully – take advantage of their diversion to turn my face toward the house of the Widow Seeley. I am only a few steps from her window. Perhaps you are sitting behind it, and we may nod to each other discreetly.

I shall then turn back quickly to my father, who is anxious not to miss the service, and he marches us on to the Unitarian Church.

There! You may limp to your chamber now, having seen

everything worth seeing in Graynier. I hope you will continue
your progress to full health, and remember with forbearance
                    Your very silly
                    and long-winded friend,
                    Jane Pettigrew

Dear Mr. Trane,
    Your sharp words pierced me to the heart. I realize now how
childish and frivolous I must seem to you. Was it only three days
ago that I paused before Widow Seeley's window and glimpsed
you through the glass? You shall laugh to know that, when our
eyes met in silent signal, I imagined us to be kindred spirits. As
usual, my fancy took the bit and galloped far ahead of my modes-
ty. How right you are to upbraid me, for I am indeed as wayward
a soul as you say, and greatly in need of spiritual instruction. Had
I but considered your religious devotion, I should never have rec-
ommended Lord Byron's volume for your reading pleasure. How
could I have dreamed that you would share the literary tastes of
a foolish, shallow, giddy young girl? Please believe that my object
was never to offend you. I desire nothing more than your good
opinion.
    Permit me, thus, to explain myself, and so gain your forgive-
ness. I know precious little of the world, craving to travel beyond
this dull and benighted town. I am naturally drawn to tales set
in exotic places, such as Lord Byron's poems evoke. How far away
from Graynier is the realm of "The Bride of Abydos"! There Turk-
ish Pashas preside over Harams, and force their veiled daughters
to marry sultans when their hearts belong to lowly slaves, all end-
ing in bloody death, and a virgin condemned to her grave! Per-
haps you are correct in calling such stories "overly heated" (as is

the Turkish climate, I infer) and admonishing me against reading such absurd romances. My father (the Pasha!) has already forbidden them. I do sometimes weep for my rebellious nature and the trouble it brings me.

Yet, if you will allow me a small protest, I wonder that you would call Lord Byron "blasphemous." To be sure, his poem depicts Moslems, whose faith is abhorrent to all Christians and whose customs are barbaric. But cannot a poet write about such things, without being thought likewise depraved? He is not to blame for the sins of the Turkish sultans, with their palaces full of slaves – he merely portrays them. He is no different from Miss Harriet Beecher Stowe, who writes about slave-owners and the evil they sow. Is it not well that people read of such things, for how can evil be reversed if it goes unpublicized? Indeed one might add that it is our duty to acquaint ourselves with evil, for the devil makes easy prey of the ignorant.

It may be harsh, then, to style Lord Byron a blasphemer. Possibly when he was alive he did not observe Christian ritual. Nonetheless, it is so hard for me to believe he did not love God, this man who wrote, in the very same poem that you decry:

"When heart meets heart again in dream Elysian
And paints the lost on Earth revived in Heaven
Soft, as the memory of buried love,
Pure as the prayer which Childhood wafts above."

You shall note that I have committed these lines to memory. Since I am forbidden to read Lord Byron's books, and can only enjoy them in secret within Mrs. Seely's wonderful library, it is only by memorizing their contents that I may carry them home, to read and read again, their pages imprinted to my mind – and no one is the wiser (except Re-

becca, who clamors for my recitations)!

Yet for you, sir, I will foreswear Lord Byron, and read no more of fevered passions and battles and virgin-filled graves. I will not even call him "Lord" for there is only one Lord, and He is the Lord our God. Only do please forgive

Your penitent friend,
Jane Pettigrew

P.S. I am also most fond of Mr. Shelley's poetry. Do you consider him godly? Dear Mr. Trane, you see how terribly I am in need of a teacher!

Dear Mr. Trane,

I am glad your shoulder has healed so impressively. I trust your prayers shall prove as successful for your leg!

Thank you for sending Mr. Artzuni's tract. It is an utterly thrilling account. How fearful and awesome, to be chosen by our Creator for such a mission, to feel the Holy Spirit actually moving and speaking inside one, to receive the gift of prophecy and the call to gather disciples. How sublime, above all, to know the <u>purpose</u> of one's life, and to follow where it leads, no matter what trials and recriminations pursue. I envy the extraordinary Mr. Artzuni, and you his followers, for your freedom to cry <u>Yes I will, Lord!</u> and leave dull existence behind. If only my insignificant life could be so lifted and ennobled by divine imperative, I would give my soul to have such faith (but who would even want my little trifle of a soul? If anyone did, he is more probably the devil than God!).

Since I first heard you speak, I have been abashed by your purity of faith. That you can believe sinless perfection to be attainable, when I can scarcely imagine it, has made me feel, in a word, lost – while you wake each day to know you belong to something great and right.

Please tell me more of Gabriel Nation. You must be so impatient to rejoin your fellow believers in Hovey Pond. I am sure Mr. Artzuni is right, that human perfection can only be achieved by retreating from the larger community of man, in small groups of the faithful, where one can intensify one's efforts to be pure. When I read these words in his tract, I felt them in my deepest self to be true: "The Almighty is assembling His chosen children for a new birth, when they will embody His angels on earth." How lucky you are to be among that beautiful brigade!

I must confess, however, I was a bit dismayed when I read of the manner of worship in your group: contortions and convulsions, falling to the ground, shrieking &c. It sounded much like the Methodists, whom I like not at all. I have read some of Mr. John Wesley's tracts, and cannot bring myself to believe that we must first be taught to loathe ourselves before we can be sanctified! I do not hold hatred to be any part of Christ's gospel. I'm certain that Gabriel Nation must be different, since in your speech you spoke so inspiringly about love. (And I suppose if I could truly, truly feel God's love in me, I too should fall to the ground!).

Will you next write to me how you met Mr. Artzuni? I notice that the printer's name at the bottom of his tract is Trane & Sons of Philadelphia. Are you related to the same?

I trust Mrs. Seeley is keeping you cheerful and well blanketed against the chill of these past days. I have instructed Letty to give you a piece of her incomparable gingerbread along with this note from

> *Your sincere friend,*
> *Jane Pettigrew*

P.S. Thank you for informing me that Mr. Shelley was an atheist. I will expunge his poems from my memory, since it pleases God that I to do so – and pleases you, too!

Dear Mr. Trane,

When I first glanced out the window this morning, and beheld a heavy gray sky, and again when I saw the first wisps of snow floating down, so benign and light, I never conceived they augured such a terrible storm! If you are like in circumstance to us Pettigrews, you have drifts piled to the casements, with their white shoulders braced against the doors. I hope you are placed well away from cold draughts, in front of a cheery hearth, with flame eternal and logs aplenty! Here on the second floor of our little house on Sycamore Street, the chamber I share with Rebecca is icy, and she has abandoned it for the parlor's warmth. I myself remain, swathed in quilts, my breath coming in white clouds, for here I may read your letters over and over again in private, as they bring me such blessed instruction, and warm me as bright coals in the grate.

I suppose it will be some days before we may go out, and so Letty will not be able to deliver this note to Mrs. Seeley's until the streets allow. I fear you have no conception of our New England winters, being from Philadelphia. They are very long, and during February, the roads are nearly impassable, and thus even if your leg heals by mid-winter as the doctor predicts, you may yet be hindered from journeying to Hovey Pond until the April thaw. Will you come to detest Graynier and its sad denizens? Even its scatterbrained young women?

But I must write on a more serious theme, because you have had the goodness to send me a second tract – again printed by your father's press! I picture you as you describe: a young man dutifully setting the type for Mr. Artzuni's pamphlet, pausing to read what it said, and how the Holy Spirit rose from the prophet's words and entered your being! How brave you were, to defy father and mother and family, to quit the comforts of home and confer your soul to Gabriel Nation. (Please do write more about the dangers facing your community in Texas when you established your tabernacle there! It makes such an exciting narrative!).

Alas, Mr. Artzuni's words did not produce such a supernatural effect in myself. Still I find some of his points to be intriguing, directing me to Bible verses with which I am unfamiliar. (I confess I am not as acquainted with the Holy Book as, for example, the works of Mr. Poe, but I have begun to reform!) In particular, I was drawn by the quotation from the Gospel of Luke, wherein Jesus said that those who will be resurrected to Heaven will not marry or be offered in marriage, and they become the equal of angels, and cannot die anymore. Does he (your Prophet Mr. Artzuni) mean that those who join Gabriel Nation, and become equal to angels in advance of resurrection, will be immortal here on earth? and like the angels in heaven they do not marry, even if they love each other? I suppose immortality might be desirable, though I must think on it more. To never be married would be sad. Were you compelled to make this sacrifice when you pledged yourself to the Gabrielites?

Your letters inspire me to read the Good Book more closely. Indeed everyone is surprised to see my head bent over its pages for hours on end. Rebecca teases me, and I cannot say rightly if Father is pleased – rather, mystified. I confess that my mind drifts often. I must bring more effort to my learning.

Your sincere friend,
Jane Pettigrew

Dear Mr. Trane,

    Today you would have been pleased with me. I received a visit from Bethesda Jarley, a friend from Miss McKeown's Instruction for Young Ladies, a boarding school in Haverhill where I was taught French and Latin languages, Music, Drawing, and Painting, as well as English studies. (I had great hopes to become a teacher myself, but Papa preferred I remain at home.) My friend had hidden in her sleeve a copy of Mr. Hawthorne's "The Scarlet Letter," proposing to lend it to me in the strictest secrecy. I reproached her indignantly for reading anything so preposterous, blasphemous and immoral. Her eyes fairly popped out of her face! For she knows how I adore Mr. Hawthorne's books. I felt proud that my change of heart, which I owe to your influence, is so well perceived by those who assume they know me well.

    "Well!" said she. "You may call Mr. Hawthorne's story preposterous, but even here in Graynier we have our own Hester Prynne!" She then proceeded to relay her gossip: that young Master Ellis Graynier has brought dishonor to a female domestic of the village and the unfortunate girl is forced to repair to Boston where she must bear the fruit of her sin alone and repudiated. (Dear Mr. Trane, if I were, like you, preferred by God to attain the power of angels, I should have a great deal of work to perform here in Graynier, where believe me Satan is prolific!)

    I would not hear the rest, but professed a headache, upon which Miss Jarley left (I did not tell her that I had previously read Mr. Hawthorne's book – at the Widow Seeley's – but this, I promise, preceded your arrival and your salutary effect on my character, God be praised.)

    I wish so much that we could continue our discourse in person. We should then have enjoyable debates over some of the Gabriel Nation principles such as the abjuration of marriage, prohibition of dancing &c. and I should advance more quickly in my understanding of your faith. Unhappily, whenever I have petitioned Father for permission to visit my dear companion Mrs. Seeley, he replies that as long as she houses a certain guest who propounds dangerously radical doctrines I must avoid her premises. I protested that if Mrs. Seeley is favorably disposed to the gentleman then he must be above reproach. Father declared that Widow Seeley was always partial to a good-looking fellow, which I thought most unchristian considering what a great friend she has been to the Pettigrews, and I said so. He did not answer, but fixed me with a look that conveyed suspicion. Perhaps I did protest too much and seemed overly eager to his eye. The consequence is that he binds me closer to the hearth than ever, and seems both anxious and mistrustful whenever I propose to go out.

I feel it unfair to be so young, and be unable to follow my own inner voice, which bids me to fly to 12 Graynier Avenue, where I might steep myself in the presence of that rare one who speaks directly to God, and perhaps receive some of that golden blessing by propinquity. And now my fingers are too numb with cold to write more!

Your devoted student,
Jane Pettigrew

Dear Mr. Trane,
Alas, our little plan did not succeed. My disappointment is keen. All seemed well, the weather warm, the snow abated, and I – seated beside good Mrs. Lang in the sleigh, her mare drawing us "at an immoderate rate," shaking her bells in a jubilation like to mine as I inhaled the pure air of freedom – I flew then, loosed from the confines of my house, with my father's permission to accompany

Mrs. Lang to the shantytown with comestibles and clothing for the needy.

The errand itself presented no obstacle: indeed the unfortunates of that appalling neighborhood fell upon our supplies like crows. Some were delirious from lack of food. We learned that, on the third day of the storm, they had to burn stools and mattresses for fuel. Doctor Pincus was there, amputating a boy's fingers because of frostbite. I cannot fathom why our Lord chooses some to receive His grace but denies it to others, His will be done. But we cannot know the thoughts of God, as Mr. Artzuni writes, unless we are in the Spirit of God, which advantage I have not yet earned.

As we trotted back through town, I quite casually asked Mrs. Lang to leave me off at Widow Seeley's to return some books (just as you and I planned). She declared she had promised Papa to bring me straight home and she could not presume to deviate from that agreement. So home I went, casting a forlorn glance at Mrs. S.'s window where I knew you waited, but even the frost upon the glass conspired to keep you hidden.

I pray your leg is improved. And now it is snowing again.

Your disconsolate friend,
Jane Pettigrew

Dear Mr. Trane,

I have lacked a letter from you for so long, with the latest blizzard smothering the streets, and moreover poor Letty has been in bed with a cold. The delivery of this note signals her recovery! She and Rebecca have both been out in the snow, but Father continues to keep me nearer than ever. I am happy to coddle him, for he does need tending to, owing to a persistent congestion of the lungs, which he attributes to breathing the glass dust at the factory over the many years – nearly 25 – he has worked for Mr. Graynier. For this reason he has been more absent from work than formerly.

But even if not for his debility, he would hold me fast. I do believe it is because of my resemblance to my mother that he delights to look upon me and has always preferred me to my sister. I tell Rebecca often that this preferment comes at the cost of my freedom, and for that she must not be envious.

How tedious is January. All seems to stand still, and one's inertia is maddening. I play the seraphine and sing until all scream at me to stop. I have darned every sock and embroidered every scrap in my workbasket. I have sketched and painted studies of every member in the household, in every angle and position – even Uli Haff, my father's foreman, who visits to give Papa news of the factory when he is ill (though I think Mr. Haff comes also to see Rebecca, and I suspect he will declare his intentions soon! Uli is not handsome but a good, hard-working man, of strong German stock, and he will provide reasonably well for my sister. I shall be sorry, nonetheless, to have her move away. She is ever my dearest companion, to whom I confide everything, excepting in the case of our correspondence, as I believe she would not approve of such deception).

And so I read, I pace, I muse, I gnaw at my cage like the little mouse I captured in a box last week. In the end I freed him. Perhaps God will note my good deed and free me, too.

In years past I endured January with placid forbearance. But now that my being has been awakened by Mr. Artzuni's prophecies, together with your dear notes of encouragement, I feel ever more restive and impatient to embrace Heaven's instruction. Whatever it may be, I await His command!

Yet for all my zeal there has been silence. I read from no other volume except the Bible, yet the words seem stale and will not animate my spirit. Could God desire to shut me out?

Last week I tried fasting, as Mr. Artzuni advises, to facilitate the onset of revelations. I refused meals, pretending dyspepsia, and made light of everyone's concern. By the third day I was compelled to take to my bed, so weak had I become. As I lay and awaited a signal of the Lord, I believe I dreamed, for I had a vision of falling into a deep pit, and a man whose face I could not discern stood above and kicked dirt down on my face. The howls of demons filled my ears as I lay in this earthen tomb, as if I were being buried alive – like the unfortunate narrator of Mr. Poe's The Premature Burial! *– and I awoke in terror, to the sound of my little mouse scratching behind the wall, like fingernails scraping at the lid of a coffin.*

I ceased fasting, yet this image of Hell haunts me still. It seems to lure me away from the light, whispering that I am unworthy of Heaven.

You say that faith alone will lead me to sinless purity. Then it must be that my faith is incomplete, and the missing element is your guidance. God's deliverance seems ever more distant in this month when the sun dwindles to nothing, and I have no word from you.

Your friend,
Jane Pettigrew

Dear Mr. Trane,

Indeed I should be very cross with you for venturing outdoors onto the ice with no accessory but a cane! I pray to Heaven the accident did not break anew your leg and that you have only bruises to tend. Rebecca heard that you fell while turning onto Sycamore Street, only a few doors from our house. I had to conceal my tears and agitation. Please reassure me that you were not on your way to visit me! I should die of guilt, if it were my selfish entreaties for your spiritual counsel that brought you out into the cold weather! I should never have complained so thoughtlessly in my last note. The moods of a young girl are beneath your regard, and you have far greater missions to pursue than the struggles of one small soul. Only send me word you are not badly hurt, and that it was not on my behalf!

In haste,
Jane

Dear Mr. Trane,

I cannot find words to express my limitless joy upon reading your letter. To know it was not my imagination, after all, that fancied a profound bond between us, that you too share the certainty that we are destined to join together, work for God's glory and seek the highest form of self-perfection! You are the star that I follow to reach the cradle of Jesus and the light of the eternal happiness! I agree that our correspondence will not suffice but we must, <u>we must</u>! see one another. And yet that event seems more remote than ever. For there has been a great upheaval here at home.

Uli Haff paid us his usual visit today. Both Rebecca and I were seated in the parlor to hear his news, as we are accustomed to do, when he suddenly asked to speak to Papa alone. We sisters repaired to the kitchen in high excitement, for we all, father included, expected Mr. Haff would make known his feelings concerning Rebecca.

After he left the house, however, it was I and not my sister whom Father summoned to the parlor. I was condemned to sit meekly – with your letter hidden in my bosom where I had folded it next to my heart – while Papa informed me that Uli had sought his permission to enter an engagement with myself, our marriage to follow in a year's time!

I'm afraid my reaction, which I could not manage to mask, was one of dumb horror. I knew Rebecca to be listening on the other side of the door, and reckoned well what anguish she was feeling. My mind filled with a kind of noise – I heard my father's voice, as from a far distance, asking if I didn't approve of Uli, and was he not an excellent man, frugal and industrious and kind (as if these qualities alone were adequate to ignite my affection), and did I know that he had purchased a plot of land, on Putman Hill, and what a comfortable house he would build for us &c.&c.

I nodded perfunctorily until my tears spilled over, betraying my true emotions. I said I hadn't thought to be married yet. When he inquired why, I replied that I was too young, being not quite twenty, and moreover I preferred to stay with Papa, at home, for he needed my company and caring. He looked pained at this. "Jane," he said, "you must apply your thoughts to practical matters now." He is afraid his lungs will not improve, and he will lose his job soon. By consequence, he worries he will not be able to provide for us. It is thus a necessity to find good husbands, at least for one of us, for if someone must stay at home with Papa it would likely be Rebecca. She is already twenty-four and no one has ever shown an interest in marrying her. Therefore, he concluded, here was Mr. Haff with a fine proposal which I should accept gladly!

I begged him for more time to consider, and after much supplication he agreed that I might have two months before giving Mr. Haff my answer. In the meantime I should see Uli often so I might know him better. Again Father urged me to be a good daughter, and consent to the engagement after Easter. Then he nearly cried too, saying that he had been excessively selfish by keeping me at home all the time – it was not healthy and had led me to become morbid and neurasthenic, or why else should I be mumbling over my Bible and refusing food for three days? To my surprise, he then told me he would no longer forbid me to go out, as long as Rebecca or some other older woman accompanied me. At that I brightened a bit, my only thought being that, with this new amnesty, I might contrive to visit Mrs. Seeley, without his being aware.

Still I could not sleep last night, as if I were on a rack being pulled two ways. One way, I have your beautiful words, your friendship, and salvation itself. On the other, I have my duty to Father and his clear wish that I marry Mr. Haff. If only I could talk face to face with you, I know you would dispel my confusion and put me to rights.

Rebecca, meantime, is cool toward me. Though she says she did not care for Uli, still I know she would have liked to be the one asked and not I. I cannot blame her. Spinsterhood is a doom that any woman fears greatly.

Pity my dilemma, good friend, and wait for more news from

> *Your despondent*
> *Jane*

Dear Mr. Trane,

It is some consolation to read that your distress concerning Mr. Haff's proposal is the mirror of mine. I am forever grateful for your solicitude, when my woes must seem altogether inane compared to the urgency of your spiritual mission. I agree that it is now essential that we meet – and without intrusion, God willing!

Father was out today, having gone back to work. I hoped Rebecca would accompany me for a walk this morning, when I planned to suggest innocently that we call on Mrs. Seeley – but she went out alone, probably to visit with her friend Mabel to whom she can disparage me for stealing her beau. Desperately I asked Letty to lend me some clothes. I put on her skirt and apron, and wrapped her shawl to cover my face as if to protect it against the cold. My notion was to appear as a servant, and to walk to Widow Seeley's alone, thus disguised. (It is a paradox, I think, that a servant who may not call her life her own is permitted to roam freely in the street while a respectable young woman with no liens on her person cannot put a toe in the outdoors without a jailer alongside.)

As I hurried along, my spirits rose, thinking I would soon encounter you in Mrs. S.'s parlor. I was only a little distance from that destination when I heard the bells of a cutter behind. Master Ellis Graynier was the driver, and he reined his horse, bidding me to jump up on the seat beside him. I shook my head, pulling the shawl tighter, but he ordered me in a sterner tone to get in. My disguise proved too efficacious, for clearly he presumed me to be a hired girl. Reluctantly I obeyed. As he urged his horse on, he pressed me with impertinent questions, wanting to know my name and where I was going. I became angry to realize that this was how he preyed upon the working girls of the town. I was frightened, also, for if I continued with my ruse I should place myself at some risk to my safety. I drew back Letty's shawl and showed my face. He laughed then, quite uproariously. "Miss Pettigrew!" he said. "Have you lost your good clothes in a gambling bet?" I snatched the reins from his hands and pulled the horse to a stop, leapt out, and ran home before anyone else could detect my ridiculous masquerade.

Forgive me for prating on about my troubles, when you have *a sufficiency of your own. I regret that your fall on the ice has delayed your recovery. Is it reprehensible to wonder if this misfortune is God's plan to hold you longer in Graynier? No matter, you <u>must not</u> try again to come to our house! Even if my father is not at home, he will certainly hear of your visit and never trust me more. Let me come to you, dear friend and teacher. I am most determined to see you as soon as mortally possible.*

Jane

Dear Mr. Trane,

Your letter grieved me, it seemed almost quarrelsome. My treasured friend, you must not reprimand me for failing to visit. More than all other people, you have the power to hurt me with a word, a frown – nay, a feather! Indeed for the past five days I have tried to escape my house, but am thwarted at every turn.

Saturday I could not leave because Uli Haff came to call on me, with a present of some soap he made. (It is so strange to sit with him now – this diffident, rather clumsy man whom I have never regarded as other than an assistant to my father. More irksome still, Papa and Rebecca make a great show of withdrawing so we are not disturbed during his visits. I must do all the talking to put him at his ease, and am quite worn out from the effort by the time he leaves. Worse, I have found out he is a Lutheran. Father has often told me I have a mad imagination, but it is he who is wildly deluded when he imagines I could ever be wedded to Mr. Haff!).

On Sunday, you may recall that it snowed. Master Ellis Graynier astonished my father by appearing at the door and inviting me to join him, his sisters, and some friends in an enormous sleigh drawn by a team of four, which he had driven over. As I started to decline, he asked Rebecca, too. She became prodigiously excited, begging me to come along, so that in the end I did go, as it is the first occasion since Mr. Haff's proposal that she has looked warmly upon me, and you must agree that we need her (unwitting) help to realize our reunion.

However, I was soon to regret my choice. Master Ellis placed me directly beside him and for the whole ride he never ceased to tease and flatter me. I have never given him the slightest signal that I regard him as anything more than an annoyance, a rich idler to whom I am obliged to be polite because he is my father's employer's son. We stopped for him to untangle the harness, and while he was about it I quickly changed places with Rebecca, who was only too content to suffer his drivel for the rest of the ride.

Monday Father was ill again. Mr. Graynier sent Uli Haff to inquire when Papa would be well enough to resume his duties at the factory. He is losing patience with Father on account of his increasing absences, and it's possible he will replace Papa with Uli before long. In truth my father seems resigned to it, and says Uli would make a fine superintendent (here he casts me a meaningful look).

On Tuesday came our invitations to the Workingmen's Ball. Rebecca insisted on going to the dressmaker for a new frock, and then the milliner for a bonnet, and I could not persuade her to any other destination. I had rather stay at home than indulge such caprices, particularly (as I told her) when we must make economies. She retorted that Father would approve of her purchases, as he wants to get rid of her and she must use any means at her disposal to attract a husband. I was quite vexed by the end of our excursion, having to hurry by Mrs. Seeley's house on the way home without a hope of visit-

ing, as it was fast growing dark.

Perhaps the next days will bring me a chance to get away. We must both pray God for patience!

Your fond friend,
Jane

Dear Mr. Trane,

The Almighty is testing our resolve indeed. He has granted our most cherished objective, yet at the same time deprived us of the communion we sought. Oh my friend, what a torture was yesterday afternoon, to be in your company at last, yet have no opportunity for discourse other than a few impersonal words of salutation and farewell, and nothing in between.

I grant that we must keep our friendship a secret, but was it necessary to avoid looking at me entirely and pay heed only to my sister? Over and over I endeavored to catch your eye, to read something within, something to sustain me, yet you never met my gaze. Were you afraid that mere glances would disclose our relation to Rebecca and Mrs. Seeley? The latter is already "in the know," having observed so many missives migrate from Letty's pocket to your hand and back again! And how could you bear Rebecca's prattling about last month's weather and next month's ball, and her silly attempts at religious dissertation, she who has scant interest in spiritual matters? You seemed instead to encourage her prolixity. I thought I would scream when she most improperly requested a fourth cup of tea, simply to prolong the visit.

When we walked home, I then had to endure her rhapsodies on the subject of your estimable character, your devoutness, your manners, and how very plausible it seemed to her

*that the Gabrielites could aspire to embody angels when you
are so angelically handsome in your aspect &c &c. From my
letters you are well aware of her intent to be engaged to any
eligible man she can espy. I boldly asked her if she envisioned
you as a candidate for husband, for if so she should be ap-
prised that your faith forbids marriage. She said she did not
believe it, and would question you on the next visit. I added
that at any rate Papa would forbid the union because of your
affiliation with Gabriel Nation. She only laughed and re-
peated that Father is unconcerned whom she marries, for his
affection has always been directed at me alone. I am sorry she
thinks so little of herself.*

*Therefore do not be amazed if she pays another call to
Mrs. Seeley before long. For myself, I had rather stay at home
than sit dumbly in Mrs. S's parlor while you and my sister
enjoy the very conversation that I have longed for, and dissem-
bled and disobeyed for, only to be ignored! I weep to remember
it! Dear Mr. Trane, why could you not look or speak to me?*

Jane

Dear, dear Mr. Trane,

*I implore your pardon, I bless you for your indulgence,
and wish I might tear to pieces that bitter note I sent and thus
you had never seen it. I never realized that, while I had ample
occasion to gaze upon your face during your lecture of many
months ago, you yourself had never seen mine, except for one
glimpse through a window on an October Sunday, when my
face was obscured by my bonnet. Your explanation for your
apparent disregard of my person during our visit is more than
acceptable – it melts my heart. If another person, such as Ellis*

Graynier, should declare he cannot look upon me because he is stunned by how beautiful I am, I should brush off his words as arrant flattery. But I know you not to be a liar or flirt, and therefore those same words produce quite another effect on me. Further, I am sure you are alluding to a spiritual beauty you perceive in me rather than a physical one, a beauty such as I see in you as well. Truly Rebecca remarks well, for one feels the light of an angel about you, and that God's grace lives with you. I cannot say it better, and thus will not try.

Yes, I will return with Rebecca, if tomorrow is not too soon! Perhaps tomorrow the two of us shall essay conversation, and even risk glances, as when one's eyes grow accustomed to the sun!

Your affectionate friend,
Jane

Very ill. Do not be concerned. God keep you –
J.

Dear Mr. Trane,

I feel as though I have climbed from my grave, and my reflection in the mirror does not belie that fancy. Truly I was completely insensible these three weeks past, and for which I am grateful, as they tell me I was in much torment, with the fever so strong, and the swelling of my throat making swallowing such an agony. Sleep was a tyrant permitting no resistance. At the worst point I seemed to quit my body – an oddly welcome sensation, of calm without regret – until the thought came that I might not see my loved ones again, at least in this world. And so my spirit hurried back to my invalid's body, and I willingly resumed my sufferings.

Imagine, I missed my twentieth birthday entirely! No matter, I am lucky to have lived past it. Rebecca delivered news of you from time to time, when I was able to sit up and drink weak tea, because she saw how it cheered me to hear of your conversations with her. May God forgive me for my envy of her who could visit and sit hours in the company of my friend and teacher, when I have only for coin the pauperly sum of one hour, long ago – an hour spent in silence! I marvel that Papa allows Rebecca such visits, and that he even saw fit to welcome you into our house when you came to call with Mrs. Seely. Perhaps Rebecca is right, and he does not trouble himself for her associations so much as he does for myself. Indeed I know from Rebecca that he has made private inquiry about your means from the Widow, and was pleased to learn of your inherited income.

I cannot fathom that my sister and father both should entertain the idea of a union! If you have told Rebecca of your faith's renouncement of matrimony, your words fell upon deaf ears, I promise you. Please assure me you foster no such alliance, or I will think my sister poorly used – but I cannot believe it of you, and it is only my imagination, so deformed by fever, which envisions such treachery.

Nay, I cannot doubt your sincerity when I hold in my hands such a gift as you have bestowed on me – and with what cunning! The others never dreamed that, concealed under the poetry volumes in the basket that Widow Seeley brought for my sickbed, and which was brought up to me by Letty, lay your beautiful present. When I uncovered it, and read your fond inscription, I truly began to mend. How good you are, to give me your own Bible! When I am too tired to read, I trace with my fingers the warm leather that has known your hands' embrace, and the stamped cross of Gabriel Nation (one day soon you will tell me the meaning of its peculiar configuration).

Your gift puts to oblivion all other presents I received while sick: from Uli a poultice he made, one of his old country's remedies, and medicinal roots he dug from the snow atop Rowell Hill; I had presents, too, from Ellis Graynier, whose questionable benevolence supplied me with a bottle of cologne, an ivory comb, and a muskrat robe which, though rich, reminds me only of the low marshes from which those creatures, and Mr. Ellis, derive! Even Papa was embarrassed by his extravagance, and wondered that young Master Graynier should bother with my health, who has never previously shown any interest in our family, or the Pettigrews should all be wrapped in ermines by now!

I am become so thin and pallid, I don't wish for you to see me until I have regained my original form, which transformation I hope will be in time for the Workingmen's Ball. Even if your religion and your injury prevent your dancing, please tell me you will attend! I am so eager to see your dear face again.

I understand that your generous gift has rendered you bereft of Holy Scriptures, so I trust you will accept my little Bible in exchange, which Letty brings you along with this letter. I have tucked in its pages a lock of my hair. I am ever

Yours in gratitude,
Jane

Dear Mr. Trane,

I profess myself amazed that you should fret yourself over the rumors of my engagement to Mr. Haff. You know from my letters that I have not accepted him, that it is beyond my power to prevent him from calling at our home, and that our

*relation is of no more substance than yours with my sister.
You yourself have explained the latter as the illusion by which
we direct the eyes of others away from our secret relation. You
wrote, too, that we must not let petty and sinful jealousy to
mitigate the power of our mission. I have endeavored to follow
your prescription. But so must you, dear mentor.*

*I promise that marriage could not be further from my
mind. Truly I am still in such a weakened state, I doubt any
man would want me for consort! Neither do I have any appetite for romance but my illness has left me strangely cleansed
of all desire, and weightless, as if my being were burned away
leaving only the soul essence. I feel God has readied me for the
redemption which only you can assist. Do not doubt me now,
savior, when I am thus exposed!*

*Rebecca says you will not come to the ball. I admire you
the more for your abstinence, though I shall regret your absence. Uli expects me to go, alas, so I must put on a show of
cooperation. Verily it comes not from the heart.*

*Your faithful
Jane*

Dear Mr. Trane,

*I may say it was the closeness of the crowd, or the music, or
my reckless exertions from dancing overmuch (the ecstasy of freedom, from the prison of sickbed and home, overtook my common
sense!) but in truth my early departure from the ball owed as
much to my shock at seeing you there, when I had not expected it.
Indeed I never noticed you enter the tavern, and it was not until
the reel with Mr. Haff that I glanced across the room, and there
you sat, so gallant in your blue jacket. Even condemned to a chair*

with your cane, you far outshone any other aspiring angels present, of which there were none!

At once I left off dancing, complaining of dizziness, and sent Uli for some punch. I thought to escape him, in the hopes of achieving some moments with you. Surely you saw me coming your way, when Ellis Graynier stepped between and would not permit me to deny him the next dance. With both father and Mr. Philip Graynier watching, I could hardly rebuff him, and upon Uli's return I had all I could manage to keep him and Master Ellis from open altercation. Ellis is aware of Mr. Haff's proposal to me, but that knowledge only seems to have swelled his zest for the hunt, of which I am the reluctant object, though it were clear to him that my scruples and station make me an impossible party to his libertinism.

In the end, Uli gave way to Ellis' superior position as his employer's son, and I was compelled to cede the rest of my dances to the man. If I did so with an "all too cheerful countenance" (as you reproach me), it was to please my father. I glanced at you often, to convey my secret unhappiness, yet each time I was met with a glare of such opprobrium that I felt as if drenched in sin – a glare so fixed that you seemed entirely to disdain the conversation of my sister seated beside you. It is well she did not remark it.

Finally I could not bear your censure any longer and pleaded exhaustion to Papa, who took us home.

I was indeed exhausted, but not from dancing. Dear Mr. Trane, do please put away your qualms regarding Ellis Graynier's overtures: it is but his fancy of the moment and not to be taken seriously, least of all by you, who knows my soul. For that is how I am promised to you, not by my hand but rather by my soul which seeks its salvation through your sponsorship. How more intimate may two mortals be? You have said so: the light of purity is more beloved in God's eyes than the bond of wedlock, which He only tolerates for the purpose of propagation. If I am ever to be pure, it will be by your tutelage. Teach me then, my friend, and may we have no more misunderstandings, which would dissolve so easily if only we could meet alone. If God intends it, He will arrange an opportunity soon.

Your own
Jane

Dear Mr. Trane,
   Our opportunity has arrived! I pray this letter reaches you in time to avail yourself of our good fortune. As I trust you have learned already, at three o'clock this afternoon there is to be a hanging in front of the courthouse, of the tragic fellow from the shanties who murdered his children. Father is going to watch, along with most of the village. Of course he made us to stay home, it being an unfit spectacle for young ladies (I do, for once, concur!). This morning Rebecca confided to me her plan to steal away, hide herself among the crowd, then run home before Papa returns. I agreed to be partner to her conspiracy, and though I voiced my disapproval, inside I was all rejoicing. This leaves me utterly alone at home for the space of an hour! Come quickly, by the alley in back of Sycamore Street, and I will let you in the iron gate behind our house.

Hurry, my friend!
Jane

Dear Lysander,
   No matter how long I shall live, indelible will be the memory of us two side by side in prayer. My knees never felt the floor,

so deep was my trance, and when you touched your palm to my brow I felt a surge of flame – my heart violently quaked – the trembling which beset my limbs was just as you described it happens when the Spirit descends!

I cry tears of gratitude to think I was, in that moment, worthy of God's grace, even if the moment was fleeting. I am puzzled, however, that when I have attempted prayer since, alone and with the same intensity, I have never again experienced such transport. It may be that your presence is the key that unlocks the Heavens on my behalf. I yearn for another chance to combine our efforts in calling down the Spirit.

I believe we may avoid discovery more easily now. Since I no longer importune Father to let me accompany Rebecca on her visits to Widow Seely, I think his suspicions have abated where you and I are concerned and therefore he may loosen the reins further.

Accordingly I have another proposal, which comes from our artful ally Letty. Now that the weather is sunnier, it is time again for her to wash all the linens of the house, beat the carpets &c. &c. She proposes to hang the sheets on the line outdoors in such a fashion as to shield the door to the cow's shelter. Now that you know the way, you may enter our yard at the same back gate as before (concealed all the while by a barrier of laundry!) and enter Emerald's domain, where I shall be waiting at three. No one will question my leaving the house to visit Emerald, as only I and Letty bother ourselves about the dear cow.

Our meeting place will be a most odorous milieu, and our prayers may be disrupted by Emerald's plaintive interjections, but perhaps you may look upon the scene as a recreation of the manger where our wonderful Savior was born! Twixt the bovine and the divine, may our worship seal a connection.

Yours in the Holy Spirit,
Jane

Dear Lysander,

Hell itself opens under my feet when I read your words. Indeed, your regret is my despair! I do not understand your turmoil over the matter of a kiss. I cannot believe it is a sin which manifests in such sweetness. Truly I felt the force of God pass through your lips to mine – when I opened my eyes I saw a ray of divine light bathing your head – joy burst in my breast until I feared it might break apart. How could this be other than an expression of God, who is all Love? When you and I were trembling and speechless in the wake of that impulse, how was it different than your Gabrielite meetings, as you describe them, when the faithful tremble and stutter upon encountering the sacred force of the Spirit? When we kissed, I drank from the stream of God's delight, and to call it a sin would seem an affront to the Almighty.

And yet you pray it will never happen again! And, more crushing to me, you suggest that we part ways, since you fear you might lose a second struggle with your "carnal nature." Oh Lysander, if you will but stay my friend I shall be strong enough for both of us, and never submit to the inclinations of the flesh. But may we not kiss, if we do love each other? I will be bold and say so: I love thee. I love thee. I love thee as I love thy faith.

I have embraced your beliefs as my own. There is nothing I want more than to become as angels are, and I have you before me as a shining portrait of that possibility. I know that angels may not marry on earth, since they do not in heaven, but must they also forfeit affection? To clasp hands, to embrace, yes, even to kiss, as brother and sister, and in the fullness of God's love? Then I must fail the test, my dearest one, before I have barely begun. For I cannot live without touch.

In sorrow and farewell,

Jane

Dear Lysander,

*I have died every day of our estrangement. When awake I
knew not how I moved or ate or spoke – my limbs and speech per-
formed their duties in some other sphere where no God showed.
Rebecca told me you did not come out of your room whenever she
called on Mrs. S., and I wondered if you suffered, too. One day
in the middle of a visit from Mr. Haff, I suddenly fell to weeping. When he became very concerned to know why, I answered
that I felt too burdened by his expectation of an answer at the
end of next week (is April really here already?) and that I was
distracted by worries about my father who has been working long
hours of late while assuming full responsibility for the factory.
(Mr. Graynier has become seriously ill of a sudden – dying, they
say – from a canker in the stomach, and thus I have seen nothing of Ellis either, who must be sobered by the likelihood of losing his father – which humbling event might produce a better
character in him – though I doubt anything would commend
either the son or the father to God as they are both irredeemably
agnostic!) The consequence of my tearful outburst was that Mr.
Haff has extended my reprieve and will not ask for my decision
until the end of the month. (He is very kind with me, and were
I not such a temperamental creature, I could be happily married to such a man.)*

*Therefore imagine, if you can, what miracle of joy irradiated
my heart when I received your letter. To read of your days and
nights of prayer and fasting, to know how you struggled and won,
and that Jesus Himself spoke to you, bidding you "go forth and
love, in innocence, thy sister soul!" Oh, Lysander, that blessed ut-
terance of our Redeemer relieves me of my guilt, when I thought
I had lost you because of my words that, while sincere, were too
immodestly expressed. I told myself, "You bared your love to him,
and it was not returned." But now I know that you love me, too,*

and moreover, that Heaven condones it!

And our fair weather, if it lasts, affords us new oppor-tunities to meet. Since you have lately cast aside your cane, a walk in the hills would be a healthy enterprise for restoring the strength in your leg. Ask directions to Mr. Quirk's farm, and an ascending path will take you to his lands, which are bounded on the east by a low rock wall. Follow this wall past a sheep meadow and then a field of winter rye. At the end of Mr. Quirk's lands, the wall turns left. Instead of following, look a little further on and you shall see a cluster of lofty white pines with low-drooping branches. They will be our curtains, to surround and hide us from view, as we meet to continue our holy work together.

My father has given me leave to take walks in the fresh air, since I have appeared so pale and dispirited of late. I expect my route will pass by Farmer Quirk's wall about two o'clock tomorrow afternoon. May the Lord give me angels' wings!

Your adoring
Jane

Dear Lysander,

I write hastily as Letty gathers her few belongings to leave us – she is dismissed – wrongly! – I will explain – we must exchange letters some other way – look for my letter in Farmer Quirk's wall near our pines – Please give poor Letty whatever money you can spare – we will never see her again – I have lost a great friend

Jane

Dear Lysander,

What a bedlam was yesterday, our small household shattered in pieces. Papa has noticed for some time that money was missing from his desk, a little at a time, and finally he accused Letty of stealing from him! She denied it, but has returned in disgrace to her family in Boston. I thank you for whatever monetary assistance you gave her, for she is now without means, and completely innocent besides. I dare not tell Papa that the thief is Rebecca. She has been surreptitiously taking a few coins at a time from his desk, over many years. She does not know I am aware of her petty theft. She conceals the money in her wedding chest, and only spends a little now and then on fripperies like ribbons. I cannot say what possesses her to steal, when Father has always provided adequately for us, but it is a kind of distemper I believe, and without logical cause. I do not wish to expose her, for the sorrow it would cause Papa. Neither should I desire to see Rebecca humiliated, for I do love my sister, and the amounts she steals are so little. I wish your influence had bestowed in her a reverence for God's laws and the path of righteousness, but she does not seem to have profited in a deep way from your many meetings.

Papa will go to the shanties on Thursday morning to find a substitute for Letty (though I cannot expect another such companion ever again!) and thus I am at liberty to take another walk up Rowell Hill. Beloved, will you be there? If your answer be yes, leave open the glass door on Widow Seeley's porch lantern, for we will be passing by tomorrow on our way to service and I shall subtly note your signal.

I have recently experienced qualms about deceiving Papa, for while Rebecca disdains the Eighth Commandment of our Lord by stealing, I forsake the Fifth by not honoring my father. Then your words return to me, and I am consoled: that I have but one Father, and He is in Heaven, and it is He who must be obeyed, and it is His Will that we be together in worship. It is strange to find myself turning from all I have been taught, yet I am filled with certainty every time you revise my thinking. Truly one feels what is right and true, in an innermost place of knowing, when it is God that speaks to our ear. How beautiful it is to serve Him.

Your devoted

Jane

Dear Lysander,

This afternoon I went to our spot, even though we had no assignation. The day was hazy and unusually warm. I removed my bonnet to feel the sun upon my face (despite knowing well that freckles would be my penance!). I lay on the spring grass, on the bosom of God's earth, and felt the rise and fall of my breath couple with the throb of nature, whose Author I praise and worship with my whole body, and I sensed divinity at my fingertips, so attuned have I become to His presence.

I spent a pleasant hour thus, in remembering our last meeting. We have covered much ground in our spiritual conference, yet I realize I am far, far from pure. Indeed, the battle against human desire is more difficult than I conceived. I have mused much on the equally natural desire to be good. I suppose it is the Devil's handiwork that slyly braids the two strands together, to confuse us, so that we incline towards our bodies' desire as if it is for our good! How important, therefore, to be forever mindful of our innocence, and while our kisses and clasped hands may construe as children's play, and thus without stain, yet at our feet the vines of lust seek purchase, at first lovingly as tendrils, and then – so quickly – as strangling coils. (How right you were, last Thursday, to end our meeting or we might have been beguiled by happiness to tempt sin. We each shall be vigilant for the other, and when one weakens we know the other will prevail.)

When I rose from the grass to turn homeward, I paused to admire the scene, which I fancied to be our Garden of Eden, wherein sin does not yet exist, and innocence claims the day, and the Father smiles on our virgin union. The Lord challenges us to protect this Eden – that it may last more than a moment – and extend into precious eternity.

Tuesday next, in the late afternoon, would suit – or Wednesday if it rains. Use our signal.

Take care of yourself, my love. I do adore to stroke your face – it is my prayer of thanks to the One who brought us together. Hallowed be His name!

> *Your loving*
> *Jane*

Dear Lysander,

Yesterday I climbed to our spot and waited in the rain, even though I knew you would not come in such weather. I paid for my imprudence, and slipped on the way down, nearly sliding the whole rest of the slope in the mud. Fortunately I was able to change my clothes before Papa came home and without Rebecca seeing – she has transferred her bed to the kitchen while she has the whooping cough.

To my surprise, Ellis Graynier called in the afternoon after the rain ended. He was very respectful and subdued when I sat with him (Papa removed to his study to read the newspaper, he said, but I rather suspect he went into the backyard to smoke his pipe, which I have forbidden him to do on account of his lungs!). Ellis seemed much shaken by his father's condition, which is very grave. You might say he poured out his heart to me – if he had a heart to tip over. But I am being unchristian, and here was a fellow human in pain, and I made the best I could of such poor material. I urged him to join me in prayer, which I promised would bring him much solace. Then he teased me, wondering who it was that decided God wished us to worship Him on our knees, and what if He had been misunderstood, and we were meant to stand on our heads, and such a mistake would account for why so many of our prayers went ignored. When he saw I did not find this humorous, he apologized. Nonetheless, you see how there is no room for reform in this young man. He cannot be blamed altogether, for his mother died when he was young, and almost immediately afterward his father acquired a Negro slave from Martinique who, it is said, is his concubine as well as his chattel – thus the sins of the father have poisoned and deformed the son's character!

My unwanted caller stayed on for more than an hour, seeming eager to prolong our intercourse. But my mind continually wandered. Truly since you and I pledged ourselves, I have felt far away from worldly preoccupations – my mundane life seems so little – I watch with dwindling interest the actions of these small figures upon a stage. No more than a snip of a scissors and I would float free of this tiny drama, just as I did quit my body when I was ill, to fly on wings to thee and the Glory.

The ground will be drier in a day or two. Let us try again to meet in our Eden – Monday afternoon, God willing, three o'clock. I await your signal as ever.

> *Always your*
> *Jane*

Dear Lysander,

I could not come because of Mr. Graynier's funeral. You must have heard the passing-bell toll all yesterday – Papa and Rebecca and I went up to the mansion to pay our respects. We were shocked to see him laid out – so shrunken and withered by the disease – which consumed him very quickly. They say the face shows peace upon the soul's departure, but that cannot be true for a soul bound for damnation – Mr. Graynier's lips were twisted as from horror, and there was an atmosphere of doom in the curtained room where he lay.

His two daughters received everyone in cool silence. I reckon they do not mourn him in their hearts, as he was rumored to be a neglectful father, showing little concern for their academic, moral, or religious education, and thus, although only 15 and 17 years of age, they are bored, enervated creatures. I believe Mr. Graynier bestowed all his affections on Ellis, whom we found sitting by himself in the corner. He had not bothered to don a cravat or jacket for propriety's sake, and though there were many visitors who wished to pay their sympathies, his manner seemed to warn them away. The Negress housekeeper served refreshments with lowered eyes. Mr. Graynier did not emancipate her before dying, so I suppose her fate is now in the hands of the young master.

I did not like to see Ellis so morbidly aloof. I approached with hesitation, but when he glanced up I saw that I was welcome. I knelt before him and took his hands, praying that a little of the Spirit that I have received from your dear hands would now pass into Ellis for it would console him. We spoke in low voices, for the others were watching us curiously. I said I was sorry for the loss of his father, yet he could take comfort that Mr. Graynier was finally free from pain.

"His torment is over," he agreed with a bitter smile. "But mine is just begun." When I asked what he meant, he replied almost an-

grily, "Jane, what shall I do with a factory?"

I drew back, for I could smell strong spirits on his breath, and I thought it likely that he was not in a rational state. I told him that he must make acquaintance with his own strength – as his father had been strong, this must be his true inheritance – and then he could meet the task with conviction. This made him laugh outright. He said when I looked at him thus prettily, and spoke such a pile of nonsense, he couldn't help believing it, and he would rather be my fool than remain a cynic, because then he might be capable of the manly exploits I imagined for him. I felt, once again, that any effort I might apply to Ellis' reformation would have no positive issue. I think God has no preferment: He may abandon a beggar to the misery of shantytown, and also abandon a rich man to a dark and soulless existence, and it is all Justice, for I think the rich man's is the greater poverty.

Today will be the royal procession and burial, and you will see the whole of Graynier done up properly for public grieving. However, I believe most will be thinking not of the deceased nor of the disposition of his soul but rather of what lies ahead for Graynier Glass with the young master in charge. There you may see praying in earnest! For everyone's fortune is bound to the factory, whether for good or ill.

For myself, I muse on the vanity of life and the powerlessness of that powerful man before the great Tribunal beyond; and how rare, how beautiful, is the path you and I are called to follow.

My mind is clear and certain now. After the funeral I shall tell Uli that I will not be his wife.

You must, for your part, most delicately but without equivocation, make Rebecca understand that you are not looking to wed any woman. My fervent hope is that Uli will next ask for her hand, and she will accept him because you have made plain your preference for a life of chastity.

They will marry, and Papa will be relieved, and soon per-

haps I may tell him of our sacred pact, and procure his blessing. Dearest, we say we strive for purity, yet there is nothing pure about our deceit. I long for the day when we no longer hide or dissemble, but instead live by our truth openly. When I looked upon Mr. Graynier's face in his coffin yesterday, I felt I knew death's most urgent instruction: to live in truth, from this time on, even if only a minute of life remains.

Your loving
Jane

Dear Lysander,

Forgive me for not coming to Eden this morning. Rebecca has been very dispirited and dependent on my company since you asked her not to visit anymore. Papa was quick to condemn you but in private he told me that she is proud and disingenuous and will stubbornly fancy a connexion where none exists, for which her lot must always be disappointment. I do believe she was more in love with you than we knew. (Adding to her woe was the news that Uli Haff was accepted by her friend Mabel – they are to be married in a month's time.)

I have been distracting Rebecca with gossip, for every village maiden is in a fever of conjecture, wondering when – and <u>whom</u>! – Ellis Graynier will marry, now that he has taken command of the factory and will doubtless want to present a more mature appearance to the community. I do think that the gossipers presume a haste that he does not himself feel, and that it will be a year – or many! – before he considers matrimony. But I suppose the girls of Graynier need a topic to match their high spirits in this lovely warm weather: thus rumors flower most pungently with the lilacs. Rebecca has allowed this topic to revive her natural energy, and by tomorrow I warrant she will be back to visiting friends

*and showing off her new hat on the avenue in case Ellis should
drive by. He will probably not – he is working long hours with
my father and Mr. Haff to learn the business of glass.*

*Papa does not speak to me much since I refused Mr. Haff.
I can tell he is not angry so much as embarrassed, and worried
on my account. The rest of the village, of course, believes me either insane or conceited or both. It is true that I hold myself high,
though to my mind I am justified, having been surrounded by
ignorance and prejudice for twenty years. I blush to realize how
ignorant I myself was, for all my airs and learning, before you
came to Graynier, my love.*

*I shall be there to greet you in the Garden of Eden at
half past three!*

                              Your constant
                              Jane

Beloved,

*I can no longer come to Eden – all eyes follow me – every-
where – daily streams of visitors to congratulate me – must trust
Widow S. to bring this note – hoping she is ever our friend – have
asked her to call again tomorrow for a longer letter – no matter
what you hear about me, presume nothing, do nothing, until I
write next –*

Dear Lysander,

*I pray my emotions, which are very turbulent, do not pre-
vent me from writing with clarity, for there is nothing I dread
more than your misunderstanding me, which might destroy your*

faith in me and in our mission together.

Everything, as you know, has changed. Yet nothing that truly matters has changed. My mortal heart and eternal soul are ever yours.

I was as astonished as anyone at Ellis' proposal. When the words left his lips, I recoiled so conspicuously that he could not miss it. We were alone, as my father had arranged it, Papa knowing as I did not what was to transpire (Ellis spoke to him privately the day before, in his manager's office). I stammered my lines, so often delivered to Mr. Haff, thanking him in all humility for extending such an honor, after which I requested some time to ponder my reply. All the while, images rushed into my mind: of myself before the altar pledging my existence to this arrogant libertine – of a life sentenced to the Graynier mansion – where no echo of God was ever heard – the vapid company of his sisters – and above all, a world of terrible emptiness, where Lysander once breathed.

Ellis did not care that I showed my aversion. Rather he seemed animated by it. I will describe his aspect without exaggeration – eyes like a hound's, when the game has burst from cover.

I fear he is dangerous.

More shocking still is that my father should force me to accept Ellis, when Papa has always championed my independence. He does not even permit discussion, but tells me sharply that ever since my rejection of Uli he no longer trusts me to recognize where my best interests lie and therefore he must decide this matter for me.

Of course everyone is amazed that Ellis Graynier would choose a bride of lesser station and no fortune. I am stared at like a bauble in a shop. Yes, it may be beautiful, but the low price tells the tale. What can he want with a paste diamond?

His sisters, it must be said, have been perfectly cordial, and perhaps their excitement is genuine, since in that dreary house any extra soul would enliven their days. They tell me how Ellis has changed, how deeply he must care for me to have achieved such a transformation of character (they freely admit his past roguery), how soberly he now shoulders his responsibilities, with the vigor of one inspired by love.

I do not believe he loves me. He hunts me.

And my sister – oh, Rebecca! She turns away so I do not see her pain. Twice now I have snatched, through no effort of my own, the object of her assiduous schemes. Worse, I do not even want what I have won. What would be her suffering if she knew there was a third one, whose heart she once coveted, who is mine – my true beloved – a union, moreover, nourished by the light of the Holy Spirit? She would never forgive it!

And my poor father – weary and unwell – what an awful wound I would deal him, if I revealed our conspiracy! I cannot imagine confessing it now. Lysander, what shall we do?

In despair,
Jane

Dearest angel,

I have no appetite, no rest, no strength, and barely enough spirit to manage this reply, after a night lying awake with the choice I must make pressing down upon me like a lid of stone.

Yesterday after Mrs. S brought your letter, and before I had a chance to read it in private, Ellis called at the house. He brought a gift – a pretty brooch wrought of gold – two roses entwined – that had belonged to his mother (who died when he was a small boy). I was happy to fix it to my blouse without the donor knowing that instead of interpreting the roses to be myself and

Ellis, in my thoughts I assigned to them our own names, Jane and Lysander entwined.

I concede Ellis has been very gentle with me of late, with no trace of his former mockery. Indeed he seems to want to know my mind, inquiring my opinion on all manner of subjects, whether music, books, or abolition. He quietly listens to my responses and then praises my intellect and character, declaring I am his better in every way and that he would make it his life's labor to be worthy of me. His first step will be to free Dorrie, his father's slave-woman! (I shall only believe this when it is done.)

Then he sought to know how many children I should like to have, adding that he fancied six. "What if I answered none?" I asked boldly – for I thought I saw a way to end the engagement right then and there. He replied that he would respect my wishes, for my reasons must be well considered or I would not have them. He finished by saying, "I cannot believe you have any flaw, Jane, I worship you so entirely. You are my faith, where before I was without any." After he left I did not know what to think. Either there was some cunning in his fair speech, or I have been wrong to detest him. How far can such a sinner change?

That question returned to haunt me after I read your letter. You offer me an escape from hell into heaven – no less. To join Gabriel Nation by your side has been my dream. You have often described the life as very hard. I am equal to arduous work and prayer, to sickness, poverty and privation, and the persecutions by those who do not accept the prophet's way. It would be easy, for the love of God and for you, Lysander – love is, and ought to be, easy. If only that were all that God demanded of His Gabrielites!

It is harder to repudiate my family, as you did. Do I have the courage? Perhaps I do. It would not matter if we fled in secret, as you suggest, or if we told them our intention openly – the blow would hurt the same. But there is another impediment to my es-

cape, against which my courage would fail if put to the test.

You have always been truthful to me about the rigors of self-sacrifice at Gabriel Nation – particularly, that all those entering must be of an incontestable chastity. I do retain my innocence, as you know right enough. But I am far from truthful, my Lysander, and I shall be honest now. I have tried so hard to overcome my weakness, when you have held and kissed me – I told myself that innocence was a matter of resolve, and of resolve I had plenty. Yet now when you propose a lifetime spent in resolute purity, I suddenly see my true fiber. It is weak and will not hold.

The truth is – I long for the love that vanquishes chastity. I would be married, and receive a husband's caresses, and bear children. All this time indeed have I wanted those things with you, though I tried to smother my desire and become the higher being you wished. But God has made me so – an ordinary sinner, unworthy of more. Do not squander another prayer on me, nor write. My love, go to Gabriel Nation alone. I will marry Ellis, and maybe I will be happy. Certainly everyone thinks I should be.

It is dawn, and the world feels unutterably strange on this new day – the first day of honesty, the first without hope. Ellis believes I have no flaw, and you have tried to exalt my purity – I am a false idol for you both. I cannot write more, my heart will break

Dear Lysander,

I hope I may trust the new hired girl with this missive. She has not been long enough with us for me to know her character well, but perhaps the money I have given her is enough to seal her loyalty. I thank God you did not follow my directive and you are still in Graynier. I could not know, when I wrote my last letter, that the most appalling reversal was yet to come.

Ellis came to see me today. Papa was at work, and Rebecca had gone out to call on someone, she said, though she mysteriously refused to say whom. I soon learned why.

The minute Ellis entered I could see his demeanor was changed. In his eyes was hard contempt, and an unpleasant sparkle of triumph. Once seated in the parlor, he requested a glass of water, and when I called for the girl he said he would rather have it poured by my own hand because he should like to know the taste of holy water. His tone was very impertinent. I ignored it – as I conceived I must often do after becoming his wife – and remarked gently that we had only ordinary water to offer whether or not I touched it.

"What?" he feigned surprise. "You're not an angel yet?" He appeared to derive an almost sensuous enjoyment from my look of confusion. He continued, "I thought you might have received your angelical diploma from the infinitely immaculate Mr. Trane."

I was overcome with dread and could not speak. He would not relent – he desired to know why Mr. Trane's kisses had not elevated me to sainthood, were they deficient? Then he laughed, saying I was beautiful enough without beatification.

I found my voice and demanded to know his reason for addressing me thus. At that he pulled from his jacket a bundle of letters. Lysander, I believed those precious pages well hidden, never dreaming anyone would look under the wedding linens in my hope chest. I did not reckon upon Rebecca's habitual larceny, or her spite. She found them – every page written in your hand to me – while I was out visiting Emerald in the shed – and then – my own sister! – straight away she brought them to Ellis.

I expect Rebecca thought this evidence of our secret relation would compel Ellis to break our engagement. On the contrary, he said it relieved him to know that I was no paragon, no miracle of virtue, and therefore he was quite content to revert to his old religion, which was to believe in nothing – and he called me a hypocrite, a minx, and a little fool – as if these were tenderest endearments.

He would still marry me, he said. He would still love me, moreover, but not as before, for I am someone he may now look down upon which was a great deal more comfortable than the view to be had on one's knees.

My temper rose at this. I retorted that the only liaison between man and woman he had known or would ever understand was one in which both are debased – that I felt no shame for loving you from a pure heart. Nay, I had only shame for allowing myself to be forced into such an abhorrent engagement with himself! I insisted he release me at once from my obligation. Then I held out my hand for the return of my property.

He thrust the letters back in his pocket and grinned, saying he liked me best in a state of outrage, it put him in mind of the day I jumped from his carriage, dressed as a servant girl – it was then he fell in love with me, knowing that life with such a woman could never be dull.

I asked him to what purpose he would marry someone who hated him. By this time I was weeping. He seemed to turn sorry for an instant, and took hold of my face and said, "Kiss me, Jane. You will forget your half-wit monk." I covered my mouth with both hands rather than accept. He let me go, and left the house without another word.

Oh Heavenly God, the difference between his touch and yours! I had rather submit to the clutch of serpents.

I cannot live without you, my Lysander – I will go with you – I renounce marriage and children – father, sister – this wicked village – only take me to Gabriel Nation and I shall gratefully assume any penance – for love of God – it is the only way forward.

Now indeed, dearest, you should follow my instruction. Depart from Graynier tomorrow, alone. Give no one an expectation that you will return. A day's walk will take you to Huxberry, where you may stay at the tavern. Wait three days there. Ellis will believe you have conceded the field. But he will watch me carefully all the same. I shall seem contrite and docile, so that he will think me broken.

On Saturday, there will be the Founder's Social on the lawn of Graynier Glass. The townspeople will all be there, with the Grayniers hosting. I shall feign a migraine and stay home. Return to Rowell Hill, taking the way through the woods where you will not be seen. Wait for me at our Eden, beside Farmer Quirk's wall. I shall come to you past noon, and never turn back to home again. God help us!

> *Forever your*
> *Jane*

PART THREE

CHAPTER TWENTY

Jack Meltzer believes in giving people a chance. That's what he had given Hoyt Eddy: every chance.

His wife Audrey was the first one to spot the huge hole in their lawn from the helicopter. On landing, she found the well nearly empty, gritty brown water flowing from the faucets, a poisoned dead mouse in the sauna, and wine bottles flung in the pachysandra. She showed the bottles to Jack, and with a sinking heart he went down to the wine cellar. The blatant gaps in the rows of prize vintages mocked him for his overly trusting nature.

"If I ever see that *shikker* again I will rip him a new one," Audrey raged, bursting into tears. When Jack left to buy groceries, she was being comforted in broken English by Silvio Pereira, their new caretaker.

"Seen anything of Hoyt Eddy lately?" he asks at the liquor store. Not for a few days, they tell him. On impulse he asks for directions to Hoyt's house. He'd rather fire him in person. Jack considers Hoyt a friend. But when an employee disappoints you repeatedly, he is asking to be dumped, and you should mercifully grant his request.

It was obvious Hoyt had problems when he came to the Melt-

zers as a handyman: why else would a highly educated, handsome
and charming man be reduced to menial work? Jack elevated him
immediately to property manager.

Now Jack will have no one to get down with on a fading summer afternoon. He'll miss their lively conversations. Hoyt had an
encyclopedic knowledge and a way of pulling obscure quotes out
of the air. For instance, when Jack mentioned a business adversary
who became tangled up in his many maneuvers and lost a deal, Hoyt
cited some Greek poet: "The fox has many tricks, the hedgehog only
one. One good one."

Maybe he used up his one good trick. As Jack reaches the dead-
end on Old Upper Spruce Lane, turning onto the twisty rutted dirt
road to Hoyt's house, he worries that Hoyt may be in some kind of
deep shit Jack doesn't know about. Rounding the bend, he glimpses
patches of red paint beneath a big pile of branches half-hidden by
the pines. Hoyt's Ford pick-up.

Why would he want to hide his truck?

Meltzer parks beside the house, trying Hoyt one more time
on his cell. As it rings, he notes that some of the windows have new
panes with stickers still on them. Others are broken, the ground
beneath glittering with glass shards.

Hoyt doesn't pick up. His voicemail announces his mailbox
is full.

Jack gets out of his car, heart quickening. An aura of failure and
incipient violence hangs over the mean lonely bungalow slumped
under the shadow of Rowell Hill. The house seems devoid of life.
He can't push away the image of Hoyt shot gangland-style, or hanging from a rafter, the overturned stool below, his sins caught up with
him at last.

At the front door, Meltzer reaches over the daggers of glass
bristling from the pane and turns the inside knob, stepping into the
house. Before calling Hoyt's name, he takes a moment to stare at an
intimate hell: sagging floor, scorched rug, abused furniture, decaying
books. Empty liquor bottles—most of them from Jack's cellar—bob
up from the depths of the sofa cushions like victims of drowning.

Mixed with the odor of the dear departed grape is something else, a sick stench coming from the kitchen: a carcass smell. Crossing the sticky, matted surface of the rug, he peers through the kitchen doorway.

The rotten smell originates from the garbage pail, which brims with at least three days' worth of food scraps. The floor is gummed with ancient spills. The dinette table, however, is spotless. A clean plate sits before a chair pulled slightly away, as if inviting someone to sit. On the plate is a supermarket cupcake in a pleated paper shell, vibrant pink frosting and bright blue sprinkles on top—an innocent, perky touch in an otherwise squalid setting.

In any case, no one is here.

Jack is about to withdraw from the kitchen when a ring of cold metal presses into the base of his skull. The rifle barrel prevents him from twisting his head to look behind, but he's pretty sure he's about to be fucked up by Hoyt Eddy.

"What are you doing here, Meltzer?" The man's breath is raspy, humid, arrhythmic; shaking hands hold the rifle barrel to Jack's neck.

Now might not be the time to fire Hoyt. Coming to the house was a mistake, like wearing a tin hat in a lightning storm.

"Hoyt, please. Put the gun down." Jack feels the cold metal withdraw, hears Hoyt reset the safety, then retreating footsteps. When he turns, Hoyt is tossing the rifle onto the coffee table, sinking onto the sofa, bottles clanking around him; he has a week's worth of beard, glazed eyes, and a maniac's calm. Hoyt asks, "Is it your habit to sneak into a man's house while he's away?"

His mouth dry with fear, Jack swallows hard. "I thought you were home. I saw your truck."

"It was supposed to be hidden. In any case, I'm not here."

The arrogance of the man! Jack can hear his wife exclaim. Angry now, he wants to loose a volley of accusations—the theft of his wine! the hole in his lawn!—yet he remembers the phrase: "You can't break something that's broken." There's no point in finishing off a man who's finished.

"Are you in some kind of trouble?" he asks.

"Why would you think that?" Hoyt's drooping eyelids snap up. Jack wonders how long it's been since the guy slept.

"You don't answer your phone, your windows are smashed, your truck's in the woods—it looks like you're hiding from somebody."

"The only one I might hide from is you. You could be a trifle peeved at me, over the state of your estate. As it happens, I'm not hiding. I am lying in wait. There is a distinction, my friend."

"Don't call me your friend." Meltzer glances at the rifle, far enough from Hoyt's reach that Jack can risk a little rancor. "You had a professional responsibility to me, which you walked away from. You owe me an explanation."

"I had an epiphany." Hoyt belches in his throat. "I spent the night in a hole and saw the Virgin Mary."

"You could at least apologize."

"You want remorse?" Hoyt grabs the gun and levels it at Jack, flicking off the safety. "Get the fuck out of my nightmare."

Driving home, Jack decides not to tell Audrey about his contretemps with Hoyt, his hasty retreat at gunpoint. An employee departs, and the vacancy is quickly filled. By the time the backhoe arrives, the sinkhole disappears, and new turf is laid, Jack will have forgotten Hoyt.

"THE MELTZERS ARE BACK," Thom Sayre mentions over the noise of the fans, draining his iced coffee and rattling the ice cubes inside his cheek.

They're passing the time with town gossip. It's sweltering inside the firehouse; even so, Hoffmann is making a pot of chili on the hot plate. The other three volunteers coming off the day shift are drinking beer. When the frankfurters are done on the grill outside, the firemen will sit around the parking lot in folding chairs, slapping mosquitoes, the sound of traffic on Route 404 dwindling as nightfall draws near.

"Thought I heard their copter," says Bern D'Annunzio, who

volunteers Friday nights. "Wonder what it's like to be that rich."

"Don't look at me." The postal service doesn't pay Thom diddly, but he still feels a secret pang of guilt for taking that money from the old guy, the P.I. from Virginia. It isn't technically a bribe; all Thom has to do is keep his eyes peeled for the girl when he makes his rounds, then call Fancher if he spots her. It isn't very much money, either, but there must be something unethical about it if he's ashamed to tell his pals.

Bern changes the subject to the Goldilocks case. Last night there was another incident down the road on Rabbit Glenn. Tisha Baxter called in hysterical, said a bear wandered in from Rowell Hill and snatched some barbecue chicken cooking on the patio. "Her husband Lonny says it wasn't a bear. He'd seen it from the bedroom and it was a longhaired woman or a hippie. 'There ain't no bears on Rowell Hill,' says Lonny, 'and even if there was, they wouldn't lift the lid up and close it after taking only one piece of chicken and some napkins.' Brenda just about hit him over the head with the spatula. 'You didn't see nothin', you been passed out in your frickin' chair in front of the TV since the ballgame ended!' She made us write it down as a bear attack just to back her up."

Their laughter gets drowned out by the bawling of the firehouse siren: it's sundown. Hoffman goes outside to check the grill.

He finds two hot dogs missing, and some napkins.

CHAPTER TWENTY-ONE

They haven't even reached the halfway point on Rowell Hill when for the third time Brett Sampson has to stop, gasping for air. He sinks onto a rock to suck on his inhaler.

Collin glances nervously around the chaos of snarled foliage and topsy-turvy trees, branches and vines so dense that the sunlight shatters into mere specks when it reaches the forest floor. The boy looks down at the half of the hill they've already hiked. Collin was given the map and the compass to carry in his backpack, while Brett hacked ineptly through the brush with his new machete.

The boy points to a bush near Brett's elbow. "Is that poison ivy?"

"Let's...assume so," Brett wheezes. "Don't touch it."

Tanned and fit from bike riding with Gita Poonchwalla, Collin hasn't broken a sweat after an hour of climbing. He'd be with Gita right now, except that her parents just got back from Mumbai and they took her shopping for back-to-school supplies.

Anyway, she seems less interested in spending time with Collin, now that Jane's gone. "Our mission is complete," she told him the other day. "Shaarinen has fled."

Collin misses her daily company, and the urgency of their

work; he'll probably never see her again after summer's end. *Our Gana Mother of Fire*...He prays to the goddess for a fresh challenge that would reunite him with Gita, at least for the remaining two weeks before Brett drives him home to his mother.

"Let me see the map again," says Brett, his breath returning.

Collin hands it over. Brett spreads the photocopied map on his knees, studying the faint property lines, the elegantly penned names of land owners and lot measurements, the wriggle of streams, the date "1848" and surveyor's signature at the bottom.

"I don't get what's the big deal about an old wall," Collin mutters.

"It's about history." Brett kneads his right shoulder where it aches from swinging the machete. "History's fascinating because you try to imagine how things used to be, a long, long time before you were born."

"But there's nothing on this map that's here anymore. Just woods."

"Then think of this as a nature walk. At a minimum you'll learn something about the woods, okay?"

Collin grunts derisively. Why is Brett so obsessed with this map, this so-called "nature walk"? *He's got some other reason he's not letting on.*

Brett adds, "I just wanted us to do something together."

Not true: his dad was forced to take him hiking because Collin couldn't go to Gita's and the boy couldn't be left home alone. Ever since Jane ran off, Brett's been mad at him. He doesn't understand that Collin saved him by betraying Jane. His dad was in danger every minute he spent with the Maximum Evil; he would have ended up as a pile of bones she'd picked clean.

"Here's where we're headed." Brett's finger marks a spot on the map. "Pease Pond."

AFTER THEY CREST the hill they come upon a small, desolate lake.

Brett looks as if he's about to pass out; his tortured breathing has worsened. Nevertheless, he busies himself with the compass and the map while Collin eyes the shimmering pond. Even though he's learned to swim, he still recoils inwardly, feeling himself dragged inexorably toward the water's baleful edge.

"It sucks here."

Brett doesn't look up from the map. "Bet there's lots of fish."

"I don't like fishing."

"Not that you've ever tried it." Folding up the map, Brett stuffs it in Collin's backpack. "We'll go 'round the pond to the other side and then keep heading west."

Brett starts picking his way around the pond's edge, balancing on precarious rocks and climbing over roots, his boots sometimes slipping into the silty water.

"This is so wack." Collin tries to keep the hysterical edge out of his voice. "We're not going to find anything, and we'll get lost."

"Where's your sense of adventure?"

Sullenly Collin looks down at his sneakers as he hops from rock to rock. The next time he glances up, his father is some thirty yards ahead. Jumping up on the trunk of a fallen tree, Collin walks its gnarled length to the root mass that, clotted with dried mud, hangs over the pond. Tempting his fear, he clambers over the roots, crawling out as far as he dares.

When he looks down at his reflection in the water, a proud, courageous boy stares back. *The avatar, mortal enemy of Shaarinen.*

"Son!" his father calls. "Hurry up!"

Collin's reflected face frowns with annoyance. Then he tenses: there's something underneath his image in the water. As he shifts uneasily, his face slides away like a mask, revealing someone else's head.

He stares into the empty eye sockets of a drowned woman.

The water over her face is glassy, motionless, her hair snarled in the pebbles and grass of the pond bottom; pale rags of flesh curl away from her skull.

Collin's scream rips the quiet. *"Dad!"*

Brett comes running. Jumping off the tree trunk, Collin clings to his father's waist. Brett strokes his curls awkwardly, patting his slender back.

"What happened?" Collin points a trembling finger toward the pond's edge. Brett peers into the water. "I don't see anything. What was it, a snake?"

"I want to go home."

"We're not turning back," Brett says firmly. "It's better to face your fears than run away."

Collin pulls away. "I'm not afraid of anything!"

"*Something* scared you."

"Nothing scares me!" Collin's voice rises to a shout. "I'm a *god!*"

Brett's eyebrows lift in amused surprise. "Cool. Then we can keep going."

PERIODICALLY CHECKING the compass, Brett leads them through a crowd of conifers. The ground cover changes to grasses and dried pine needles.

A little distance further, they find what he's been searching for: an old, tumbledown stonewall. Brett practically breaks into a dance. "It's still there—right where the map said it would be!"

"So what." Collin sits on the wall, which stretches in both directions, snaking out of sight.

His father ignores him, puzzling out loud, "Which way do we go from here, though? Right or left?"

Collin notices the ground slopes gently downward to the south. Downhill means home. "Left," he says quickly.

As they trek south, the wall sometimes crumbles away, stones scattered and hidden by overgrowth; further on, it magically reassembles, like a film forwarding and reversing.

Collin's mind drifts back to the woman in the pond. His heart beats faster; a confusion of images crashes over him: all his nightmares of tidal waves and undertow and plummeting down dark water, mixed in with the corpse's submerged face, the vacant eyeholes.

She wasn't really there. It must be Shaarinen filling his head, messing with his courage.

But Shaarinen is gone. They chased him off.

Gita could explain what happened at the pond. She always fits the pieces together.

"Over here!" Brett beckons with the machete.

Pushing through the trees, they arrive at a clearing. In the center is a primitive lean-to shack made of old splintered planks.

Brett approaches the latched door, putting his finger to his lips. Knocking lightly, he calls, "Anybody home?" He presses his ear to the wood. Getting no response, he lifts the door latch, flashing a conspiratorial grin. "Let's check it out."

Collin can't see much of interest inside the shack. Just a bench and some camp stuff: utensils, a folding stove, a large skillet, a box of glass jars, measuring cups and spoons, coffee filters, and plastic gallon jugs of water.

Propping up the hinged flip board to let in some air, Brett starts poking around under the bench. Finding a metal footlocker, he tries the catch; it's locked.

Collin moans impatiently, "I gotta pee."

"Go outside. I'll be out in a minute."

Only too happy to comply, Collin goes behind the shack. Pointing his stream at the base of an oak tree, he lifts his eyes to the leaves overhead.

He spots a sliver of pink showing through the rich greenery. Pulling up his shorts, he ducks under the oak's canopy, pushing aside branches for a better view. Something is squashed into a crook of the tree, at arm's length. As he rises on tiptoes, reaching toward it, his fingertips touch nylon fabric. With a little jump, he catches hold of the object, tugging; it falls into his hands.

Jane's duffel.

He listens for his dad thumping around inside the cabin, then opens the zipper on the duffel, finding her toiletry kit and balled-up purple anorak inside. His knees tremble; an ecstasy he has never felt seizes him: rapture mixed with rage.

All along his father has been looking for *Jane*. He is still possessed by the demon. Even though she's been gone from their house for almost a week, Brett's concern is all for her, with none left for Collin.

But now, with Jane's duffel in his hand, the power of knowledge is Collin's, with none left for his dad. Because Collin will keep it a secret. He stuffs the bag back in its hiding place.

When Brett emerges from the shack, Collin is squatting on his heels, pretending to examine a bug. His dad looks deflated. "Not much here. Guess we should keep following the wall."

As they set off downhill, Brett points out the flattened grasses alongside the stone wall, trodden by someone making numerous trips to the shack: "Probably a hunter. That shack was a hunting blind. You can tell by the flip board. That's how the hunter makes an opening so he can see game approaching and stick his rifle out to shoot it."

I am the hunter. The reincarnation of Yenu Krishna, the Tawny One destined to track down and defeat Shaarinen.

You'll never find Jane. Not until we destroy her.

Can't wait to tell Gita.

CHAPTER TWENTY-TWO

Jane scrapes dirt from the rock with the spade, then slips her fingers underneath, exerting all her strength to dislodge the big stone. Her nails are broken to the quick from digging a little further down every day. By now the hole is four feet deep, the rim almost to her shoulders as she stands in it to work.

Over in the shade sits the leather satchel she unearthed last week. Inside she found, wrapped in a silk square, Jane Pettigrew's crumbling letters.

She has read and reread the letters, each time finishing in tears and clamorous questions. *Did Lysander come for me that day? Did we run away together? Why did I bury my bag? What happened to me? Why can't I remember?*

She digs because she does not know what else to do. Perhaps she will find something else that might provide answers, something that was buried further down, beneath the satchel.

She climbs out to drink from the water jug. Her empty stomach is growing fretful. When the sun is low, she will take the battery lantern from the shack and climb down Rowell Hill to look for food, searching the outskirts of town for an unoccupied house with an empty driveway and unlocked door.

As she continues digging, the shovel clanks against something, meeting resistance. When she clears the soil away, she finds yet another rock. Wearily she scours more dirt off it, then realizes: this stone is bigger than any of the others. To uncover its edges she will have to widen the hole. Even if she is able to do so, how will she lift it by herself?

Despondent, she pulls herself up from the hole, lying on her back in the grass. A pine tree looms sympathetically over her, brushing her face with cool shadows.

Eden, we called this place. Truly it is heaven.

She closes her eyes; feels the vague weight of the gold brooch over her breast where she pins it to her shirt every morning before leaving the shack, wary of leaving it in her duffel in the tree. *Ellis gave it to me...*

Light and shadow play on the carmine underside of her eyelids. As she melts into drowsiness, a shivery wave ripples from her toes to her head.

She feels lifted infinitesimally from her body and then gently settled back again, somehow rearranged.

The ground throbs under her head: a sinister drumming sound reaches her ears.

A horse's galloping hooves, fading away.

Then a fiery pain explodes in her abdomen. Her eyes fly open. She sits up, momentarily blinded by dizziness, hand moving to her belly.

When she looks down, she is wearing a long white skirt, its linen fabric wrinkled, crushed, and the front drenched with fresh blood. Is it hers or someone else's? Her chemise is torn away from her bosom.

The pain in her abdomen intensifies, burning. *Help—oh, help!*

Struggling to her knees, she looks about desperately. She is in a maze of low scrub trees, her blue-ribboned straw bonnet lying nearby in the dirt. Her satchel is flung onto a patch of grass, striped by the amber rays of a descending sun.

Must move. Walk to safety, before nightfall. Shan't think

about the blood. God has spared me—I am alive. And help is near—Lysander waits—in Eden—!

She reaches for her satchel and bonnet, stumbles to her feet. Each step brings agony; yet she wills herself forward.

She must find her way back to the wall.

The distant bleating of sheep guides her to a breach in the trees, where she sees the familiar rock fence bounding Farmer Quirk's acres of pasture. Summoning the last of her strength, Jane follows it north, too intent to acknowledge her pain or weep for her terrifying condition.

A horse stands tethered inside the glade ahead.

He is there.

Only a few more steps, and she is pushing the branches aside, staggering into the clearing.

To her shock, it is empty, except for the plastic water jug by the stump where she left it. The shovel leaning in the hole. Her pants covered with dirt from her labors.

The bloody skirt, the pain that cleaved her—gone. His horse gone. A cry in her heart: *Lysander! Where are you?*

CHAPTER TWENTY-THREE

Pearl stands anxiously in the corner of the curtained hospital cubicle while a resident examines her mother. He pokes the mole on her cheek with his plastic-gloved finger. When he brings it away, there's a smear of blood on the tip.

"When did it start bleeding?"

"This morning."

Marly hadn't wanted to go to the hospital, arguing that they couldn't afford the time off from work to drive all the way to Quikabukket.

Pearl can't very well tell Marly that she quit her job weeks ago.

Already she has made more money off Seth Poonchwalla than she could have earned in six months at Valyou Mart. Seth brings her pleasure, but she doesn't love him—maybe because the whole thing started off as a money transaction, or because he's going off to college at MIT in a few weeks. Whatever the reason, love is not in the equation. But she is happy. All her life Pearl has personified her mother's folly, her error in judgment. Now she is somebody's idea of a sex goddess.

She still keeps up the pretense of working, allowing Marly to drop her off at the Graynier Outlet Center every morning. She spends the day at the food court, or in the multiplex, or shopping for clothes for her going-away wardrobe. Soon Pearl will be so gone from this nasty bunghole town.

The only thing that might keep her in Graynier is her mother's alarming decline. Plagued by nightmares, Marly stays up until dawn. The woman who used to be all sun and bubbles, who never left the house without a pound of makeup on, is now surly and secretive, and never even looks in a mirror, as if afraid of what she'll see. Pearl was the one who noticed the black blotch growing on her mother's cheek. Then this morning it started to leak blood.

The resident sends them upstairs to the chief of dermatology, a woman with minty breath and binoculars on her eyeglasses. She measures the mole, calling it "remarkable," takes several photos, then dictates rapidly into a cell phone.

She turns to her patient. "In all probability this is a melanoma. It must be excised at once. A biopsy will determine if it has metastasized."

Then she schedules Marly's surgery for the following morning.

HER EMPLOYER AT the Graynier B & B is not happy to get Marly's call. "You want another entire day off to have a *mole* removed?"

"It's an outpatient procedure. I'll be back at work in the morning."

Mrs. McBee snorts. "What's next, liposuction?"

"I might have cancer."

In the silence that follows, Marly can almost hear the gears clicking in the old woman's head: runaway hospital bills...rising employer insurance premiums...

"Don't bother to come back."

"You're—you're firing me?"

"I'm downsizing."

On the drive home Pearl rages, "The old bitch. I hope she clocks out for good."

Sending her mother to bed, Pearl brings her a bowl of chips and a cold beer on a tray. "Want your vibrator, too?"

Though Marly knows Pearl is just trying to make her laugh, nothing can stem the tide of anguish flooding her body. *Things could be worse.*

And now they are.

"If they cut this thing out, I'm going to look like a monster."

"Mom, you have to do it."

Marly turns her face to the pillow. "I'm so ashamed."

"For what?"

"Pearl..." She brings her eyes back to her daughter. "Honey, I'm a whore."

"So?" Pearl shifts nervously, reaching for her mother's untouched beer. "Like, what's your point?"

"I am a bad person."

"Mom!"

"Why else would God be punishing me?"

Pearl rolls her eyes. "Shut up with that religious crap."

"I've tried to bear up my whole life the best I could. But He has it in for me." Marly starts to cry. "It must be for something bad I did."

"You mean, like having *me*?" Rising from the mattress, Pearl snatches back the tray. "God's a crock. Your life sucks, that's all." She stomps out of the room.

There must be someone else Marly can talk to.

Reverend Crowley would be unsympathetic.

Her lovers? Face it, there's no love there.

What about Hoyt?

She has been thinking a lot about Hoyt lately. Every time she puts her hand in the drawer for a pair of undies, her fingers encounter the cool metal of his gun. And every day she waits for the mail to bring the results of the DNA test she sent for, using Hoyt's pubic hair and a hair from Pearl's comb.

Once she proves Hoyt is Pearl's father, he'll have a change of heart. He'll beg her forgiveness, embrace his daughter, take his place as the head of the family, get his act together to support them, have the front of her car repaired. No more toting her cross alone. This is the one hope that hasn't died with Marly's former optimism.

Like the sermon used to go: *"For the Lord is a God of Justice."* So her luck is way overdue to turn around. It's only fair.

FIGHTING THE EFFECTS of four days without sleep, Hoyt has been lying in wait for the intruder's return when, at 6 p.m., the electricity goes off in his house.

He duels with the fuse box, in vain. Then he realizes he hasn't paid the electric bill in a while. He picks up the phone handset to call the utilities company.

No dial tone: the phone base is dead.

His cell phone battery is out of juice. He could charge it in his truck, but he'd have to remove all the tree branches covering the vehicle. He's too tired; the sleep he has resisted for so long threatens to capsize him. He reaches for a bottle of whiskey.

Moonrise finds him passed out on the couch, shirt unbuttoned to his belt, sweaty chest rising and falling, the neck of the Dewar's nestled in his open hand, when something wakes him.

A sound. Not the usual wall creaks, or Pete barging through the doggie door after a night of hunting. It's the sound of something alien, inside the house.

By the time Hoyt breaks through layers of drunken sleep to consciousness, the house is quiet again. His scotch-addled brain decides the sound was in a dream, though he can't recall dreaming anything.

His mouth is open and dry; he wets his lips with a nervous swipe of the tongue. His bladder is about to pop. Padding into the bathroom in the dark, he lifts the toilet lid. The rocketing stream of urine meets the water in the bowl, waking his senses.

Then he hears the noise again. Coming from somewhere in the house.

The scrape of a chair, the faint rattle of silverware.

Someone's in the kitchen.

The trespasser is back.

Hoyt tucks his dick back in his jeans, then steals to the bedroom; training an ear toward the kitchen, he reaches into the closet for his .22.

He knows the intruder couldn't have come through the front door; he tripwired it: a blast of pepper spray would blind anyone entering. No, the guy used the kitchen door, where another kind of trap awaits.

Hoyt grins. The cupcake on the table is a bit stale by now, but the bright pink frosting still beckons to a hungry soul, and the blue sprinkles on top—pellets from a box of D-Con mouse poison—should give the guy one bitch of a stomach ache.

Hoyt releases the safety on the rifle and begins his silent trek through the shadows of the living room. The sounds of his guest heedlessly moving around the kitchen reach his ear curiously amplified, hyper real.

His rage building, he nears the kitchen doorway. There's a vague glow within: the light of the half-moon shining through the window.

Hoyt peers carefully around the doorframe to see the indistinct shadow of his guest, bent over the sink.

He expected someone taller.

He raises his rifle and points it at the intruder. Before he can growl, "Don't move," the figure suddenly wheels around and dives toward him.

Without thinking, Hoyt squeezes the trigger.

In the echo of the gun's blast, he realizes the intruder wasn't attacking him, but rather collapsing to the floor.

The form at his feet moans softly. Hoyt grabs a flashlight off the shelf beside the door and shines it on his prey.

A thin young woman is jackknifed on the linoleum tiles, vomiting. Blood spurts from the bullet entry in her upper arm, drenching the fabric of her shirt and pooling into the vomit. Raising a face whiter than the half-moon, she gazes at him with the same meek acceptance as the animals in his traps.

She's not much more than a child.

Appalled, Hoyt flicks back the safety and hurls the gun aside, sinking to his knees beside her. "Oh shit—oh fuck—I'm sorry—"

Her eyes roll back. In an instant, she is unconscious, her head lolling on the floor.

She must be in shock. Grabbing a roll of paper towels, he rips off handfuls, wadding them into the bullet wound. After twisting a dishtowel around her upper arm as a tourniquet, he jumps to his feet.

"Stay there," he says, unnecessarily. "I'll be right back."

As he dashes to the kitchen door, he nearly stumbles over the girl's battery lantern lying on the floor. He kicks it aside. He sprints down the driveway in the moonlight, his legs pumping robotically, the grainy circle from his flashlight jiggling on the dust ahead.

He tears apart the tangle of branches heaped over his truck for camouflage, parks the pickup with headlights aimed at the kitchen door, and rushes in to gather the girl in his arms. Kicking the screen door open, he carries her to the truck, her body pressed ardently to his chest. Her blond hair drifts over his arm; her legs sway limply.

She is light and delicate, a puzzle of bird bones.

Just a kid. An innocent kid, a runaway, harmless, hungry.

Propping her in the passenger seat, he fastens the seat belt over her. She sags to one side. Blood seeps through the paper towels wrapped around her arm.

You fucking idiot, Hoyt, you fucking failure. Worthless son of a bitch.

He drives one-handed, steadying the girl as the truck bounces over the ruts on Upper Old Spruce Road. By the time he hits the hardtop on Rabbit Glen, he's babbling, "Are you okay, honey? That's a good girl. Everything's going to be all right."

Then, later: "Please, please, don't die."

The Quikabukket Hospital is twenty-five minutes away; if he defies speed limits, he might make it in half the time.

Speeding through red lights, he steals quick glances at her. In the passing light of street lamps, her profile looks carved from a seashell, like an old-fashioned cameo.

"We're almost there. Hang in there." *If I've killed her, dear God, never forgive me.*

He spots the blue sign with the big 'H' for Hospital and a left arrow. He can't chance running the red light, with the Quikabukket police station on the corner. He rolls to a stop.

Turning to the girl, he lays his hand gingerly on her head and smoothes her hair back from her temple with his thumb. Remorse floods his heart, suffusing his tissues, his bones.

Her lips part. A bubble forms. She vomits on her lap, and Hoyt notices the white foam at the corner of her mouth.

Oh God. She ate the fucking cupcake.

Chapter Twenty-Four

"**I**t was an accident. Somehow the gun went off."

He repeats this to the emergency room receptionist, then the aide, then the intern on duty. They mostly ignore him. Locked in their professional ballet, they rush the unconscious girl into a curtained cubicle, barking orders, paging personnel who dash in, wheeling machines. They undo the purple anorak tied around her waist and cut her bloody shirt away. Hoyt watches, transfixed, as her fragile white torso comes into view.

"Sir!" An officious nurse notices Hoyt. "You can't stay here unless you're a family member."

"I'm her uncle," Hoyt blurts. "She also needs her stomach pumped. I think she ate some mouse poison."

The intern glances up, one eyebrow lifting.

"Just a few pellets of D-Con," Hoyt adds. "She didn't mean to. She thought they were—it was an accident."

The intern and the nurse checking the girl's blood pressure exchange a look. "Another accident?"

When the stomach pump arrives, the nurse steers Hoyt firmly from the cubicle. "Go outside to reception." Her tone forbids protest. "You've got to check in."

Hoyt retreats.

A weary-looking receptionist poises black-enameled finger-nails over the computer keyboard. "Patient's name?"

Hoyt squirms in the molded plastic chair beside her desk, casting about for a name to give. *Jane Doe.*

The woman looks up from the screen, annoyed. "Patient's name, please."

"Jane," he stammers.

"Last name?"

"Jane Eddy. E-D-D-Y. She's—my niece."

"Date of birth?"

"I don't know. I don't have that on me."

"Do you know her social?"

"Not offhand."

"Does she have insurance?"

"I don't know. Her parents are away. In Africa. Can't be reached."

"Who is the responsible party?"

His tormented brain hears: *who is the guilty party?* "I am," he confesses. "Don't worry about insurance, I'll pay everything in cash."

A uniformed police officer approaches alongside a grim-faced nurse, who lifts her hand to point at Hoyt.

"WHAT IS THE NATURE of your relationship to the victim?"

Sitting in a private corner of the emergency waiting room with the police lieutenant, Hoyt tries not to get rattled. "I don't know what you mean by 'relationship.' She's my brother's kid. I already said that." It's too late to back away from the lies he has told.

"Have you contacted them?"

"They can't be reached. They're in Africa, on safari."

Hoyt knows how he appears to the cop: unkempt hair, twitchy eyes, filthy work shirt and jeans, unlaced boots, dirt under his nails, pickled breath.

"What year was she born?" The officer's tone is neutral, his expression neither friendly nor accusing. He jots notes on his pad.

"I'm not sure." The nurse must have called the Quikabukket police station, interpreting the "accidental" shooting and poisoning as possible signs of child abuse. The lieutenant must be angling to find out if the girl is a minor. "She's around 22 is my guess. She just graduated from university—St. Andrews in Scotland. She was going to bum around Europe this summer, but I guess she decided to come home early without telling anyone. She's impulsive that way."

His imagination gallops ahead of his mouth as he embellishes the life of young Miss Jane Doe Eddy.

Born and raised in Lexington, Kentucky, Jane was a troubled adolescent. Abused drugs and alcohol; a couple of times she tried to kill herself, once using rat poison. His brother sent her to live with Hoyt, who succeeded in straightening her out. (This is the least credible segment of his story; stinking of liquor, Hoyt hardly looks the part of a savior.)

Uncle and niece became very close through the worst of times, and now he is so proud of her: a college graduate, clean and sober, sweetest girl you ever want to meet.

"I didn't even know Jane was back in the country. I guess she decided to surprise me. Or maybe she tried to reach me but my phone was busy. The dog knocks it off the hook sometimes."

She must have hitched a ride from Boston, gotten in late, seen all the lights off, and, not wanting to wake her beloved Uncle Hoyt, she slipped in the unlocked kitchen door to look for something to eat. Hoyt heard noises, couldn't turn on the lights with the electricity out. He's been robbed once before, so he always keeps a loaded gun handy. He saw a movement in the kitchen, fired into the darkness...

"I would never hurt Jane." Hoyt remembers the slight

weight of the girl in his arms, the half-moon's shimmer on her face. "I mean, I love her."

He glances at the lieutenant's pad. The guy has the lid flipped up so Hoyt can't read his notes.

"The admitting nurse told me there was no ID on her person. I assume her identification is back at your house?"

"I have no idea. I don't know what she brought with her. There was no time to look, I had to get her to the hospital as fast as I could."

"Mr. Eddy, do you have a license for your gun?"

"Yes, officer. It's at home."

"Do you own more than one gun?"

"Yes, sir. All licensed."

"I can check that. Would you object to my accompanying you to your home? I'd like to see your niece's ID."

Hoyt laughs harshly, his deference evaporating. "You can do anything you want. If you get a warrant."

"I'm surprised you don't want to cooperate."

"You're intruding on my grief."

"I apologize." The lieutenant rises, closing his pad. "I will have to ask you to come with me into the parking lot to take a breathalyzer test."

"Happy to oblige." Hoyt stands. "I consumed half a quart of scotch nine hours ago, I was fully sober by the time the accident occurred six hours later, and I doubt I would blow over .02 now."

"Mister Hoyt Eddy," comes a voice over the loudspeaker, "please report to emergency reception immediately."

Excusing himself, Hoyt leaves the frustrated cop and heads to reception, where an aide waits to escort him into the ICU.

The trauma unit doctor stands in the corridor outside Jane's room.

"What's happening?" Hoyt is shivering with dread. "Is she going to make it?"

"The bullet went through the lateral deltoid, just missing the bone. She's fortunate no nerves or artery was involved, though she's lost a lot of blood. We're hydrating her to keep her pressure up, and she's on an antibiotic feed in case of infection."

"Can I see her? Is she awake?"

No, Hoyt will have to come back in the morning.

WHEN HOYT COMES out of the hospital, the lieutenant is waiting with the breathalyzer kit. Hoyt comes within a tenth of a point off his prediction, measuring a blood-alcohol content of .01.

Disgruntled, the cop follows Hoyt's truck for a few miles, then turns off at the Quikabukket police station.

Hoyt drives through darkened streets.

He almost took an innocent life. What does his own amount to? He imagines chomping down on the muzzle of his .22, the gun wedged between his knees, the eager obedience of the trigger. His pointless life bleeding out through the back of his head: a life precious to no one, least of all himself.

A mysterious, knowing voice echoes in his mind: *See what you've done to your soul.*

At that moment, he's passing by the First Calvary of Innocents. It's three a.m., but the Pentecostal church's lights are still on. First Cavalry is popular with Graynier's meth addicts, who can repent and save souls all night long until the drugs wear off. The windows are open, releasing the holy-roller throb of bass, drums and tambourines into the night.

Hoyt himself has refused to go near a church since his mother deserted him for her faith. Now he wonders, could he be born again? Is it possible a laying on of hands could remove his sin, cast his devils out? What if he turns the wheel, pulls a U-ey, walks into the tabernacle and gives himself to Jesus?

And if he backslides to his old ways, what then? Could he be born all over again? And again and again?

No way, the knowing voice tells him. There's a limit to the Lamb's patience, and you have exceeded it.

It's time to pay.

CHAPTER TWENTY-FIVE

As his father pores over dusty volumes in the museum's reading room, Collin follows Elsa Graynier through the door marked "THE HISTORY OF GRAYNIER GLASS."

They enter a gallery of framed photos, documents and engravings, lit by low-hanging glass chandeliers and glass sconces. With all the lights on and no air conditioning, the room is as hot as the tropics. Beads of sweat trickle from Elsa's hairline, damp patches spreading across the back of her blouse; her lipstick is smudged.

"So, young man! You're here to learn all about Graynier!"

Collin grunts. He's here because his dad made him come.

She ignores his disinterest. "My great-great grandfather Philip founded Graynier Glass in 1828. The Graynier family were wealthy plantation owners in Louisiana. But Philip wanted to try his hand at industry. He came north, bought land to build the factory and to house his workers. He began with two furnaces, twenty-five cutting mills and a pressing machine..."

If Collin were at Gita's, they could be figuring out a plan soon, before Jane—She Who Is He—decamps from the hunting blind.

"Then Philip brought over the finest glassblowers he could find from Italy." She leads him to grainy 19th century photos of workers holding strange tools, gaunt-framed in grimy clothes, posed before hulking machines. Their haunted eyes make them look hungry and sick.

"The factory produced eight tons of leaded glass weekly," she is still talking, "which was cut and shipped to Boston for sale. Maybe you saw some of these beautifully-finished pieces when you came in."

How will he and Gita get away from their parents for the hours it will take to climb up and down Rowell Hill? The Poonchwallas are making Gita do her summer reading at home before school starts. And Brett has been "supervising" Collin ever since the cop brought him home, managing to keep his son close while still completely ignoring him. Like today, dragging him to the Historical Society and palming him off on this weird lady.

"...Then, in 1853, Philip Graynier died of stomach cancer. His son Ellis Graynier—my great-grandfather—took charge."

Why are they even here? It must have something to do with Jane. Everything his dad does these days comes down to Jane.

They stop before an oil painting of a family posed in a richly decorated parlor, a handsome, dark-browed, unsmiling man seated at its center. "That's Ellis." Two younger women languidly play cards, their mountainous hoop skirts wedged under the card table. "Those are his two sisters."

Collin looks over at a pasty, blond, blank-faced woman standing in the corner as if cringing against the picture frame. Elsa explains: "And that is my great-grandmother Ophelia. Her family owned textile mills all over New England. When she married Ellis, her money added considerably to the Graynier fortune. Eventually she went insane."

Collin pricks up his ears. "She was crazy?"

"I think her heart was broken. All her children died in infancy, except my grandfather Faro." She nods to a ringlet-haired child crouched on the carpet of the painting, playing with a wooden elephant on wheels. "His maiden aunts named him after their favorite card game."

The whole family looks crazy to Collin, starting with the old lady beside him flapping her mouth.

"Business declined once Ellis took over the factory," she continues as they move toward more exhibits. "The forests were depleted, and coal was expensive. And then, so many men were lost to the Civil War..."

Collin is drifting toward the exit when his gaze falls on a daguerreotype hanging beside the door. The boy stops to stare.

A wrinkled, white-maned old man, face bracketed by muttonchop whiskers, glares fiercely at the camera. There is a deep whorled scar under his cheekbone: it looks as if half his face is being sucked into a hole.

"Who's that?" Collin asks, creeped out.

Elsa comes alongside. "That's Ellis Graynier, too, but much older."

"What happened to him?"

"A gunshot to the face. The factory laborers were threatening to strike and Ellis hired guards to raid the shanties looking for unionists. Somehow a fire got started. Several children died trapped inside the shacks. The father of one tried to assassinate Ellis. Fortunately, the town had an excellent surgeon, and Ellis lived to the grand old age of 83."

"What happened to the guy who shot him?"

"He was hanged, I suppose, like the other one." She lowers her voice. "Someone tried to kill Ellis once before, over a factory girl he'd got in the family way. Ellis was a naughty man, I'm afraid."

What did it mean, "the family way"? If the Graynier family way was insanity, then did Ellis make the factory girl go insane too? Was craziness like a virus that the Grayniers spread around?

He backs away from Elsa Graynier so he won't catch it.

"Are you going to the St. Paul's fair tomorrow?" she asks.

"What's that?"

"The church puts on a carnival every August. The fair is held on the same grounds where the glass factory once stood."

"What happened to it?"

"The government took it over for the manufacture of munitions during World War Two. Afterwards my father closed it for good. Later some vandals set fire to the building and it burned down." She sighs. "It's just a field now. But the fair is very jolly! There are rides and games and lots of food. Crowds of people attend from all over the county."

Crowds. An idea starts forming.

"...So if you go, you can walk around imagining what it looked like in the old days."

Collin abruptly heads back to the reading room, where he announces to his father, "I have to go to Gita's."

Brett doesn't look up from the book he's paging through. "I'm not finished yet."

Elsa joins them. "We had a fine time, your little boy and I. He was awfully interested in the exhibit."

Collin says loudly, "It's boring here! I don't want to stay!"

For the first time that afternoon Brett focuses on his son. "Apologize to Miss Graynier for your rudeness."

"Sorry," Collin says to the floor.

Elsa looks deflated. "It seems few people are interested in the story of glass."

With a sharp jerk, Brett pulls Collin down on the seat beside him. "Sit down and behave. You're not going anywhere." He turns to Elsa. "Do you have something for my son to look at while we're working?"

"I have a lovely book of gravestone rubbings, sweetheart."

"No, thank you." Collin kicks his father's chair leg angrily.

Ignoring him, Brett beckons Elsa over to his open volume. "I found a Jane Pettigrew listed in the 1850 census, but not 1860. Does that mean she moved away sometime during those ten years?"

"Possibly. Or she stayed, but got married and changed her name. Or she died."

Just as Collin thought: his dad is trying to find Jane. But why here, in a museum?

"The church registries recorded deaths and marriages," Elsa says. "Unfortunately we have to look through ten years of them for all six churches in Graynier, unless we know which denomination the Pettigrews belonged to. What does the 1850 census give as her birth date?"

Brett reads aloud, *"Pettigrew, Jane. Date of birth: March 2, 1833. Place of Birth: Graynier, Massachusetts."*

"That makes it easier. We'll assume she was baptized in the same year as her birth. Let's look through the six 1833 registries until we find her, and that will tell us which church we need to focus on. Give me a moment to pull the books from the archive." She leaves the room.

Collin asks, "Who's Jane Pettigrew?"

"A lady who lived a long time ago. I don't know much about her yet."

"Why're you so interested in someone you don't know anything about?"

Brett is quiet for a moment. "Is Gita a Hindu?"

"Why?"

"You know what that is, right?"

"Yeah. She told me her parents used to be Hindus but now they go to a Christian church."

"Does Gita ever talk about something called reincarnation? Where somebody dies and comes back as another person, or a dog or whatever?"

You are the reincarnation of Yenu Krisnu. Don't tell anyone. We have to battle in secret, or all is lost, the fate of the world and everyone in it.

"Gita never said anything about that," Collin lies.

Elsa returns, unloading large books stamped with gilt crosses onto the table in two piles. "You check the Catholic, Unitarian and Christ Church registries and I'll do the Presbyterian, Methodist and Universalist."

Brett reaches for the first volume.

"I wanna go to Gita's *now*!" Collin explodes.

Brett starts turning pages. "What is it about 'no' you don't understand?"

"It's just down the street! You let me go by myself a hundred times!"

"Stop bothering us." Brett and Elsa bend their heads over their task, as if Collin isn't even there.

The boy walks over to the display cases. What could be more trivial than these bottles and goblets and plates and little glass birds, when *evil* is about to swallow the whole world?

The door of one case is slightly open, the key still in the lock. Studying the array of stemware on the shelves, Collin eases the door wider, then carefully picks up a delicate pink cup. The display card says *"Blown Stem Cordial Glass."* He studies tiny bumps of purple grape clusters decorating the cup.

He opens his hand and lets it drop.

The splintering crash brings Elsa rushing over. "Oh, no! Oh, no! You bad, terrible boy!"

Brett marches Collin out to the sidewalk. "Go to Gita's and wait for me there. No going off on bikes, understand? And don't think you won't be punished just because you got what you wanted."

Shaking his arm free, Collin hurries off to the Poonchwallas' motel without a backward glance.

NO ONE IS AT the motel reception desk. Collin presses the bell. After a minute Mrs. Poonchwalla comes out, her orange sari whispering, her long gray braid grazing her butt.

Gita can't come out; she's busy doing schoolwork in her room. "Maybe tomorrow you'll see her," Mrs. Poonchwalla says kindly. "Are you and your father going to the fair?"

"Yeah."

"We'll look for you there."

She withdraws behind a beaded curtain. Peeking after her, he can see her padding barefoot down the hallway into the kitchen. Collin waits a few minutes, then slips into the corridor.

He peers into the kitchen. Gita's mother bends over the stove, her elbow working hard. The swish-swash of a spatula, the sizzle of steam, and the whirr of a portable fan cover the sound of Collin tiptoeing past the doorway behind her.

At Gita's door it occurs to him: her mother might hear if he knocks. He tries sending a mind-message.

He hears a toilet flushing. Gita comes out of the bathroom into the corridor. When she sees Collin, her eyes open wide. Putting her finger to her lips, she pulls him into her bedroom and quickly shuts the door.

His eyes take a moment to adjust to the darkness. Her curtains are drawn; the room is lit only by the blue screensaver on Gita's laptop, and some candles set before the shrine to Gana. He smells sweat and leftover skunk.

When he tells her his plan, Gita's eyes glow with approval. "Yes! We can do this."

"But what do we do when we get to Jane's hiding place? How do we fight Shaarinen?"

"We'll ask the goddess."

A soft knock at the door: "Gita?"

Motioning toward her bed, Gita lifts the dust ruffle so he can hide underneath. Collin curls up alongside their summer stash of stolen items: the Episcopalian psalter, the Jewish blue-and-white braided candle, the Catholic altar bells, the Calvary of Holy Innocents tambourine, the Meltzers' tiki torch.

He can see Gita's bare feet retreat as she goes to the door. Opening it a crack, she speaks with her mother in their language.

Hearing the door close, he crawls out. Gita is swallowing some pills with a glass of water.

"The doctor says I have an ulcer. Just another one of the trials a warrior has to go through. Did you bring an offering?"

"I couldn't. Dad doesn't let me do anything except what he wants."

"Never mind. Let's write our questions." Gita tears a page from her school notebook in two.

They each write a question, then fold the paper into small squares, placing their petitions on the shrine amid the candles.

Gita turns off the light so they can meditate before Gana.

Collin stares into the flame, repeating the prayer he has learned— *"Tell Me O Gana"*—until the goddess answers his question.

Afterward he turns to Gita. "I asked if my plan would work and she said, 'Yes.' What did you get?"

"I asked her how we destroy Shaarinen. She said: *'By blade or by fire.'* "

Gita has an idea for the fire. And Collin can steal his dad's machete, so that takes care of the blade.

"Tell me again what will happen after we complete our mission." He never gets tired of hearing her tell the story.

When the battle is won, Gita and Collin and the other avatars scattered about the planet will shed their color. Their skin will go white, then transparent, then invisible. They will walk among the people unseen, potent and infinitely wise.

Chapter-Twenty-Six

I *am Jane Pettigrew.*
     Her words echo in Brett's mind. They are all he has to go on.

This was my home almost two centuries ago.

Now that he has lost the Jane he knew, the only thing left is to delve into the past, and find the Jane he doesn't know.

With Elsa's help, Brett turns up a record of Jane Pettigrew's baptism in 1833, at the Unitarian church.

Child: Jane Amelia Pettigrew. Parents: Benjamin and Sarah Pettigrew.

Later the same year, the registry reports Sarah's funeral. Elsa sighs, "Poor girl, to lose her mother so young. At any rate, now we know the Pettigrews were Unitarians."

They wade through the next twenty-three years of the Unitarian registries but find only Benjamin Pettigrew's funeral in 1854. No weddings for Jane or her sister Rebecca; no funerals for them either. By 1860, all the Pettigrews have disappeared from the Graynier census.

What happened to the two sisters?

What if Jane married someone from another church, and left

the Unitarians?

Brett resigns himself to flipping through the other five churches' records. The leather bindings powder his fingers with dust which coats his sinuses as he turns the stained pages, poring over the spidery script that reports arrivals and couplings and final departures of the human faithful.

There is no trace of the Pettigrews in any of them.

He has always assumed reincarnation to be horseshit, a way for nobodies to boast they used to be somebodies. You can claim you were King Arthur or Cleopatra in a former life, and who can prove otherwise? Funny how no one ever says he was a garbage collector, or an aardvark.

Fragments come to me and I don't understand them. But they have a certainty—I know them to be true, as I know my name is Jane and I was born in Graynier. If they come not from my memory, then where?

How could she know which was the Pettigrews' house? The detective said she had lived in the autistic facility for most of her life. Where did she get her memory of a wall, and the name Quirk?

Elsa pipes up from the corner where she is studying local cemetery records: "I've found the headstones!"

She brings the book over to Brett's table, pointing out the entries. He reads the first: "Pettigrew, Sarah. Location: Beacon Unitarian Cemetery. Description: marble monument, side border of vines, flowers, and fruit, crowned by weeping winged head. Inscription: 'Sacred to the memory of Sarah Mayhew Pettigrew, our cherished wife and mother, born in 1807 and died on February 6, 1833. *I am the resurrection and the life/ He that believeth in me/ Though he were dead/ Yet shall he live.*'"

Underneath Sarah's entry is "Pettigrew, Benjamin. Location: Beacon Unitarian Cemetery. Description: simple granite slab. Inscription: 'In memory of Benjamin Leviticus Pettigrew who died March 21, 1854 aged 48 yrs. *Calm & resigned I do give over/ My life for one that shall never end/ Death has no terrifying power/ To those who find in Christ a friend.*'"

Turning the page, he sees the last listing is Rebecca. "No

headstone for Jane?"

"I'm sorry, dear. Perhaps she moved away to live with rela-
tives, after her father and sister died. But go back and look at
Rebecca's entry, because there's something odd about it."

He returns his eyes to the page. "Pettigrew, Rebecca. Location: Crompton Field plot. Description: sandstone slab, broken at
base. Inscription: 'Rebecca Pettigrew, died April 1854, aged 24.'"

Brett looks up at Elsa inquiringly. "What's strange about it?"

"Rebecca's headstone isn't in the Unitarian cemetery along
with her parents. There was no funeral recorded in the church registry, either. She's in Crompton's Field, where they buried the or-
phans, the servants and shanty workers. To be in Crompton's Field,
you were poor, or an outcast of some kind."

He doesn't care about Rebecca. "But what about Jane?"

"I believe we're at a dead end on Jane Pettigrew." Closing the
book, Elsa rubs her eyes, smudging her mascara into ghoulish whorls.
"Is there a reason for your curiosity about this particular person?"

Because I love her. "She's, like, a distant relative."

She glances at her watch. "I'm afraid it's closing time."

Dispirited, Brett follows Elsa to the door as she locks up.

"I'm still curious about Rebecca's death," she says as she lets him
out. "I think I'll have a look at Doctor Pincus' journals. He was both
doctor and coroner back then, and he cared for nearly everyone in
Graynier. He made notes about all his cases, so maybe there's some
mention of the Pettigrews. Leave me your number and I'll call you if
I find anything."

A FOOL'S ERRAND.

"Well, that was a wasted day," Brett says on the drive home.

Collin, riding beside him in barbed silence, is even further beyond his reach than when they left Connecticut. Brett feels a growing
contrition; he has squandered their summer.

At dinner he tries to engage his son, chattering inanely about
software and sports. The boy, staring at his plate of takeout ribs, doesn't

even bother to grunt.

"Maybe we should use our last days together to take that fishing trip I promised you."

"I don't like fishing."

"How do you know if you never tried it?"

"'Cause I know."

Right back where they began.

Collin rises abruptly, takes his plate into the kitchen. Brett hears water running in the sink, then the clank of the plate as the boy places it in the dishwasher.

I've lost everyone now, Brett thinks. *The two Janes, and my son.*

"Dad?" He feels the kid's hand on his shoulder.

He looks up. Collin's brown eyes are round and sweetly supplicating.

"Can you take me to the fair tomorrow?"

Even in the short time that's left, they could change things around, Brett thinks. He needs to give the boy his full attention.

"Awesome! Great idea, son."

They'll have fun. And maybe the love he's supposed to feel for Collin will emerge.

And then he could forget about Jane.

Later he kisses Collin goodnight, and finds his kiss miraculously returned. He arranges the mosquito netting around the boy's bed and turns out the light, climbing upstairs to work at his computer.

Instead of working, however, he goes online and enters "jane amelia pettigrew" in a search window. The results return instantly: "0." He tries other search engines, with no luck.

His cell phone rings.

It's Elsa Graynier. "I hope you don't mind my phoning so late. I was paging through Doctor Pincus' journals and I found several notes on the Pettigrews."

"Great. Anything new?" Brett asks, his hopes roused.

"In 1833 there was a scarlet fever epidemic. That's how the mother died. And here's the death of the father: *'March 21, 1854. Attended bedside B. Pettigrew. Death past midnight. Phthisis.'* I had to look the word up. It's what they used to call tuberculosis."

"And...anything on Jane?"

"There's only one entry about her. The doctor treated her for a serious bout of the grippe in 1853, which she survived. She would have been about 20."

"That's it?"

"I'm afraid so. But then there's Rebecca. Listen to this: *'September 20, 1854. Examined body of Rebecca Pettigrew. Death by drowning in Pease Pond. Decay indicates more than a month in water. By her own hand.'* It would explain why she was buried in the paupers' field. Although I thought the Unitarians were more charitable toward suicide than the Catholics. I do hope your Jane had a happier life."

Brett thanks Elsa and and hangs up.

He wants to cry; his heart feels leaden. Turning off his computer, he goes downstairs to his bedroom and lies down in the dark. *Jane, where are you?*

Then he remembers the vision he had, here in this same bed, that night she first knocked at his door.

A doctor, bent over his wasted dead body, closing his lids. The blood flecks on the sheet about his chin. Phthisis. Tuberculosis, coughing up blood, wasting away...

He wishes suddenly that he could conjure that scene again, like a dusty volume that he could reach down from the shelf and open, to learn...

He feels a shifting in the darkness as his body grows heavy. He finds he can't lift a muscle. A febrile heat spreads through his limbs, and a dim light blooms on the ceiling.

My Jane, my own dear Jane, where are you?

The voice is no longer his own. Another man's tortured cry issues from his throat: *Jane! My daughter!*

He tastes blood in his mouth; feels a suffocating pressure in his chest, his body immobilized on fever-soaked sheets. He manages to rotate his head a few degrees, and sees a kerosene lantern beside his bed. It throws a weak halo of light on the ceiling.

Suddenly the light is blocked: a face bends over him. A young woman in tears. She touches her hand to his, weeping, "Papa...I'm sorry, Papa..."

He musters enough strength to push her hand away.

She retreats from his view. "Oh! He won't forgive me," she sobs to someone else in the room.

He doesn't want her. She isn't Jane.

He hears her retreat, the door closing. A man's head comes into view, looking down upon him. Rimless spectacles, a high stiff collar: the doctor.

He's dying.

Again.

IT TAKES ALL Brett's effort to force the images away, and pull his consciousness away from the dying man's. The scene dissipates.

He is Brett Sampson, splayed on the musty bedcovers in the dark, in Father Petrelli's bedroom.

It was his bedroom, too—Benjamin Pettigrew's. He died here, calling for his daughter Jane.

Where does that knowledge come from? The strange certainty, the unsought images.

If they come not from my memory, then where?

CHAPTER TWENTY-SEVEN

Toward dawn, Jane returns from the Realm, flying swiftly over land and sea, unfettered by flesh and bone; her being is weightless and lambent. She pauses to hover over 53 Sycamore Street, pining for home and the man she deserted. But her body is waking; and so she travels on to the hospital bed.

She slips back into her form, then awaits the conscious day.

She wakes with no memory of the dream. When she opens her eyes, she is gazing up at a harsh, flickering rectangle of bluish light on the ceiling. The air is cold. A dull buzz of pain in her shoulder comes alive with the rest of her. She cannot move her arm. Her left shoulder is covered by a thick bandage; there are tubes extending from her hand, attached to the needles taped to the back.

What has happened to her?

She is naked under a patterned cotton shift; her clothes are gone. Her first thought is of her gold brooch, missing along with the shirt it was fastened on.

She feels something encircling her right wrist. She lifts it to her eyes.

A plastic bracelet. It tells her she is Jane Eddy, date of birth unknown, in the care of Dr. Kashishian, ICU ward.

A nurse peeks in. "Good, you're awake." Entering, she takes Jane's temperature and checks the empty IV bag. "How are you feeling this morning, Jane? Any pain?"

"My shoulder," Jane whispers hoarsely. "And—" she touches her hand to her throat, then her abdomen.

"That's from the stomach pump. Do you feel like you can get a little broth down? Some Jell-o?"

"I shall try."

The nurse presses a button beside the bed, tilting Jane up. Detaching the needles, she frees the girl's injured arm.

"If you please, where are my clothes?"

"We had to throw out your shirt. Your uncle has the rest of your things. He's waiting outside to take you home, after the doctor checks you."

Uncle? Home? Jane watches the nurse leave. Fear mounting, she wonders: could "home" mean Virginia? Is her "uncle" that detective, masquerading as a relation to take her back to her false parents?

The door opens again. A strange man carrying a shopping bag steps inside and approaches her bed.

"Hello," he says softly. "Do you remember me?"

"No, sir," she murmurs, bewildered.

Lean, tanned, freshly shaved, he smells of soap. Sun-streaks rake his brown hair; bloodshot whites rim his brilliant blue eyes.

"You were in my kitchen last night."

"Was I?" She has a vague memory of eating a pretty cake in the moonlight. Then the punishing stomach cramps...

"I didn't mean to shoot you."

"Am I shot?" She looks at her bandaged shoulder, understanding now.

"I thought you were an intruder." He shakes his head ruefully. "Jesus. I could've killed you."

He could have killed me. She shivers as if enveloped in a shroud of cold: she feels danger behind his transparently blue eyes.

He has killed before.

"I'm sorry," he is saying, "I'm so sorry."

Voices in the corridor approach. The stranger puts his mouth to her ear, hastily whispers: "Please don't get me in trouble. Tell them I'm your Uncle Hoyt."

"Uncle Hoyt," she repeats, shifting her head away. His nearness, his breath on her cheek, alerts her to a different danger: a sudden erotic heat climbs up her body, unfamiliar and frightening.

"And your name is Jane, okay? Like Jane Doe." He straightens up as the door swings open.

A hirsute man in a white jacket enters briskly, clipboard in hand. "Good morning, Jane. I'm Dr. Kashishian. I'm going to examine your wound."

The man who calls himself Hoyt steps aside so the doctor can sit on Jane's bed. She winces as he gently peels the bandage off her shoulder, revealing a livid gash.

"Not bad," he remarks. "You shouldn't have a problem with infection, if you follow preventive protocol at home." Rising, he turns to Hoyt. "She's good to go. The nurse will show you how to dress the wound for the next three days. After it's had a chance to drain, bring Jane back and we'll put in stitches."

"Will do."

"She's lucky, you know. I hope you'll be more careful with firearms after this."

Hoyt starts to speak when Jane interrupts: "It's not his fault."

The men look over at her.

"Uncle Hoyt believed I was an intruder," she says, her voice surprisingly vehement.

The uncle rewards her with a grateful glance.

A volunteer brings in a tray of Jell-o; behind her, the nurse carries pills in a paper cup.

The room feels crowded; the man named Hoyt backs toward the door. "I'll go check you out while you eat and get dressed." He puts the shopping bag on the chair. "Your stuff's inside. I bought you a new shirt and some jeans. Hope I got the size right."

"Thank you." She is careful not to look in his eyes; they have too troubling an effect on her.

As soon as he is gone, Jane asks the volunteer to bring her the shopping bag. She rifles through the contents with her good hand. Underneath the new clothes are her bloodstained purple anorak and dirty sneakers zipped in a large plastic bag. A smaller bag contains the gold brooch.

Her fingers close around the pin. It fortifies her; her pain fades away. She knows what she must do. An unfinished task awaits her return: the half-dug hole in the glade, at the top of Rowell Hill.

HOYT PAYS THE HOSPITAL bill in cash—nearly all he has—without a second thought. He hurt the girl; he must make it right.

On his way out of the office, he sees Pearl Walczak counting cash onto another bookkeeper's desk, paying a bill of her own. Her cheeks are tear-stained; she looks thinner than he remembers. He hesitates, wondering if Marly is here, sick, in the hospital.

He could ask her, but Hoyt has always avoided contact with Pearl, annoyed by Marly's pigheaded insistence that he fathered the girl. He might have taken her seriously if he and Pearl bore the slightest resemblance. He would have bolted, for one thing, and left Graynier. But Pearl looks nothing like him, and Marly's full of shit.

He takes the elevator back up to the ICU where Jane is dressed, alert, and ready to leave. She keeps pace beside him as they walk down the corridor, moving briskly despite her injury, her pale brow furrowed with some private problem.

They ride the elevator to the lobby in awkward silence. The jeans he bought that morning when the mall opened hang off her slender hips; the T-shirt is loose as a sack, humped up on her left shoulder over the bandages. A gold pin of twined flowers is fastened to the chest pocket.

He cups her right elbow to guide her toward the exit. "What's your name?" he asks gently.

She evades his touch. "I am Jane."

"No, your real name. Now that we're done pretending."

"Truly, my real name is Jane." She sounds impatient.

"No kidding." He laughs. "Pretty lucky guess."

"Indeed it is."

A little lady. The stilted speech and grave manner are odd on someone so young. He mimics her formal tone: "Jane, may I inquire why you were in my kitchen last night?"

"I was hungry, and I found your door open."

"Are you homeless?"

"No."

Outside, they pause on the sidewalk under the glaring morning sun.

"Can I give you a ride home?"

"If you please, Mr. Eddy."

He walks her to where his truck is parked. Clearing the clutter from the passenger seat, he helps her up into the cab and starts the engine. "So where are we going, Miss Jane?"

She stares forward, her hands folded neatly in her lap. "To your house."

"You want to stay with me for a few days?" He likes the idea, wanting to care for her, to make up for his wrong.

"No, sir. I would like to return home, and your house is nearby."

He steers the pickup out of the lot, searching his memory for names of neighbors whose child she might be. "Why don't I just take you straight to your place?" He fishes for information: "I guess I owe your parents an explanation."

"My parents are long dead."

"Sorry to hear that." Actually, he's overjoyed. He'd rather eat glass than explain to some parents how their little girl got the hole in her arm and the ache in her belly. "Where do you live, then?"

"On top of Rowell Hill."

He's taken aback. "It's all woods."

"Nevertheless, for the present it is my home."

"Raised by wolves, eh?" He makes the turn onto Route 404

heading for Graynier.

"I have not seen any wolves." She seems displeased by his joke; her voice hardens. "I live alone in a small shelter, where I do not want anyone to find me. I am forced to confide in you, Mr. Eddy, because I will need your help to get there. It is a long walk uphill, and I am not in superior health, owing to your carelessness."

He is incredulous. "Let me get this straight. You want me to carry you all the way up Rowell Hill?"

"Only on occasion, when I am tired," she says matter-of-factly. "And there is something else you may do for me. There is a heavy stone I must move, which I cannot manage on my own. After that you may go. But you must promise to tell no one where I am. I trust you will keep my secret as I have kept yours, *Uncle Hoyt*."

"You win," he says to mollify her. "But as long as we're sharing confidences, you might tell me what you're hiding from."

"I may not!" she retorts. "You are importunate."

Hoyt breaks out laughing. "In my entire life I've never used that word."

"Perhaps your entire life has been useless."

He grins at her. She keeps her gaze forward, but he sees a smile tweak the corner of her mouth; her cheek flushes, pink spreading across the pallor. She suddenly looks pretty. He's embarrassed to find himself aroused...

...then has to slam down the brake to avoid hitting a car stopped in front of them.

Stalled traffic snakes around the bend, the cars blinking left signals. Ahead, a policeman holds up the opposite lane, beckoning Hoyt's line forward.

"It's the St. Paul's fair." Hoyt points out the Ferris wheel looming over the trees. "Ever had a corn dog?"

"Is that an animal?"

"No, it's food."

"Then I think not."

She "thinks not." Flaky kid.

THOM SAYRE ACHES to get to the St. Paul's Fair. This is his favorite day of the year, when the Graynier Volunteer Fire Brigade hosts its traditional Dog 'N' Patty Grill stand; he was up all night hand-molding hundreds of his famous burgers.

After rushing through his rounds, he heads toward the post office to ditch his truck, only to get stuck in the traffic turning onto the fairground. As the cop ahead releases the opposite lane, a stream of cars slowly moves past his window.

That's when he sees the girl sitting alongside Hoyt Eddy in his pickup.

Taking Fancher's card from his wallet, Thom punches the Virginia number into his cell phone.

"HERE WE ARE." Hoyt holds the door open for Jane. "The scene of the crime, as it were."

She steps inside.

Hoyt is uncomfortably aware of what she must see. This morning he swept up the remaining glass shards from the broken panes, washed her blood off the kitchen linoleum, kicked the piles of books behind the sofa, and vacuumed until the bag split open. When he opened the back of the machine, it regurgitated its contents back onto the carpet. He had no replacement bag, so he swept the mess under the sofa.

Now Jane is surveying the putrid rug and pull-out couch, which have absorbed every spill and excretion of his tireless debauchery. He used to bring women home from O'Malley's Mare just to watch their nostrils quiver at the smell; then they'd get that pained rumple on their foreheads as they debated whether they could actually go through having sex in this sewer.

Jane's gaze travels to the shattered panes. "Those are the windows you broke," he says dryly.

"I?" Her gray eyes are wide with protest.

"Wasn't it you?"

"On my honor, no."

"Doesn't matter. Water under the bridge. Anyway, I thought you could sleep in here on the sofa. Or," he offers reluctantly, thinking of his stain-speckled sheets, greasy pillows and dented mattress, "if you want more privacy, I could give you my bed."

"I shall not be sleeping here." Her voice is cool. "We should embark right away on our climb. The trail begins behind your house. At the end of it, you continue straight up until a stonewall appears. It marks a path to the shelter—"

"You're not going."

Her eyes flash indignantly. "You gave your word!"

"Jane." He folds his arms. "You're still at risk of infection. I would be derelict in my duty if I left you up there all alone. You can't clean out your wound by yourself, and then you need someone to drive you back to the hospital to get stitched up. When I know you're better I will take you uphill and move your stone, whatever you want. Right now you're going to lie down and rest."

Jane sits on the couch. Her expression is veiled. "If that is your wish, then please leave me alone to sleep. I am indeed quite tired."

They are interrupted by Pete exploding through the doggie door, smelling of carrion. Jane cowers; Hoyt grabs the animal's collar, drags him into the kitchen and thrusts him out the door with a bowl of dog chow to keep him occupied.

Returning to the living room, Hoyt is happy to see Jane lying curled on the couch, shoes off, her head on a cushion. "Atta girl, take a good nap. Pete won't bother you." He locks the dog flap on the front door. "I'm going out to fill your prescription at the pharmacy and get us some lunch. There's orange juice in the fridge if you get thirsty." Hand on the doorknob, he adds, "I think you know your way around the kitchen."

"I do." She doesn't return his grin.

Driving to the mall, Hoyt congratulates himself on getting the upper hand. *Not as fragile as she looks, my Jane,* he thinks, then scolds himself for using the possessive for a girl he knows nothing about. But there it is: right or wrong, he feels as if she belongs to him now. His mistake, his responsibility, his guest—his.

On the radio, the weather report promises a cold front coming down from Canada—a break in Graynier's record 56 days of drought. After months of unrelenting sun, the browned trees and leached grasses carry an enamel glaze. But now, overnight, all the humidity has been sucked from the air. The sky blazes azure, as bright as if it has just been invented. The dimpled moon still hovers clearly across from the sun, and the lawns and forests of Graynier wait for rain.

"Can you believe it?" Behind the pharmacy counter, the ponytailed druggist rings up Hoyt's gauze bandages, adhesive tape, and antibiotics. "Rain, finally. Everybody's running to the fair today, 'cause tomorrow's supposed to be rained out. You been yet?"

"No." Hoyt's gaze wanders to a corkboard beside the register, where people post notices for sublets and yoga classes.

"I gave my kids a fifty-dollar limit for the whole two days. They already called, crying poor. They get hooked on those games, just to win some crap prize they don't even want."

Hoyt is no longer listening, transfixed by a missing-persons flier on the corkboard: "HAVE YOU SEEN HER?" The kind of poster you see at the post office and liquor store and never really look at.

Unless you recognize the person in the photo.

"What's this?" He tries to keep his voice calm.

"Some old dude was in about ten days ago and put that up. You recognize her?"

"Can't say I do," Hoyt lies.

When the druggist's back is turned, he snatches the flier off the board and hurries outside. Standing in the parking lot, he scans the description under Jane's blurry photo.

Height 5'5", blond hair, gray eyes, age 22. *"Missing since 7/20, last seen at the Winchester Mall in Deer Run, Pennsylvania."* Then, *"Has a mental development disorder that requires medical care,"* heavily underlined. Below is a telephone number, area code 703.

JANE PEERS OUT the kitchen door's stickered pane, looking for the dog.

Pete is asleep on the grass in the noonday sun. The barrel of his ribs swells with each breath.

She returns to the living room, fishing her sneakers from under the sofa. A small book slides out with them.

Bound in cracked black leather with gilt-edged pages, the volume bears a stamped gold symbol.

Her fingers tremble as she turns to the flyleaf. *The Holy Bible*, King James version, 1851.

A thin, threadbare ribbon marks a page.

And in the sixth month the angel Gabriel was sent from God unto a city of Galilee, named Nazareth, To a virgin espoused to a man whose name was Joseph, of the house of David; and the virgin's name was Mary. And the angel came unto her, and said, Hail, thou that art highly favoured, the Lord is with thee: blessed art thou among women.

The angel Gabriel. The Gabriel Nation Bible.

She can barely breathe for joy. She holds the precious volume, no longer imaginary, but real, in her hands. It is a gift, like the brooch, inviting her: *Come closer, Jane, you are very near to the truth. You have only to climb the hill.*

She slips on her sneakers, ignoring the pain in her shoulder. Feeling the breath of angels at her back.

CHAPTER TWENTY-EIGHT

The first thing Seth Poonchwalla notices when he arrives at the clearing is that the shovel is missing.

Panting from his trek up Rowell Hill, he slips off his backpack. His load isn't heavy: only hundreds of decongestant cold capsules in zip-lock bags and two empty plastic soda bottles.

The last time he'd been to the shack, a month ago, he left the shovel leaning next to the door. Or did he? Maybe he put it in the crawl space.

He needs it to bury the coffee filters and matchbooks and lye cans—whatever is left over from cooking. He goes down on all fours to look. The shovel isn't under the cabin.

Someone was here.

Getting to his feet, Seth scans the ground with misgiving. No tracks, human or animal. The ground is baked rock-hard by drought. But the dried grass seems matted in places. Probably from his own footsteps...

A vagrant wind sweeps through the clearing; branches on the surrounding pine trees flail. Seth's anxiety increases: rumor has it that the Graynier cops have sent for extra detectives to help solve the town's drug problem. Still, they're probably looking for meth labs in houses and trailers in town, not in an old hunting blind everyone's forgotten. But his intuition persists. *Destroy the lab and go home.* Let the crank addicts of Graynier turn into shrieking psycho insect-hallucinating bales of exposed nerves. Already tweakers like Googie Bains and Graynier's mayor Sharon Sperakis are texting him every five minutes, getting antsy for delivery.

But...Pearl.

She wants more money. Unlike her soft-brained mother, Pearl gives nothing for free. The funds he kept stashed in the pool robot are gone, spent like his seed inside her luscious cunt. His cock hardens, remembering the squeeze of her sugar walls when he comes, and the full-body trembling that seizes him afterwards. (He's trembling right now; he will have to beat off before he can manage the volatile chemicals with a steady hand.)

Inside the lean-to, the room is in the same condition he left it. Whoever came to the clearing didn't go inside the shack. Pulling his footlocker from under the bench, he unlocks it with the key from his backpack. The contents are untouched: ten boxes of matchbooks, rubber gloves, engine starter fluid, lye crystals, Heet, muriatic acid, digital scale, skillet, coffee filters, surgical tubing.

Propping open the cabin's flip board to give himself some air, he gets down to the tedious work: scraping the red striking strip from each matchbook to make red phosphorous; soaking the cold capsules in Heet to extract the pseudo, wiping the wax coating off each pill with a towel... And then it will be time to cook.

The soft pink hills of Pearl float through his mind. He is a fool to love her. But he is addicted to her extravagant flesh. Like his clients, he will pay anything to feel that happy.

In ten days he'll have to kick his habit, though, when he leaves for freshman orientation at MIT. This will be his final batch of crank. Then he'll dump the evidence into Pease Pond, and close up shop for good.

RUPA POONCHWALLA GAZES around the fairground, feeling a wave of nostalgia. Every year they have the same rides: the Ferris wheel, the Dragon, the Sizzler. So many summers have passed since Gita and Seth were little!

The little ones used to ball up cotton candy and pelt each other, and fish for prizes at the Frog Bog; the two would beseech Rupa and Harish to stay long after sundown, until the tattooed roustabouts pulled the brakes on their rides and the strings of bulbs festooning the concession aisles were switched off.

And the Convoy. Before Gita was born, Seth used to race around on his short chubby legs, finally choosing the best color truck to sit in. So solemnly, he'd pull the rope on the bell that didn't ring, as the trucks wound slowly around the track. He truly believed he was steering the whole convoy with each masterly turn of his wheel.

But Seth hasn't even bothered to come today, and Gita looks like she'd rather be anywhere else. Such a strange child, with her moods and whims. And so unfeminine.

What goes on inside that head? It's been ages since Rupa has been inside Gita's bedroom, even to vacuum. Her daughter won't allow it. She says she will clean the room herself, but as far as Rupa knows, the girl has not used so much as a dust cloth. Rupa can't help worrying that all Gita's candles dripping wax on the carpet will set the motel on fire.

Rupa was granted no such freedoms when she was a girl—in India, independence did not come with Independence Day! That is an American delusion. What do either of her children know about self-sacrifice? Americans act as if they alone control their fates. But they are strapped to the wheel of karma like everyone else.

Her willful girl sits now on an artist's stool while Rupa looks on in dismay. Gita has insisted on having her face painted; at her request, the artist layers a military camouflage pattern on her face: olive green and tan smears, black stripes under her eyes, even black lips! Horrifying. Wait until Harish sees her, he will throw a fit. Then Gita will backtalk. And Harish will come unglued. Daughters know all too well how to dismantle their fathers.

Rupa and Gita are to meet Harish at the Daffy Dress-Ups

trailer, and have their photographs taken in funny costumes, like cowboys and hippies and harem girls. She hopes Gita won't put on the G.I. Joe outfit to go with her face paint!

It's true the girl has been seeing a great deal of the Sampson boy. That she likes a boy is a good sign. But Rupa will feel relieved when Collin goes home. Gita is better off choosing a husband from Mumbai.

Or will her daughter demand to have her way there, too? Will Rupa and Harish then crumble before their child as American parents seem to do? There may be peace and prosperity in this nation, but in families it is a land of war.

THEY'VE DONE THE SCRAMBLER, followed by the Sizzler and the Howler. But Brett can't tell if his son is having any fun. Collin seems distracted. At the Quack Attack, when he knocks a duck down on the third beanbag throw, and wins a bright yellow duckbill hat, he doesn't even crack a smile. Maybe he's afraid moving his face will ruin his makeup.

The artist hadn't been surprised when Collin asked him for army camouflage instead of clown paint or cat whiskers; the guy told them he'd already done camo for someone else ten minutes ago.

Seeing his black lipstick in the mirror, Collin smiles for the first time that day. Maybe the kid will be a goth in high school.

On their way to the next amusement, they pass Elsa Graynier running the Historical Society booth, which the crowds seem to be spurning.

Brett imagines what the fairground must have looked like, when the Graynier Glass factory was on this same spot. They might have sponsored an annual company picnic on a day like today.

The lawn would have been dotted with blankets and baskets. Brett can picture women of all ages strolling about in straw bonnets and flounced summer dresses...men in shirtsleeves and vests, their Sunday-best frock coats cast on the grass, hacking watermelon slices for the children...young men dashing by in a foot race, to flaunt their prowess before the girls selling pies and boiled ham at a communal table.

And Jane Pettigrew, in a picture hat with a blue satin bow, laughing on Brett's arm...

"What about the Rope-A-Dope?"

Collin is pointing to a rope ladder stretched over an inflated cushion. A carny barker motions to a stack of toys: "Get to the top, you get to shop!"

"Go on, Dad, win me something!" For the second time that day, the boy grins, his teeth flashing white. "I dare you!"

Brett considers the Rope-A-Dope dubiously. Handing two tickets to the carny, he climbs up on the cushion, plants one foot on the ladder.

He is thinking about his vision of Jane at the picnic, when the ladder pivots and flings him onto the inflated bolster with a thump.

Under the yellow bill of his hat, Collin is laughing. "Go again, Dad! Bet you'll win."

Brett flushes with embarrassment. He fell because he was thinking of Jane, when he'd promised himself to think only of Collin. This time, he'll concentrate on impressing his son.

Paying more tickets, he studies the contraption. He concludes that putting weight in the middle of the rungs activates the pivot. If he grabs the side ropes only, not the rungs, and keeps his weight evenly distributed as he climbs—by grasping with the left hand while stepping with the right, then grasping with the right while stepping with the left—he will be able to maintain his balance.

He tries out this technique on the first rung. The cords tremble, dying to flip, but Brett is balanced...moving up...hearing voices behind him as people congregate to watch.

Gathering speed, he reaches the top, where he triumphantly clangs the bell.

A cheer erupts below. He rolls off the ladder onto the air cushion, sliding easily to the ground. A couple of teenagers high-five him; the barker tells him to pick a prize.

Brett's not listening. His head jerks from side to side, frantically looking around him.

His son is gone.

RUPA POONCHWALLA'S SIDES ache from laughing. Harish looks so funny as a gunslinger, tripping over his spurs, with his stiff bowed chaps and ten-gallon hat tipped over his nose. Rupa declines the skimpy dancehall hostess outfit, then slips into the cowgirl costume the young photographer found her.

It's Harish's turn to convulse with laughter as his wife stumbles out of the dressing room, a gun in her holster, pointy Western boots on her tiny feet. "You are dangerous, woman!"

They pose before a white backdrop, while the photographer props a fiberboard cactus behind them. He is a wiry boy not much older than Seth, with oiled hair flopping over his brow. His sleeveless T-shirt shows off tattooed biceps as he adjusts the digital camera on the tripod.

Behind him a plump girl in a short babydoll sundress shows off her soft round thighs. The candy apple in her hand glistens with her saliva.

Rupa recognizes her: the daughter of the local whore.

"Look in the camera lens, please. Point your pistols at each other like it's a shoot-out."

Rupa lifts her gun to Harish's chin. "Careful, husband, I will kill you!"

He aims his gun at her temple. "I will give you such a headache!"

The photographer snaps the picture, and goes over to a printer in the corner. The plump girl joins him, leaning so her breasts graze against him as they watch the photo slide out. He turns and hooks his arm around her neck, kissing her candy-stained lips. She giggles.

The daughter already turns into the mother. Rupa looks away, unbuckling her holster.

Harish approaches the curtain of the dressing room, where

Gita is taking forever to change into a mermaid costume. "Gita! It's your turn!"

There is no answer from the girl.

"Gita!" Rupa opens the curtain to peek her head inside.

The dressing room is empty.

"COLLIN SAMPSON," a voice blares over the P.A., "please come to the Ferris wheel ticket booth where your father is waiting."

Collin darts quickly through the crowd, keeping his face down.

"Anyone who sees a boy ten years old, in a dark green tee-shirt and a yellow duck hat, please bring him to the Ferris wheel."

Ditching the yellow hat, he cuts between the Dog 'N Patty and the Buttered Cob, then sprints for the exit. Gita is already waiting.

They dodge through backyards, avoiding main roads, and blending into the foliage in their camo makeup.

At the motel, they retrieve their bikes and weapons and begin pedaling toward Rowell Hill.

Pumping beside Gita, Collin is breathless, ecstatic. They are cosmic commandos. Their mission is underway; there's no turning back.

CHAPTER TWENTY-NINE

Marly is dying.

She can tell from the doctor's aloof expression: she is as good as gone.

While she was out on the table, they scooped out her mole and the surrounding flesh; then did some kind of dye test that lit up the tumor's progress.

It had branched out to the lymph nodes. The doctor removed those too.

She has to wait four days for the biopsy, but the doctor is 99.9% sure that it will confirm melanoma; it has probably spread too far to treat, and there's only a 1 in 10 chance that radiation will work.

Sure, if I felt like going through agony and then dying anyway and leaving Pearl with a pile of hospital bills.

Dying.

She couldn't say the D word to Pearl when she emerged from the doctor's office. (She couldn't say much of anything, with half her face still frozen from the anesthetic and her cheek taped up in bandages.) Pretending she was fine, she made a show of lying down for a nap once they got home. She sent Pearl off to the St. Paul's Fair to have herself some fun.

Alone, Marly bursts into tears.

She shuffles to the kitchenette, opening a can of beer. She'll have to take food through a straw for a while; barely more than a membrane remains of her outer cheek. She's afraid to touch the spot with her tongue for fear it'll break through.

The beer makes her have to pee. But if she goes to the bathroom, she will catch sight of herself in the mirror.

Someone put a curse on me.

It all started going bad that summer night—can it be only six weeks ago?—she swerved to avoid a girl in the road, and crushed her bumper on Hoyt Eddy's pickup. Ever since then, it has been one woe after another, eroding her spirit; despair metastasizing like the cancer in her face.

Outside, Thom Sayre's brakes screech; she hears the thud of the mail in her box, the lid squealing shut. He's gone by the time she comes out on the stoop.

She surveys her pathetic slice of lawn, an overgrown mess of chickweed that's also metastasizing. Pook's food bowl lies near the corner of the picket fence; she never had the heart to throw it out.

Pook is gone. In a little time she'll be gone too. Then who will take care of Pearl?

All because of a girl in a purple anorak who appeared out of the dark and walked into Marly's headlights...

Whatever happened to hope?

She retrieves her mail, flipping through collection notices. Then she sees the envelope from the lab.

Here it is: one last hope.

She sits at the dinette table. Breathless, she tears open the envelope.

Skimming over all the confusing numbers and columns, she skips to the interpretative section.

The alleged father, Hoyt Eddy, is excluded as the biological father of the child named Pearl Walczak. Based on testing

results obtained from analyses of 4 different DNA probes,
the probability of paternity is 0.0%.

Stunned, Marly rereads the paragraph so many times the words blur. She pictures her younger self in the bar, in her apron and miniskirt, flirting with the blue-eyed boy named Hoyt, thinking of his trust fund as he fucked her, hopes flying like colored flags: *he'll take me to Boston, introduce me to his family, lift me up into a life of riches…*

An idiot to her dying day.

She probably knew all along, deep down, that Pearl's father was the fat man who stocked convenience machines along the Interstate, Marly's once-a-month customer until he moved to Michigan.

She stares at the official envelope. Her last hope can't be dead on arrival. There has to be another last hope.

HOYT FLINGS OPEN the bedroom door. He already knows Jane won't be there. There were too many signs when he got home: the kitchen door hanging open, her battery lantern gone. He picks up her purple anorak lying on the rug where she dropped it in her haste to leave.

He shouldn't have left her alone.

Tossing the anorak and flier on his bed, he quickly changes into his hiking boots. He knows just where she's gone. How much of a jump has she got on him: 30 minutes? 40?

He wonders what the words mean on the flier: "a mental development disorder." Is she retarded? Crazy? Or just eccentric? It's plenty bizarre to live alone in the woods and move stones for fun. No matter: she asked for his help, and he refused, and now she needs rescuing.

As he grabs a water bottle from the fridge, he hears a car careening to a stop outside.

Seconds later, someone knocks.

Marly stands there holding out his Magnum. "I'm returning this," she mumbles, one side of her mouth constrained by the large bandage taped to her cheek.

"Thanks, I'd appreciate your not pointing it at me." He takes the revolver, checks the safety, then chucks it on the sofa. When he turns back, she has stepped inside, blocking his exit.

"Marly, I'm on my way out." He tries to get around her.

"I brought your gun back 'cause I'm scared, Hoyt." She looks up at him with the abject expression that always makes him want to clock her. Except it looks like some surgeon got there first. "I'm afraid I'll use it on myself."

"Look, can this wait? My niece is in trouble. It's urgent."

Her hand flashes out, gripping his wrist. "This is urgent. I've got skin cancer. In a month I'm gonna be dead."

"Oh, Jesus. I'm sorry." He fights off a wave of disgust. He has always been heartless when it comes to Marly; she pisses him off even more when she's dying. He grits his teeth, faking sympathy, "God, that's so tough. But why come to me?"

"I just want to talk."

"Go talk to someone who gives a shit!" He shakes his arm from her grip. "You've got a daughter."

She narrows her eyes. "So do you."

"Not that again."

"I have the proof! I got the test results."

Her eyes skate away from his face; she's lying. "Show me."

"I left it at home." More eye wobbling.

"Too bad, when you went to all the trouble to type it up. Probably lying about the cancer, too. Christ, now she's going to cry. You're such an asshole, Marly."

She flings herself on his sofa, weeping. "You have to take care of Pearl when I'm gone! There's nobody else! Can't you care about anyone but yourself?"

"Least of all myself." Hoyt snatches the bottle of gin off the bookshelf and sets it on the coffee table in front of her. "Boo hoo, have a drink. I'll be back in an hour. Make sure you're not here."

THE TRAIL BEGINS *behind your house. At the end of it, continue straight uphill until a stonewall appears...*

The trail Jane mentioned begins behind his dump. Fear driving him, Hoyt climbs Rowell Hill by leaps and bounds. He has already forgotten Marly; there is only Jane, struggling up the hill somewhere above him, weakened by a wound that he made.

Spotting the old rock wall, he stops to catch his breath, chest heaving.

He hears a crackle in the underbrush, then silence. "Jane!" he calls.

A flutter of wings answers, as a thrush bursts from cover, rocketing to a high branch up the hill. As if Jane is beckoning: *I'm up here. Come find me.*

Hurrying alongside the wall, he realizes the miracle that is taking place. He cares about someone.

That he hurt Jane has awakened the Catholic in him, his mother's legacy, and now he is in the heady thrall of atonement. A lifetime of buried tenderness gushes up like the Holy Virgin's spring at Lourdes, rushing from his pores, a sacred river carrying him to Jane...

He arrives at the clearing. In his overexcited state, the shack seems to shine like the Grail. Except, as he creeps closer, it emits a powerfully noxious chemical smell.

Hoyt puts his ear to the door. There are movements inside: faint metallic clanks, glass dings, a cough.

He knocks lightly.

The sounds abruptly cease.

He pushes on the door, which opens a crack, then stops, latched from the inside. "Excuse me," he calls through the crack, "I'm looking for a girl named Jane. Is she here?"

Whoever is inside remains silent, pretending there's no

one home.

Hoyt tries again. "Have you seen a girl in a white tank top and jeans?"

"Yeah," comes a gruff, impatient voice. "She went by."

Hoyt glances across the clearing, then sees where the wall picks up again, snaking through the trees. "Sorry to bother you."

He moves on. Behind him the voice says, "Don't come back."

Chapter Thirty

Jane's energy is flagging fast. With every step the battery lantern in her grip weighs heavier. Without a hat or anorak, she is at the mercy of the sun; it has made a feast of her bare arms and face, inflaming her open wound under the dressing. As her head swims, her resolve wavers; she fears she will never get to the pine grove.

She had planned to rest in the shack after her climb. But when she arrived, the open flip board told her a hunter, or a fellow fugitive, had claimed her shelter.

Not wanting to alert him to her presence, she crept along the shack's wall, ducking below the opening. Before she could reach the tree where her pink duffel was wedged, she heard a scuffling movement inside; footsteps approached the lookout. Panicking, she broke from cover and fled the clearing, aware that the stranger's eyes watched her.

She did not stop running until she reached the pond. Gasping for breath, she knelt to splash water on her face and arms. Her shoulder hurt terribly. Peeling away one side of the bandage, she cupped water in her hand to clean the wound.

Now the bandage will not stick to her moistened skin. It flaps open as Jane walks on, her livid wound bared to the sun. The brooch fastened to her T-shirt seems to glow with heat, as if the twin roses are on fire.

At length she reaches the place where the firs grow closer together; she leaves the wall to avail herself of their shadows, only to retreat when their sharp needles brush her exposed shoulder.

She will have no place to sleep tonight.

Another sanctuary lies ahead, she tells herself: the glade of white pines. Eden. She pleads with her body to soldier on, take another step, another. One more...

The lantern is the first to fall. Then she is on her knees, collapsing to the grass, her strength entirely drained. A veil moves over her mind, as her blood pounds in her ears, faster, louder...

JANE'S HEART BEATS *faster as she redoubles her pace, gathering her pelerine tight about her shoulders. A low-hanging holly branch knocks her bonnet askew; straw and ribbons snag on the thorny leaves. She picks up her white skirt to hasten her stride. Her blood drums in her ears, the sound growing louder...*

No, not her blood drumming. A horse's hoof beats.

Peering through the branches, she can see Farmer Quirk's grazing field beyond the stonewall, where the sheep are fleeing before a galloping horse. Its rider, coatless, shirt cuffs pushed above his elbows, hunches low over the big bay's neck.

Ellis.

Someone has betrayed her.

"Rebecca," she breathes. Her jealous sister must have returned from the Founders' picnic to find Jane gone, then rushed to tell Ellis.

Desperate, Jane casts about for a place to hide. Behind her she hears the horse's sinister rhythm, the brief caesura and landing thump when it leaps the stonewall. She darts to where the trees are most dense, hoping the branches will be too enmeshed for a horse to follow. Instead they yield, thrashing as the rider forces his animal through. Jane dares not look back as she flees, the bay's moist panting growing closer until she has no choice but to whirl around and face her pursuer.

Ellis pulls his horse up short; it rears, bulging eyes showing white. Vaulting off the saddle, he advances, jaw set tight, teeth clenched. His dark curls swarm over his brow; his cheek is hatched red where pine needles and twigs have lashed it.

Jane has never seen any human face so distorted with rage: as though eyes could pour fire.

"Ellis, go back." She tries to keep the fear from her voice, dropping her leather satchel as she steps back. "I have made my choice."

His hand shoots forward. With a blow of shocking force, he hurls her to the grass.

Dropping to his knees, he straddles her waist. His fist closes around his mother's brooch at her neck; he wrenches it away, ripping open her collar.

Her mind flies up into the trees, hovering in bewilderment while, down on the grass, hands tug and tear at her clothes. She hears the sound of her own whimpering; feels the air startle her breasts as her chemise shreds away. Her white skirt rises, then descends over her face like a strange benediction.

Awaking from her daze, she kicks out, blindly striking him with her fists.

Ellis pins down her limbs with the length of his body and seizes a nearby rock, holding it over her face. "Do you want to live to see him again? If you fight, I will crush your head to powder."

She shuts her eyes and makes herself inert, a thing. She tries to hold a picture of Lysander in her mind—his gentle eyes, his arms held out to her in tender compassion, haloed like the Lamb of God—while Ellis pulls her legs apart. Making a blade of his fingers, he thrusts his hand inside her.

SURELY IT IS OVER and Ellis has finished what he came to do. Her eyes are still closed, but his hot curses no longer spew in her ear; she can hear the inane chatter of birds; the horse grazing contentedly nearby, snatching grass with its teeth. She feels the wet flow of what she has lost on her thighs.

She opens her eyes to the sight of Ellis sitting back on his heels, his expression one of triumph mixed with disgust. The length of his member is smeared with her blood; his hands and forearms are crimson with it.

She starts to roll on her side, gathering her shame.

But he is not done with her. Flinging Jane on her back, he takes her a second time—plunging still deeper, as if to mine a brighter blood.

She remembers Lysander saying that God is on high, and beyond mortal reach. She would tell him now: there is God, too, in that low place deep within her, where God is without defense, where God is wounded, and weeps, and no comfort is possible.

After he finishes, Ellis wipes his bloody hands on her skirt. "Now go to him. See if the pious hypocrite will have you now."

Jane stares at the sky. She hears Ellis' boot clank in the stirrup, the creak of leather as he hoists himself onto the saddle. Then the horse wheels and rackets through the trees, carrying away her destroyer.

She burns inside, a column of fire rising to her abdomen. Yet she must get up. Move forward, walk to safety before nightfall. Lysander is waiting in their secret spot.

In Eden.

Chapter Thirty-One

I t doesn't take long for the gin to topple Marly. Within ten minutes she's out cold on Hoyt's couch, welcoming unconsciousness: the day has been almost too much to bear, with its steady march of humiliations.

Then she is on top of a hill, astride a horse, her boots clamped to its flanks, and her trousers taut over her thighs. She touches her hand to her face where there is pain, encountering a hole gouged in her cheek, and whiskers, surprised to find that she is a man.

She is a man gazing down at a valley below, where a cluster of shanty houses bursts into flames.

She is a man listening, unmoved, as people scream, the fire spreading too fast for them to flee.

A solitary figure appears, emerging unharmed from the conflagration: a beautiful young woman with auburn hair, climbing toward Marly. She wears a long, old-fashioned, white dress from another age. A spot of blood appears on the skirt, bright red on white, expanding rapidly. The woman's eyes pierce her, the woman's voice sounds in her mind: *You did this to me.*

In defiance Marly replies silently, *Only what you deserved.*

Ellis. The woman stares straight into her soul. *I am taking you to die.*

I'm not going anywhere with you! Stay away.

It's time. You agreed to this.

Never.

Spurring her horse, Marly gallops down the slope to trample the woman. The horse turns into a car; Marly presses the pedal, bearing down.

The woman stands her ground, impassive.

Marly is almost upon her when she recognizes the face: the same one she saw that night on the road, when her headlights swept over a pale girl in an anorak coming toward her.

Shrieking, Marly swerves the wheel.

And crashes awake.

Shaking from her nightmare, Marly raises herself from the depths of the couch. Her head wobbling on its axis, she doesn't recognize where she is. There's something hard she's sitting on. Groping under her buttocks, her hand finds the contours of a gun, stuck between the sofa cushions where Hoyt tossed it.

Hoyt said he'd be back by now. She was supposed to go home. She doesn't want to go there. Doesn't want to be here either—or anywhere. Even sleep is a minefield. *Nowhere*, that's where she'd like to go.

The anesthetic has worn off; her cheek throbs with pain. Another slug of Hoyt's liquor should take the edge off it.

But the gin seeps like venom into her tissues. Scorching vomit rises in her throat.

She dashes to his bathroom and drops to her knees before his toilet, hurling into the water. A bitter taste of bile in her mouth, she rises unsteadily.

She glimpses herself in the sink mirror: not as bad as she feared. Except for the gauze bandage: the adhesive tape tugs her eye down, making her look deformed. But the other side of her face is okay, if greenish in the dim bathroom light.

There's crusted sleep dribble at the corner of her mouth. She wets a corner of Hoyt's towel and wipes the uncovered half of her face.

Her hand moves irresistibly to the bandage, lifting up the corner to peek at the surgeon's work.

Where her cheek used to be is a crater, nothing left but glistening pus and blackened blood. Her mouth forms a second crater as she screams.

I'm a monster!

Another dash to the toilet, only dry heaves this time. Leaving the bathroom, she sits on Hoyt's bed, trembling with horror.

God, why do You hate me? What did I do to deserve all this? Tell me!

She pats the bandage back in place, hiding the terrible hole in her face. But the image remains in her mind.

She remembers the day she was cleaning the Ellis Suite at the Graynier B & B, and she glanced into a mirror, when a face appeared in place of her own: an old man with muttonchop whiskers, a hole in one cheek gouged out. He glared accusingly at her, until—

Monster! Marly's mouth opens and she can't stop screaming.

When she has no voice left, her shaking subsides. A strange torpor sets in. Her body is an insignificant mass denting the bed, of no importance to anyone. Her mind hovers over the bed, dispassionately appraising her circumstances. Her eyes range over the room, Hoyt's wall, Hoyt's room, Hoyt's bed. Discarded sneakers on the floor, a purple windbreaker tossed on the blue sheets...

A crumpled flier lies beside her on the mattress. A familiar face stares up at her, beneath the headline "HAVE YOU SEEN HER?" She picks the flier up, looks closer: it's the girl.

The girl from the nightmare, the girl from the accident. The purple windbreaker flung onto the bed is the anorak she wore that night.

Pain explodes in Marly's head: the same agony she suffered after the crash, only much worse. Intolerable: she drops the flier, gasping, her hands clutching her skull.

Something wet trickles down her temples from under her palms. She brings her hands away.

They are drenched in blood. The red flows from under her fingernails, climbs up her wrists, toward her elbows.

She can bear no more.

There is only one last hope left.

Marly retrieves the gun from the sofa. No hesitation: she drops her jaw, lodges the muzzle on the roof of her mouth, her finger curled tightly on the trigger. *Deliver me from evil.*

She squeezes.

CHAPTER THIRTY-TWO

"**J**ane."

The girl's shallow breathing barely stirs the tendrils of hair trailing over her sunburned face. Hoyt kneels over her huddled form in the grass, brushing the strands from her forehead. Her skin is cool and damp to the touch: feverish. Her suppurating wound is laid bare on her shoulder, the bandage fallen away.

He jostles her gently. "*Jane.*"

Her eyes fly open, wide with fear; she recoils, one arm flailing to ward him off: "Don't touch me!"

"Easy, easy. I won't hurt you."

Dizzy and disoriented, she blinks rapidly, as if unable to bring him into focus.

"It's Hoyt."

She struggles to her feet. Facing uphill, she goes back to stumbling along the rock wall.

Hoyt overtakes her. "Where are you going?"

"Eden...I...to Eden..." Her words are jumbled.

He grasps her good arm. "This is insane. You're delirious."

"I have to go!" She writhes in his grip. Her strength surprises him.

"Jane! Listen to me. You need *help.*"

The fight leaves her. Hoyt sits her on the wall, then rummages in his knapsack for the water bottle and antibiotics. "If that thing gets infected, you'll wind up back in the hospital, and getting sunstroke's not going to help matters. I'm amazed you got this far before collapsing. You're made of some stern stuff, I'll give you that."

She shivers as he dresses her wound and administers pills.

Casually he says, "You do know there are people who are looking for you."

She goes rigid, her eyes mistrustful.

"It's not my business, okay?" he adds quickly. "I just want you to get better so I don't feel like such a shit. Then you can run off to Bora Bora for all I care. But right now you're coming home with me." He stands, shouldering his knapsack, and retrieves her lantern.

She accepts his proffered hand. He turns her to face downhill. "Here we go. Take your time."

After a few obedient steps, she abruptly reverses direction. "Please, I cannot go. Not yet."

"Why?" He's exasperated. "Honey, you're out of juice. For Christ's sake, you just fainted."

"I feel stronger now, and it's only a little way from here."

"Jane—hey!"

She's already moving off.

"Where are you heading?"

She points toward a stand of pines silhouetted on the rim of the hill.

He understands now. "Is this about your damned stone? If I move it, then will you go back with me?"

"Yes."

"What's underneath?"

Her solemn gray eyes are fixed on the grove ahead. "Truly, I do not know. The rest of my memory, I think."

"I DON'T SEE THE TRAIL anymore." Carrying the tiki torch, Gita hangs back, dragging her feet. They haven't been climbing more than twenty minutes. "We're gonna get lost."

"No, we won't. I know where I'm going." Collin can tell that Gita's never been hiking. Now he is the teacher. He takes the lead, whacking branches and vines with great sweeps of his dad's machete.

"Shit! Is that poison ivy?"

"Yeah, don't touch it."

"Oh, snap. Like I didn't know that, foo."

To entertain her, Collin tells her the story of the kid in camp who got poison ivy on his hands and then got it on his pecker when he held it to pee. He had to show it to the nurse so she could put pink medicine all over it. He was so embarrassed he cried like a little baby.

But Gita doesn't laugh. He can feel her cranky mind-waves as she climbs silently behind him. She hates the woods, tripped up by hidden logs, startled by birds in the underbrush, her long braid snagging in holly bushes.

Stretching up to slice some foliage high overhead, Collin arcs the blade downward, neatly bisecting the swag of vines. The handle suddenly flies out of his grasp.

The machete sails end over end into a dense thicket of poison ivy.

"Whoa," he says, mortified by his blunder.

She puts down the torch, breathing heavily. "You gonna get it?"

"No way." He's wearing only shorts and a T-shirt; he'd get a rash all over his arms and legs if he went after the knife.

Sweat is pouring off Gita's brow. "Then we gotta go back. Mission aborted."

"Why?"

"We don't have the right weapons."

He sees relief flickering across her face. *She's scared.* Not of the woods, realizes Collin: of the mission itself. The great battle ahead.

"Gana didn't say to kill him by blade *and* fire," he says, "She said blade *or* fire. We still have fire."

Leaning the torch on his shoulder like a rifle, he points to a vague hump of rubble further on. "There's the wall. Let's go."

He doesn't look back as he climbs, hoping she'll find her courage again. He can't fight Shaarinen alone.

In a minute he hears her feet shuffle in the dry leaves as she follows.

CROUCHING, THEY CIRCLE the hunting blind, careful not to rustle leaves or crack twigs. Collin points out Jane's pink duffel wedged in the tree. They creep close to the hinged lookout.

There is movement inside the shack. A strong rotten-egg smell reaches their nostrils.

They nod to each other: the demon is in there, stinking of the underworld.

Gita has said that when Shaarinen drops his human shape, thinking he's alone, he looks like hardened smoke. *But he's still Jane*, Collin thinks bitterly. He remembers how she sucked his dad's heart out. Then it was like his father shut the door in Collin's face. Like in his nightmare: pounding on a door that won't open, and the flood sweeping him away, and then he drowns. Because of Jane.

His hatred stoked, Collin readies the torch. Gita takes the butane lighter from her pocket. She flicks the wheel once, twice, her hand trembling.

She shakes her head beseechingly: *can't do it.*

Collin starts to recite the Valor Prayer silently, moving his lips: Gita taught him to do that if he gets scared before an important battle. She joins him shaping the soundless words: *O great Gana, I consecrate my sword to Thee. I destroy the destroyer, in Thy name...*

Collin kisses the tiki torch. Gita kisses the butane lighter, her hand no longer trembling. She flicks the lighter again, this time kindling the spark. Collin leans the torch to it.

The instant before wick touches flame, Collin feels the real world flare to life with an immediacy he has never known. A ray of sun bursts through the branches to vibrate on the shack's weathered wall. The metal stem of the torch seems icy cold in his hands. The cicadas' volume abruptly rises. Inside the cabin a floorboard crackles; the strange brimstone smell intensifies.

Gita's eyes signal him. Collin rises quietly from his crouch, taking his warrior stance, the flaming torch readied like a javelin.

HIS BACK TO the window, Seth tips the Mason jar into the separating funnel; gloves and surgical mask protect him from the corrosive gases. He doesn't see the tiki torch sail through the lookout.

Before it can hit the floor, flame meets hydrogen chloride gas with a thunderclap. The explosion blows out the walls of the shack, hurling the roof into the trees and driving fiery sparks into the dry brush.

Within seconds, the dead grass comes to life, reveling in flames.

The demon is released.

HEARING THE DISTANT thump of the explosion, Jane lifts her head. Birds desert the white pines for the sky, swirling raucously in alarm.

"What was that?" Hoyt stands waist-deep in the pit, digging around the edges of the long flat stone. He leans on the rusty shovel. "Did you hear something?"

"No. Hurry, please."

"Yes, ma'am." He smiles wryly, taking up the spade again. "It's your show."

Watching him bent over his labor in the hole, Jane feels a strange dread creep over her.

How have I seen this before? A man, in this very pit.

The memory hovers somewhere close, gathering.

Her ominous feeling grows as Hoyt levers the long end of the stone up from its bed in the ground. She watches him kneel, sliding his hands beneath the edge, groaning as he lifts. Now he puts his shoulder underneath, straining the stone up, but for all his exertion he can't tip it past the vertical. Instead, bracing it upright with his whole body, he grunts, "I can't hold it here for long. So take a quick look at whatever you came to see."

On her hands and knees, Jane peers over the rim to gaze into the shallow trough left by the stone.

Tears of recognition film her eyes. The past rushes over her, and the voice that will not be still: the voice of poor, reckless, passionate Jane Pettigrew.

CHAPTER THIRTY-THREE

*T*he sun is gone and my tears blur the way. Beloved, for your sake I force my feet to move, as I stagger over roots and stones to Eden. I hold my fire inside, the burning pain he put in me.

I push away the memory of him grinding me into the earth, his shirt buttons scraping a livid path on my breast. His hands bathed in my blood.

I come at last to the glade—I'm parting the pine branches—Yes, you are here.

How the sight of you kindles my spirit—your noble face and halo of fair hair—like a holy revenant. You rise from the grass, putting aside your Bible, and your beautiful blue eyes attach to mine.

I expected it—your horror. How could you not stare aghast? I've no cape, no bonnet, my blouse in tatters, my bosom as naked as Eve's. My skirt with his red victory splashed upon it.

"Ellis." I choke on his name. "He forced me—"

Then my words fall to pieces, and I come to lay my head on Lysander's breast, to cover it with tears, and mourn my dead innocence.

How can you thrust me away?

Your eyes are ice, your anger unconcealed. "You are defiled."

"Defiled?!" I cannot hold back my protest. Violated, mutilated— wronged!—but "defiled"? "Am I a thing of filth? I was attacked, sir! Where is your charity?"

(Ah Jane—impulsive, hot-headed girl. If you had not provoked him, you might have lived.)

I see your fury rising. It frightens me, and I beg you to forgive me, but you will not. I petition your goodness, saying Ellis may have riven my body but he did not breach my heart. It is all I have left to offer, but it is whole and loving and red with my blood—

You glare above me like a judge, holding no mercy. "You schemed to make two men go mad with lust. I fought against it. But Ellis was weak, and you lured him on, and now you cry for a loss you don't feel. You ask my pardon? God Himself abominates you!"

Where has my Lysander gone? Who is here, with fists clenched and eyes inflamed with hate? Does God hate? Can angels be cruel?

"I don't care what God thinks of me. Only—do you hate me, Lysander?"

"You threw away the only thing that mattered! You have ruined everything—everything!"

I understand at last. Because I am no longer pure, you will not have me.

Suddenly I cannot drink air: your hand strikes like a snake, gripping my throat, tightening—my hair tangled in your fingers. Then you bring both hands to the task.

You have no need of two. My neck is slender; a man may easily break it with one hand alone.

The twilight deepens; your face is fading.

Life ends with a snap of small bones, a head cracked from its stem, and a spirit unmoored.

SHE WATCHED HIM then. Lingering in the glade, she saw him pull branches over her body. The next day he came back on a horse, and a spade to dig the grave. The night creatures had already begun their business in her poor flesh. Turning his eyes away, he dragged her to the pit.

She witnessed all of it: herself flung in the grave, the horse hauling the stone from Farmer Quirk's wall, Lysander toppling the stone over the edge, to be the lid of her tomb. He threw his satchel on top, burying all her letters.

He wept when he had finished smoothing the earth over the spot. *God help me. Forgive me*, he prayed.

Then she was called to the Realm.

Still she continued to visit the burial place, and watched as the small, delicate body fed ravenous maggots and beetles. Only a jumble of bones remained, shattered apart by the great stone.

Over time she watched Lysander's soul eaten away by his secret, his hollow prayers mounting to heaven, as he trudged with the stubborn little band of Gabriel Nation toward their fate. She saw them leave Hovey Pond for the western territory, their covered wagons creaking across the plains.

She came again at the end, to the snowy mountain pass, when there wasn't much left of him but breath and bones, and he was long past hunger.

A burst of wind brought the sound of wood creaking: the ribs of the covered wagons groaning, forsaken in deep drifts. A clatter of wings nearby. Though he could not turn his head, he knew a dark bird had come down to peck a crumple of rags in the snow. Many like him lay about in the limitless white. It had been a long time since he heard their prayers.

All of Gabriel Nation were dead now, except him.

His eyes beheld the canopy of heaven as he stared fixedly upward. The sky seemed to sink lower; its burden of snow would be his shroud.

Flakes big as thistles came down, no warmth left in his cheeks to melt them. The snow fell straight into his eyes. A curved film of ice prevented his eyelids closing; a white mask formed on his face, snowflakes meshing over his sight.

She knew his last thought: Jane.

And then she visited no more.

When it came her turn again, to quit the Realm for the Colony, she begged her teachers: *Do not make me forget. I want to remember, when I see him again.*

JANE LOOKS DOWN into her uncovered grave. Among the scattered bones pricking through the soil are small vertebrae, which alone have maintained their fragile row for more than one hundred and fifty years.

"Hope you're done now," Hoyt calls over his shoulder as he strains against the stone. "'Cause I can't hold it anymore, kid."

Jane gets to her feet. Something troubles the air. Black smoke billows across the sky overhead. The atmosphere has grown suddenly very hot, hazy; it smells strongly of wood ash.

But there is something that disquiets her much more. She moves around the perimeter of the hole to stand over Hoyt.

His chest pressed against the rock, he glances up.

She stares into his blue eyes.

I want to remember, when I see him again.

"I remember you." She chokes on the memory, as it bears down like a thunderhead. "You put me in this grave." Backing away in horror from the rim of the pit, she cries, "It was you! You!"

"What—?" In his surprise, Hoyt relents his pressure on the rock for a brief moment. A moment is all that is needed for the stone to fall.

He tries to scramble out of the way, managing to move his upper body clear; but not in time to drag his legs out of the way. The stone crashes down; he hears both thighs snap.

He hollers in agony, "God damn! Fuck!" He tries to push the stone off, to no avail. "Holy Christ! Jane, get help!"

Jane is already running away, lantern in hand, vanishing into the woods.

"Jane!"

Hoyt's cries follow her, but she holds no mercy.

Chapter Thirty-Four

Down at the St. Paul's Fair, Bern D'Annunzio is the first to see the thin furl of smoke from Rowell Hill. He pulls Thom Sayre away from the firemen's grill to come look.

"Oh, shit," says Thom.

"Maybe it's somebody's camp."

"I've never heard of any hikers going up Rowell," Thom says. "There's no trails, no access, not even a fire road." The land belongs to Elsa Graynier, not the state.

"Let's hope nobody's up there," says Bern. "That's a lot of dry timber."

"Uh-huh. All it needs is wind." As Thom says it, a sudden gust flutters the bunting above the Dog 'N' Patty stand. The cold front is coming in.

The breeze picks up; the smoke on Rowell Hill blooms. As the first orange ribbons of flame erupt above the treetops, Thom calls the firehouse.

FIRE TRUCKS FROM FOUR surrounding counties arrive, sirens weaving through the air.

People rush to buy tickets for the Ferris wheel: an excellent vantage point to watch Rowell Hill burn. Others simply stand with their mouths open, never having seen a wildfire up close, as their children slip away unnoticed and run about in overexcited packs. Country-western songs play over the PA, warring with the carousel's recorded calliope music. As the drifting smoke from the forest blaze dries people's throats and eyes, the concession stands run out of soda.

Someone thinks to console Elsa Graynier, whose hill is burning.

"I'm only happy no one lives there," she says, blinking back tears. "The forest will grow back. Though maybe I won't be around to see it." She manages a philosophical smile. "When you get old you know that everything comes and goes and then comes along again."

Smoke floods the sky with the darkness of night, as the north wind builds to twenty miles per hour. Driven by its force, the flames are boiling down Rowell so fast there is no time for the fire teams' bulldozers to cut breaks on the hill.

To protect the surrounding property and houses, they decide to contain the fire at the base. Crews string out along Upper Old Spruce to meet the advancing fire, using the road as a natural firebreak.

Then Thom Sayre remembers Hoyt Eddy's isolated bungalow at the foot of the hill. He sets off with a small team on foot.

When they arrive, the house is alight, its flames too intense to approach without hoses.

By the time they return with trucks, it has burned almost to the ground. Hoyt's pickup is in the driveway, as well as someone's beat-up Cavalier. Then his dog appears out of nowhere. Eyes scared, tail wagging incongruously, he attaches himself to the crew, following them everywhere.

Thom assigns two volunteers to search the house for bodies. The others set spot fires to keep the runaway blaze from sweeping into the town.

At sundown, the wind abruptly reverses, propelling the flames back uphill. More trucks and dozers arrive on the opposite side of Rowell to light a backfire.

With any luck, the two blazes will meet at the top and burn each other out.

HERE HE IS IN A PIT again, unable to climb out. *Sinkhole redux.* It's almost funny.

Hoyt knows Jane isn't coming back. The look on her face told him, when she cried, "It was you!"—what did she mean? Why was she so angry?

That's what you get when you finally care about somebody. When you finally give a shit. She runs out on you, no reason.

He slides in and out of lucidity, his trapped legs alternating between numbness, pins and needles, and searing pain.

All he can do is wait, lying in a mess of someone's old bones, his own broken bones mingled with the shards of a stranger. *Sacrum, femur, patella, tibia,* he recites. Absurd to know a lot of nothing, for nothing.

He stares up into darkness. How can it be night so soon?

He smells smoke. Hears distant sirens, shouts.

The wind changes abruptly, now seething up the hill. It scoops into the pit, buffeting Hoyt's face and driving thick smoke down his throat into his lungs. The sky fills with an eerie apricot glow, soon spinning into a glory of scarlet, orange, and rose.

His lungs labor as oxygen is sucked from the air; he chokes, throat squeezing shut. The air scorches his nasal passages.

A second roar comes from the opposite direction. Fire is closing in on both sides.

It's over. To state the obvious.

Then thought ceases.

A slender thread of mercy raises his soul out of Hoyt
Eddy's doomed body, just before it perishes; sparing him his
own end.

WILDFIRE AND BACKFIRE meet. As awestruck firemen and townspeople watch, curling crests of treetop flames merge, in a shimmer
of gaseous heat. Then comes the crash, and a tremendous gyre of
flames whooshes up: the death spiral.

The fire begins to destroy itself.

Rain starts before morning. Four hours later, when the rains
slacken, the fire is all but dead. The bleak scorched stubble of Rowell
Hill stands revealed. Ninety acres in all have burned.

Awake more than thirty-five hours, stretched to their physical limits, Thom and Bern refuse to shuck their gear and go home
to bed. The conflagration is in their blood; they don't want it over.
They join the volunteers climbing Rowell Hill to put out spot fires
and assess the damage. Hoyt Eddy's dog trots anxiously alongside
them.

To walk the ashy terrain is unsettling; it's a world of phantom limbs, gaunt specters of trees, blackened and still smoking. The
crew finds it comforting to follow the track of a human element:
a centuries-old tumbled stone wall, whose meanderings used to be
concealed by living greenery, now burned away.

They pause in a small clearing when someone treads on metal
objects among the cinders: butane canisters. Sifting around, they
find a pot, a camp stove, and the upper half of a patio torch.

The fire may have originated in this area. Several of the men
stay behind to collect evidence and look for human remains.

Soon they will find the charred body parts.

Hoyt's dog suddenly breaks ahead, galloping over the crest of
the hill. They find him in a second clearing, where he's sniffing excit-
edly around a pit.

They are afraid to touch the body they find in the hole. It's
wedged under a heavy stone that takes two men to lift. One guy

argues that it's not a body at all, but a charred log. A metal belt buckle embedded in the shape decides the matter. They call for a forensic team.

Bern and Thom leave their comrades to puzzle out the scene.

Bern says he feels disconnected, like his head is separated from the rest of him; maybe it's the adrenaline, or too much coffee.

It's like being in a movie, Thom says.

The woods are utterly quiet: no insects or birds. The men's boots crunch on the still-smoldering residue on the forest floor. They follow the stonewall mechanically as their amazement fades into stupor.

Then they hear the child's cries coming from Pease Pond.

CHAPTER THIRTY-FIVE

"**W**hat were you doing there?"

They can't get anything out of him. Police, fire forensics, the trauma specialist, the grieving Poonchwallas, his grandparents—they've all tried to find out why Collin was on Rowell Hill that day.

The boy won't say a word. All he does is grunt.

"He's waiting on his mama," says his grandfather. Veronda is on her way back from Ghana. They've barred Brett from visiting his son in the hospital.

Everyone agrees Collin is severely traumatized.

No one suspects him of starting the fire. The newspapers report that it was caused by a chemical explosion at a homemade meth lab in a hunting shack: not a rare occurrence, unfortunately, in economically depressed rural areas.

Three people are dead.

The body parts found at the site of the meth lab were identified as belonging to Seth Poonchwalla, an honors student with a bright future in robotics. Everyone is shocked except Graynier's crank addicts, now going through withdrawal.

The forensic specialists are waiting to do tests on the second body, believed to be Hoyt Eddy. They are waiting for a DNA sample from his brother in Kentucky.

At first there is some confusion over the Jane Doe found roasted beyond recognition in Hoyt's house. A detective from Virginia claims it is Caroline Moss, a fugitive autistic who was spotted in Hoyt's pickup on the day of the fire. However, the Chevrolet Cavalier in his driveway is traced to Marlene Walczak.

Her distraught daughter Pearl confirms the vehicle is her mother's. She has not seen Marly since the day of the fire, when she went to the carnival, leaving her mother asleep in their trailer. After spending the night with a roustabout, she returned home to discover her mother missing and her car gone.

The police take a cheek swab from Pearl. The body on Hoyt's floor is confirmed to be Marly Walczak's.

Later the medical examiner will report that Ms. Walczak did not die of a self-inflicted gunshot wound. The bullet took out her left eye and a piece of skull but missed the brain. She would have been conscious, though unable to move, when she died of smoke inhalation.

Gita Poonchwalla is also missing. Since no fourth body was found in the ashes of Rowell Hill, her parents remain hopeful she's alive. They could not survive the death of both children. As it is, the Poonchwallas are now pariahs in Graynier: greedy upstart aliens whose son turned a clean, law-abiding community into a cesspool of vice, nearly burning down the whole town in the process.

The police, for their part, believe Gita ran away from home. Judging from the strange contents of her room, she seems to have been a troubled adolescent and a kleptomaniac besides. They put out an Amber Alert. Posters are distributed nationwide: "HAVE YOU SEEN HER?"

It is one of many questions that will never be answered.

All of Graynier is wracked by the tragedy. Saloons are full of the shocked and sad, made sadder still by the weather. They take no joy in the rain that falls relentlessly, filling the reservoirs and coaxing new growth from lawns and forests.

COLLIN REMEMBERS EVERYTHING. The deluge of images engulfs him, over and over, asleep and awake, extinguishing his power of speech.

He recalls waking sprawled in a blackberry bush, choking on torrid smoke-filled air. His eyes stung from the thick, suffocating haze, and his eyelids were sticky with blood seeping from cuts on his head. But he was alive and whole: he had been thrown wide of the hunting blind when it exploded.

He pried himself from the bush and rose to his feet. The upper air was so hot, the smoke so intense, he had to drop back down on all fours.

A moan came from the base of an oak, its crown on fire.

"Gita!"

Another moan.

She was alive.

Crawling over, he passed a bloodied shoe, then a broken rind of skull with black hair and clods of brain still clinging to it. Stuck in the branches of a pine was a severed human arm, its skin melted away. Collin had no time to wonder whose life was strewn about so horribly, but the images would return to him later, in the hospital.

He found Gita where the explosion had flung her headfirst into a tree trunk. Dazed and bleeding from a head wound, she gazed up at him in mute fear.

"Can you get up? We gotta run!"

She nodded once, uncertainly. Stretching his T-shirt over his nose as he'd learned in fire-safety class, Collin tugged frantically on Gita's arm, forcing her to her feet. "Stay low!" he shouted, though she was already bent double, whimpering with pain.

He scanned the clearing for an exit: maybe they could take the stonewall path back to the bottom of the hill.

But leaping flames blocked the way, as strong winds pushed the wildfire downhill. More flames surrounded the shack's skeleton, swarming up the trees and irradiating the forest in demonic red light. Pine needles, ablaze, snapped as they disappeared; bright cinders rained.

Beside him Gita began to choke on the air.

Where could they go?

A loud crash in the brush: they froze.

Something large was drawing near.

Shaarinen! Collin pulled Gita down, trying to duck out of sight, hoping their camouflage paint concealed their faces.

An antlered deer burst into the clearing; three more deer followed. Their white tails lifted, they vanished as quickly as they appeared, heading toward—

The pond.

Grabbing Gita's hand, Collin ran after them, hunched below the dark miasma of smoke as he followed the stonewall leading to Pease Pond. Gita gagged and stumbled. Clutching her hand more tightly, Collin willed her forward.

When they reached the banks of Pease Pond, she collapsed and curled up, holding her stomach. He knelt beside her, shaking her shoulders. She took her hands away, and he saw a metal fragment of pole protruding from her abdomen: the base of the tiki torch.

Without thinking, he grasped the end and pulled it out. Her shriek echoed across the water. More blood than he'd ever seen surged from the hole in her stomach.

At that moment a wallop of heat hit his back, singeing his nape. The wind had changed; the fire was now advancing in his direction, and would be here soon. He heard crackling in the dark sky; the wind had sucked the flames up to the treetops, and the crown fire was racing along the dry canopy, far ahead of the conflagration on the ground.

"Coll…," he heard Gita whisper hoarsely.

He turned back to her. "We have to go in the water."

She shook her head. "You go."

"I can't!" The terror he'd been holding in exploded. "I can't without you! You have to come!"

Ignoring her cries, he dragged her into the shallows. The cool water seemed to revive her; as they waded to their necks, she moved her arms in a feeble swimming motion.

Collin peered through the smoke. The water was choppy ahead, oscillating strangely from the center.

At first he couldn't comprehend what he saw: the water's surface was stippled with darting silhouettes, like tiny skaters, some with arms outstretched. Through stinging tears, he saw the arms were antlers. The skaters were the heads of deer, alongside other animals, all swimming to the pond's center to escape the coming flames.

He turned back to see Gita swimming slowly away, into the deeper water.

"Gita!" He took a step, and the pond bottom fell away. His old fear of water flooded him; he flailed for traction, but there was nothing to support his sneakers. Straining his chin above the surface, he paddled as Gita had taught him, breath coming in frightened gasps.

He followed the shape of her head until it disappeared behind a billow of smoke. He paddled faster. At last the haze parted and he could see her again. "Wait!" he shouted, suddenly angry with her. "We have to stay together!"

Then she was swimming towards him.

Except it wasn't Gita. A dark animal of some kind clawed the water, swerving away when it saw Collin.

Crying, he yelled Gita's name over and over. She never answered.

He lapsed into silence, then started paddling toward the shallows. But the water at the pond's edge was too hot; the wildfire had encircled the banks, throwing off gaseous fumes. He swam back toward the center.

Treading water, he stared at the boiling hell he and Gita had summoned with the flick of a lighter. The evil god Shaarinen straddled the lake and unfurled his red cape of flames, laughing in great gusts of smoke at the boy warrior quailing in the pond.

An impenetrable darkness settled over the water as the fire

raged. Collin felt things bumping against him: paws scratching at him as they pedaled past, long ropey muskrat tails or snakes raking his arms, blunt noses nudging him.

He couldn't help thinking of what he'd seen beneath the water, weeks ago when he and his dad had explored the lake.

The drowned woman's skull, her empty eye sockets, her long hair drifting...

Suddenly he felt her.

Long wet strings brushed against his arms under the water, tangling in his hands...smooth, spongy flesh and the knob of a nose met his fingers...his sneakers kicked against the soft trunk of a submerged body...arms and legs interlaced with his.

She's here! She wants to drag me down!

Screaming, he pushed the horror from him, thrashing through the water, swimming to a spot far away from her clutches.

Looking up, he saw the fiery tsunami roaring away from the pond toward the horizon. Another fire seemed to be approaching from the opposite direction. Maybe he and Gita would be safe soon, and could go ashore.

"Giiiii-taaaa!!"

All at once, the knowledge came to him: it wasn't the lady's corpse, the phantom body he'd felt under the water. It was Gita.

Drowned.

IN TIME, HE couldn't feel his arms and legs. The idea of sinking offered comfort: he only wanted to rest. He imagined lowering himself into the embrace of the silky scarves he used to play with from his mother's bedroom drawer.

His head sank beneath the water; it flowed into his mouth and nose.

Then a voice spoke sharply inside his ear. A memory of Gita's voice:

Float!

He broke to the surface, flailing and puking water. He fought not to sink a second time, his head spinning.

Float!

He remembered that first lesson in the pool, Gita's hand under his back as she supported him in the dead man's float. He lay spread-eagle on top of the water and concentrated on staying awake. Sleep meant sinking.

After what seemed like hours, rain pelted his upturned face. He closed his eyes against the drops.

Later the air got cooler and the smoke ebbed. He turned over, treading water to watch the fire dim as it gradually lost its life to the rain.

He swam to the shallows. Hauling himself up on a rock still warm from the blaze, he fell asleep until the firemen's voices woke him.

COLLIN WON'T SAY his secrets to anyone. Even when he recovers his speech, three months later, he will claim to remember nothing of the entire summer.

He will never go swimming again.

CHAPTER THIRTY-SIX

Brett hasn't packed yet.

Although he has ten days left on his lease, there is no reason to stay. Now that Jane and Collin are both gone, he doesn't really know anyone in Graynier. Of course, now all kinds of people recognize him, especially since the fire: the druggist, the supermarket cashier, the mailman.

Like the rest of Graynier, he avoids the Poonchwallas.

There's no one to talk to, except perhaps Elsa Graynier. He runs into her on one of his habitual walks through town.

"You haven't been to see me, dear." She wags a finger at him. "I've been wondering, did you ever find out what happened to your Jane Pettigrew?"

"No." They say their goodbyes; he walks on, relieved she didn't ask after his son. She didn't like Collin; after all, he had deliberately broken her glass goblet. That was a piece of cunning: it got the kid what he wanted, to be expelled from the museum so he could visit Gita.

But no one believed Brett when he said the boy was crafty.

He explained to his in-laws how he'd lost sight of Collin at the fair, how the kid had persuaded him—begged him—to climb the ladder and then taken off the minute Brett's back was turned.

"He set me up."

Rolling her eyes indignantly, Veronda's mother asked her husband, "I'm-a ask you, can a little ten-year-old boy '*set you up?*'"

"And I say the only one who thinks that is a damn coward."

Then they tore into him. Brett was banished from his son's life, maybe forever.

Brett knows he is a terrible father. Worse, he's fine with turning his back on Collin. From the beginning, the boy was weird, not letting Brett in, which made it hard to care about him. He's sorry about Collin's trauma and everything, but—

What had he been doing up there on Rowell Hill?

If Brett could really speak his mind, he would say the boy got what he deserved. Except what kind of father thinks that? A damn coward.

He's just too young to be a parent; he doesn't have that unconditional love stuff in him. Maybe one day he will, if he ever has a child by someone he loves, who loves him back, or at least likes him, or is just nice to him.

Back in the house on Sycamore Street, Brett works at the computer, makes French toast for his dinner and washes up, then climbs the stairs to the garret, finishing work around 10. Too early for bed. He should pack, leave in the morning, get back to Brooklyn, sleep in his own bed.

But he doesn't want to leave this house. He doesn't understand why, but it feels like his home.

That first day, driving the RV full of camping equipment, his little boy beside him—strangers then, destined always to be strangers now—what made him turn the wheel and enter an obscure town? He could just as easily have kept going.

He would be hard put to describe that feeling: when there is no decision made, you're just doing exactly what you are supposed to do. Being in this house is like that: being exactly where he is supposed to be. It's a feeling of clarity, of pure grace, as simple as turning his face to the sun.

Nevertheless, he lays out his T-shirts, slides his pants off the hangers, and starts to pack.

Collin's room has already been thoroughly cleaned out by Brett's in-laws. As a kind of rebuke, they left the bed unmade. Half-heartedly he draws the bedspread over the rumpled sheets, then proceeds to Jane's room, though he knows she left no trace, and he promised himself he wouldn't think about her.

The volume of romantic poetry he bought her is on the bed. Had it been there before? He thought she took it with her.

It's lying open to a poem.

"*To Jane,*" by Percy Bysshe Shelley.

He snatches the book up, switching on the bedside lamp, and begins to read.

> *The keen stars were twinkling,*
> *And the fair moon was rising among them,*
> *Dear Jane.*
> *The guitar was tinkling,*
> *But the notes were not sweet till you sung them*
> *Again.*

By the time he reaches the last stanza he is reading the corny words out loud:

> *Though the sound overpowers,*
> *Sing again, with your dear voice revealing*
> *A tone*
> *Of some world far from ours,*
> *Where music and moonlight and feeling*
> *Are one.*

It's no use trying not to think of Jane. Now he permits himself an orgy of remembering.

All evening long, her image envelops him.

Switching off the kitchen light at midnight, he gazes into the backyard, where he first glimpsed her. A different moon, low, swollen and coppery, shines behind the sycamore tree. But there is no silhouette of her beneath its branches.

Thinking back to that night, he feels the eerie rightness of their meeting. Just as when, in the rented van, he turned the wheel toward Graynier: the same sense of clarity. The same way he feels about mathematics, when he encounters the immutable, somehow loving, perfection of things.

There is a perfect order to these events, hidden behind the riotous sprawl of the universe. So of course he found her. Of course she found him. Of course she knocked on his door.

Now comes the *tap-tap* on the etched daisy panel of glass.

Of course he is racing to open it. Of course she stands there on the stoop, gazing up at him. What could be more right?

"Jane!"

She looks even thinner, a wraith, her skin drawn tighter over her cheekbones, mauve hollows carved around her eyes. Her jeans are torn and filthy; a tank top hangs loosely from her delicate shoulders, one of them swathed in a bandage; bruises, scrapes, and black charcoal smudges cover her face and bare arms. In her hand is a battery lantern, its weakened light almost dimmed out. A gold brooch of twined roses, fastened to her top, gleams incongruously through the grime.

Her gray eyes are alight, as joyous at the sight of him as he is to see her. She lets out an exultant laugh, white teeth radiant in her sooty face. The sound echoes through the empty street, its landscape now transformed into a world of music and moonlight and feeling.

"Papa! I have come home!"

Acknowledgements

MY GRATITUDE TO Grey Swan Press for taking a chance with me. Thank you to Christopher Schelling and Helen Eisenbach for their crucial help in shaping this yarn. Love to James and Phoebe Lapine for indulging my writing addiction. Thanks to Colette Baron-Reid for reminding me what I came here to do.

Colophon:

This book was typeset using Garamond, a classic 16th century typeface interpreted by type designer Robert Slimbach and released in 1988. Originally, Claude Garamond created the roman form and Garamond's assistant, Robert Granjon, designed the italics face. Together, this font family is considered to be among the most legible and readable serif typefaces because of its fluidity and consistency.